THE KILLING HOUSE

The Big Shilling Book One

GOMERY KIMBER

PROCURSUS PRESS, LONDON

'There are, however, many murderers for whom this description would be quite inadequate. Some are intelligent and, in many respects, self-disciplined. The case of Robert Irwin illustrates this class of murderer . . . Prior to the murders, Irwin had been preoccupied with a notion that he called 'visualising.' It had struck him that before a sculptor could create a piece of sculpture, the work had to be visualised in the artist's mind. For Irwin, the function of imagination was to allow a man to close his eyes and 'see' whatever he wishes to see . . .'

P.151, 'THE CRIMINOLOGY', 'COLIN WILSON – THE MAN AND HIS MIND,' BY HOWARD F. DOSSOR

'The secret is to imagine to the point of self-persuasion.'

NEVILLE GODDARD

PROLOGUE

They were an odd couple, strolling in one of London's royal parks that foggy Sunday morning at the beginning of spring. He was tall and narrow and stooping, and she was a fresh-faced dumpling in a black hijab.

The young woman was eating nuts, and the noise she made when she chewed them was getting on her companion's nerves, not that anyone would have known, since the man's charming expression never changed. He was a diplomat, and a spy, and the woman munching nuts was a junior employee of the British Secret Intelligence Service, also known as MI6.

'Code name BASKERVILLE,' said the diplomat, appreciatively. He was an aficionado of the Sherlock Holmes stories and he was enjoying his walk in the London fog.

The woman looked at him blankly.

'Please go on,' he said.

'So,' said the woman, 'I got to see the file before it

went back to Registry. It was written by a psychiatrist, or a psychologist – anyway, a lot of it was about his parents. His mother died when he was quite young. She was psychotic and killed herself in a mental hospital. His father was known as Spyker Hanratty.'

The woman looked up at him again to see if the strange name meant anything to him, but the diplomat merely smiled politely at her. He made her nervous, this middle-aged patrician with the handsome face and elegant manners. Whenever she spoke to him she tried to make her London accent posher than it was, and the effort of doing so made her weary. She wanted to sit down and have something proper to eat, but it was too cold to sit on the park benches they passed, and she'd brought nothing more substantial with her than a bag of mixed nuts.

'I didn't know who it was. I had to look it up – I didn't do that at work,' she added quickly.

'That's very good,' said the diplomat.

'Do you know of him?' she asked, a little overawed. In her limited experience, the diplomat seemed to know everything.

'Yes. He attempted to assassinate the South African Prime Minister, I think. As I recall, he was deemed unfit to stand trial due to insanity and was sent to a secure institution. It is not unusual, of course, for Communism and violent insanity to go hand in hand.'

The woman blinked, as though this were news to

her. She was certainly intelligent but had been educated at one of Britain's most prestigious universities, where, thought the diplomat, she had been indoctrinated by progressives. She was a strange mixture, undoubtedly a devout Muslim, but also in many ways a western liberal.

'Spyker means nail,' said the woman. 'He had schizophrenia. I can't remember the percentages, sorry, but there was something about the chances of their son inheriting mental illness from the parents. He fought against the Portuguese in Angola, and before that he'd been in the British Army in North Africa, and Italy. He received a head injury in the war and they thought that might have contributed to his mental illness.'

'And does Rickardo take after his parents?' asked the diplomat. He was being provocative, certain that the woman believed a person was a blank slate, and that inheritance counted for nothing.

'Well, he did spend time in a psychiatric hospital in New York State in the 1980s, and when he was in prison in Australia in 2002 he was diagnosed as a psychopath.' The woman paused for a moment, trying to recall the medical jargon and acronyms: 'A psychopath with attention deficit hyperactivity disorder, callous and unemotional traits, and displaying high levels of Machiavellianism, impulsivity and aggression. He scored 38 on the PCL-R test for psychopathy, out of a maximum of 40.'

'Very good,' said the diplomat, praising her. She beamed up at him, before abruptly covering her smile with a pudgy hand and quickly turning away.

'Tell me more about Petra,' he said, as though nothing had happened, 'about when she returned from the meeting with the Director General.'

The young woman scowled, as he thought she might: she detested her boss, Petronella.

'She headed straight for the whisky, innit,' she said, contemptuously. 'She looked like she'd seen a ghost, all the blood had drained out of her face.'

The diplomat made sure he didn't sound the least bit sceptical when he said, 'This happened once before?'

'Yeah, 'wet jobs' they call them. Petra looked all queasy then as well. I've heard her talking on the phone to the guy who carries them out. His wife's moved to Tel Aviv with their little girl. She told him the British will help get the girl back for him if he dealt with BASKERVILLE.'

'He has to be bribed in this way to carry out an assassination?'

'I don't know. I think he might have retired, but he knows BASKERVILLE personally. He can get close to him.'

'Interesting,' said the diplomat, 'very interesting indeed.'

He was thinking what a dirty business he was in, and wondered how many would die before BASKERVILLE was himself killed. He was thankful that he himself never had to get his hands dirty. He pitied those that did.

'Shall we go back?' he asked the woman. 'It's getting cold.'

CHAPTER ONE

It was God who killed Aias Pneumaticos. That's what the Big Shilling told American Troy when they arrived at the safe house in Antwerp, Belgium. American Troy was an intelligent kid, he knew what Shilling meant, or thought he did: that if Pneumaticos hadn't been religious he'd still have been alive. But Shilling spelt it out for him anyway. The Big Shilling was like that – he had a compulsion to talk.

'I've known a lot of guys like him, hey, gangsters who believe in God. Gangsters who believe in God,' he repeated, as though he couldn't fathom it. 'Me, I believe in nothing, nothing that I cannot imagine, nothing except my own prowess, my own strength, my own self-belief. Did you see how his head exploded! Man, that was a shot. Wind blowing a gale, only two seconds to make the hit, and boom! Did you see it? His head exploded like a watermelon.'

Then Shilling slapped himself on the forehead with the flat of his hand.

'What am I talking about? What am I talking about? Forget God. It wasn't God who killed that Greek, it was me, the Big Shilling. I killed Aias Pneumaticos, I did it. I killed that dumb son of a bitch, eh? I am God, that's who I am!'

This kind of talk was typical Shilling and American Troy hadn't been paying him much attention, just waiting for the chance to speak.

'You were right,' he said in admiration. 'You said he'd leave the compound over the holiday weekend.'

The kid realised Shilling was looking at him quizzically and didn't know why, but the moment passed and he forgot all about it.

'I told you. I told you he would and you didn't believe me. Didn't I tell you? I said he would leave the house, hey?'

Right from the start, the Big Shilling had insisted that the mark would go to church at Easter. Aias Pneumaticos was in Holland to supervise a big drug deal for his boss, the Russian exile. He and his bodyguards – there were four of them, all Russians – were holed up in a big, walled mansion in the countryside somewhere east of Rotterdam. Shilling and American Troy had spent five long days observing the house. Pneumaticos never left. Instead, he had his underlings come to him.

'What if he doesn't leave?' American Troy had asked. 'What if he stays holed up and only gets in that armoured limo to take him back to the airport?'

'He'll leave,' said Shilling. 'Put your money where your mouth is. On Good Friday, Easter Sunday or Easter Monday, he will leave. You want to bet? I bet you he leaves. I bet you your cut he'll leave.'

'A hundred big ones? You want me to bet a hundred thousand bucks he won't leave?'

Shilling could see where American Troy was going. He interrupted, 'He doesn't leave, you won't see a penny, is that what you're thinking? Don't worry, my boy, you'll get your money. It's as good as banked already. The guy will leave that house. Believing is seeing. Because he believes in God, he will leave that house, eh?'

American Troy didn't say anything. He was thinking of the new BMW motorbike he was planning to buy with his share.

'Are you listening to me, boy? Believing is seeing. I've got a new bet for you. I bet he leaves on Good Friday. Not Easter Sunday or Easter Monday: Good Friday. I bet you half your fee he leaves on Good Friday.'

American Troy could tell this time Shilling was serious. Fifty thousand bucks! The American's greed kicked in but immediately it was cancelled out by the thought of losing.

'No,' he said. 'I'll bet you five hundred.'

'Five hundred? Five hundred! What the hell's wrong with you? Five hundred's not a bet. Five hundred's a joke. Either you bet big shilling or you don't bet at all.'

Big Shilling.

It was one of the Big Shilling's favourite phrases. He used it so often that it had become his nickname. American Troy had heard him say it on the phone to the Turk when the Turk had offered six hundred thousand dollars for the assassination of Aias Pneumaticos.

'Six hundred thousand? Six hundred thousand is nowhere near where I want to be. Pneumaticos is protected, Pneumaticos rides around in an armoured car, Pneumaticos is second in command of one of the biggest crime syndicates in Europe. To take him out you're going to need the best. That is why you've come to me, my friend. I am the best. I am the best, most experienced hitman in the world today. No one is better than me, no one. Six hundred thousand? Man, that's nowhere near where I want to be. You want Pneumaticos dead, my friend, you're going to have to pay big shilling.'

And so the Turk had paid big shilling, one million US, plus expenses. American Troy's cut was a very generous ten per cent. His job was to handle the logistics, Shilling's job was to kill the mark. Troy had carried out his tasks diligently. He'd stolen identities, he'd procured the vehicles – two cars and a motorcycle – he'd rented the house and garage in Amsterdam, and the Antwerp apartment, he'd even sourced and built the incendiary device. Yes, he'd done it all diligently and professionally, the way his Uncle Nathan had taught him to commit crimes, but all the time he wished it was he who was pulling the trigger and not Shilling, for it was American

Troy's life ambition to be a professional killer.

The one thing he'd really wanted to procure was the rifle, but there was no way the Big Shilling was going to allow him to do that. Shilling always procured his own weaponry, of course he did. He'd been away for almost a week, and when he came back to the Amsterdam house he was uncharacteristically close-mouthed, refusing to say where he'd been or who he'd seen. In his suitcase was the smallest sniper rifle American Troy had ever set eyes on.

'You didn't tell me you were dropping by the toy store.'

He said it without thinking, and when he realised what he'd said he checked Shilling to see how he'd taken it. But Shilling was in a good mood. There was a smile on his pale, freckled face, and his whole attention was focused on the rifle. Shilling loved weapons. So far as Troy could figure, weapons were the one and only love of Shilling's life. Guns, knives, he handled them like other guys handled women.

'Compact, isn't she?' said Shilling, hefting the rifle in his small hands. 'A bullpup - you see the magazine's there behind the trigger? The Stealth Recon Scout, eh? The Stealth Recon Scout. Stupid name, but you expect that from the Yanks, eh? Twenty-six inches long, just twenty-six inches long. Look, two different barrels, two different calibres, one for vehicles, one for soft targets.'

'Would it take out the armoured car?'

'Forget about the armoured car, boy, just forget about it. He's going to church, and I'm going to take him out as he walks into the building. That's what's going to happen, you mark my words, my boy. Believing is seeing, oh yeah, believing is seeing.'

Believing is seeing – that was another one of the Big Shilling's favourite phrases, but to American Troy it was illogical and slightly irritating – seeing was believing, right? - and so he never thought about what it meant.

Shilling picked up a carton of cartridges. '308s,' he said. 'Hit him with one of these babies and his head will explode like a fucking watermelon, like a fucking watermelon, eh?'

He tossed the carton to Troy who caught it. Then Shilling raised the gun to his shoulder and took aim at the TV on the other side of the room. Yes, it was short for a rifle, thought Troy, but it still looked big when compared to the diminutive Shilling who stood barely five feet three inches tall.

To say that Shilling was sensitive about his height was something of an understatement: for him it was an open wound that never healed. In Troy's experience, barely a day went by without Shilling taking umbrage at some slight, imagined or otherwise, relating to his lack of inches. Even if someone used the word 'short' in an entirely innocent context it was sometimes enough to goad the Big Shilling into a confrontation. And in the underworld, Shilling's reputation for violence was legendary. The joke was, if you wanted to suicide yourself just call the Big Shilling a short ass.

In fact, American Troy had a theory about why

Shilling had agreed to kill Aias Pneumaticos for the Turk. Shilling was freelance. He killed people for cash. You went to him, told him who you wanted wacked and agreed the price. But sometimes, for no good reason, the Big Shilling turned you down. Troy had heard on the grapevine that the Russian exile had approached Shilling to sound him out about killing the Turk, and that Shilling had nixed him. Troy's theory was this: the reason Shilling had taken the Turk's contract and not the Russian's was because the Russian was six foot five and the Turk only five four.

He had no proof, of course, and he wasn't about to ask Shilling for confirmation, especially not after the Big Shilling turned around and aimed the sniper rifle at him in the Amsterdam living room, saying, 'A toy, is it, a fucking toy? You saying I'm a kid, are you, boy? You saying I'm no taller than a little kid? Is that what you're saying? You're calling me a fucking midget, eh? Is that what you're doing? Is it, you punk? I'll tell you what I'll do. You give me one of those cartridges and I'll load this toy and you can call me a fucking dwarf and we'll see what happens.'

It was a good five minutes before Shilling calmed down and dropped the subject, but to American Troy it seemed like half an hour, and so he was mightily glad when Shilling ordered him to get on his bike and ride out to Pneumaticos's mansion. He was glad even though it was going dark outside and pouring down with rain.

'Stay there till I tell you you can come back,'

ordered Shilling. 'You understand me, eh? I know how you love the great outdoors.'

'Yes, boss,' said American Troy, trying to sound contrite. 'I got it.'

'That's right. I'm the boss, the fucking boss, and you will do as you are told and fucking like it. Now get out of here. I've got work to do.'

It was after one in the morning before the Big Shilling called American Troy and told him he could come home. It was April in northern Europe, and Troy was freezing his ass off, sheltering from the rain in the lee of a wall about two hundred yards from the Greek's hideout, but Troy didn't mind too much. He had a tolerance for cold that the Big Shilling, raised, so they said, in the West Indies, did not share.

'And you'd better not be at that McDonalds drive-in,' Shilling said to him over the phone.

'I'm here, I did what you told me.'

'I know, my boy,' said Shilling, laughing. 'I can see you through the night sight.'

Troy smirked. It was typical Shilling. It was shit like this that made him love the guy, kind of.

'What day's today?'

It was after midnight, so Troy said, 'Friday.'

'Wrong. It's Good Friday. What time did the lights go out?'

'A little after eleven.'

'An early night. I reckon today's the day, my boy, I reckon today is the day. In fact, I know it is.'

'Good luck.'

'Good luck? I make my own luck, boy. Seeing is believing, remember.'

Big Shilling made the hit when Aias Pneumaticos got out of the armoured Mercedes, right outside the door of the Greek Orthodox church. It was a relatively easy shot, in spite of the rain and the gusty wind. The Big Shilling aimed for the bottom of the occipital bow and he saw a pleasing spurt of blood and brains and bone as Pneumaticos's forehead exploded.

Ignoring the screams of the women and the shouting men, he laid the sniper rifle on the passenger seat, started the engine and drove the Peugeot around the corner to where American Troy was waiting astride the motorbike with a spare helmet.

A couple of Aias Pneumaticos's guards gave chase, of course they did, but their car was no match for a motorcycle driven by a champion rider like American Troy. As they sped across Museums Park, the Mercedes left far behind, blocked by metal bollards, Shilling glanced over his shoulder and saw the Peugeot burst into flames as the incendiary device detonated.

'I told you,' he shouted, 'I fucking told you, eh? I told you he'd leave the house and go to church. What an idiot, what an idiot. That's one less fool in the world, eh? That's one less fool in the world. The kingdom of heaven is within, it's within. Didn't he know that? I sent him back, I sent him right back to the beginning.'

And the Big Shilling kept on talking, even though

his words were drowned by the noise of the motor-bike engine and American Troy couldn't hear a thing he was saying.

CHAPTER TWO

When they left Antwerp early on the morning of Easter Monday, American Troy and the Big Shilling travelled separately. Shilling took the train to Geneva, Switzerland, and Troy hired a car at the main railway station using the fake ID his Uncle Nathan had provided, and drove.

American Troy was feeling somewhat deflated. After the tension of the stake out and the exultation of the successful assassination, he was depressed and bad tempered. Driving the ridiculously small and underpowered Suzuki Swift, which Shilling had insisted he hire, did nothing to improve his mood either. It was almost as if Shilling wanted to humiliate him.

Once the death of Aias Pneumaticos had been confirmed by the Dutch authorities, as reported by the mainstream media, Shilling had logged on to his Swiss bank website via the encrypted server Tor and discovered that one million US had been deposited in his account by the Turk. If American Troy had expected an immediate transfer of a hundred thousand to his own account then he was to be sorely disappointed. Shilling didn't even mention Troy's money. In the end, Troy had to bring it up himself.

'What about my share?'

'What about your share?' Shilling demanded, lolling in the armchair in the Antwerp apartment and toying with a Zippo lighter and a Cuban cigar.

'Hey, I did a good job, didn't I? When do I get paid?'

'When do you get paid? I'll tell you when you get paid, my boy, you get paid when I'm good and ready. And I won't be good and ready until I know you're good and ready, if you understand my meaning, eh? If you understand what I'm getting at.'

But Troy, in this as in so many things over the past few weeks, didn't understand what the Big Shilling was getting at, he didn't understand at all. He was looking at that Cuban cigar, that single Cuban cigar, thinking, dude, I would have liked to have had a celebratory smoke. Next, he looked at the bottle of tequila, and the single glass that Shilling had brought in from the kitchen and slammed down on the coffee table.

'Fuck it, man, what did I do wrong?' Troy asked.

'Not much,' the Big Shilling admitted, uncapping the tequila and pouring himself a large measure. 'You did a pretty good job all round. Yes, even if I say so myself, you did a pretty good job all round.'

'So where's my goddamn money!'

The Big Shilling didn't answer right away. First, he got that cigar alight to his satisfaction, next he drank the tequila down in one, and then refilled his glass, smacking his lips and making loud noises of appreciation.

'Let me ask you a question,' he said, eventually, sitting back in the armchair with a sly look on his face. 'What are planning to do with your slice?'

'You know what I'm planning to do. How many times did I tell you? I'm gonna buy myself a motorcycle.'

'Here in Antwerp?'

'No, not here. There's a dealership in Brussels. I rang them. The guy didn't speak good English but he can get the model I want, the right colour and specs.'

'You rang the dealership,' said the Big Shilling quietly, then without warning he threw the lit cigar at Troy's face and yelled, 'you rang the fucking dealer!'

Troy was on his feet. Not to fight, but to get the burning cigar off of his shirt, which happened to be one of his favourites. He ducked suddenly as Shilling hurled the glass of liquor at him. The glass shattered against the wall behind him.

'You dumb punk,' shouted Shilling, and even from three yards away hot spittle flecked Troy's face.

'What did I tell you, eh, about not attracting attention? What did I fucking tell you, hey? The cops are looking for an ace motorcycle rider in connection with the killing of the Greek, and you rang a fucking motorcycle dealer and ordered a fifty-thousand euro BMW a couple of days before the hit! Has it occurred to you, brainbox, eh, that the cops might just have contacted every dealer in the Low Countries and told them to pick up the phone if some fuckwit walks in with a big chunk of change to pay for the ritziest machine in the shop?'

And as the Big Shilling was saying all this, he was at the same time gripping American Troy by the throat with a hand of steel, and Troy was choking and gasping and wheezing, and utterly determined not to apologise for his stupidity whatever Shilling did to him.

But, as he crawled through eastern France in the misnamed Swift, American Troy kept telling himself that the Big Shilling – the animal - wasn't all that. He was an old guy, he'd lost his edge, he was too cautious, and anyway what was the point of being a fucking criminal if you didn't get to enjoy your ill-gotten gains? That's what he kept telling himself, but every time he imagined arriving at the dealership in Brussels, the cops were waiting for him in ambush, and he knew that the Big Shilling was right and he Troy was in the wrong. Not that he would have admitted it to anyone, of course, least of all BS. And what the fuck were the Low Countries, anyway? What did that even mean?

In any case, all of this was forgotten when, later that afternoon American Troy arrived at his destination. As he drove into downtown Geneva and saw the famous fountain in the lake lit up in the gathering, glittering darkness, American Troy was excited and looking forward to meeting up once more with his stern tutor. This was more like it! This was how he'd imagined it to be, back home in Hicksville, Illinois, the life of the international jewel thief or high class hitman. He remembered the poster on his bedroom wall, Steve McQueen leaping a bike across the barbed wire fence into neutral Switzerland. 'The Great Escape,' that was the name of the movie. That poster, Jesus, it summed up all the yearnings of his teenage years - the effortlessly cool McQueen, the motorcycle, the escape to freedom. And now he was here, in Switzerland, with the whole world at his goddamn feet.

With the help of his phone he found the Hotel Reichenbach without much difficulty, and not even the sight of the pension's rundown façade and its location in a side street in the blandest part of town could dent American Troy's mood. Shilling had chosen the place, and he'd chosen it for a reason. Keep a low profile for a couple of weeks, then they would start to enjoy themselves and spend some of that money they'd made. It's what real pro's would do, right? Right. He parked the Swift, planning the evening ahead. First, food. He'd grab a pizza and a couple of beers, then a Steve McQueen movie maybe. His stomach rumbled. There was something else that needed urgent attention as well. He hadn't jacked off for at least forty-eight hours. As he got out of the car, his balls ached as though in reprimand.

The hotel turned out to be tiny. There was a tiny reception desk in the tiny entrance hall, and a tiny dining room off to one side. A petite and terminally bored female receptionist asked to see his passport, and returned it after copying the passport's number on the registration card. Feeling like he was acting in a spy movie, American Troy recorded a false address along with his false name. (There would be no comebacks: Uncle Nathan was a true professional). The elevator was tiny as well, a notice warning in three languages that no more than two persons should ride the car at any one time. With his bags there was barely enough space for a single person, never mind two. American Troy checked the key card – room 51 – and thumbed button five. The narrow doors juddered closed and the elevator began its dilatory ascent.

The fifth floor proved to be at the top of the building, and room 51 appeared to be the only room on the floor. American Troy shouldered open the heavy fire door, entered the narrow lobby and slid the key card into the slot. Nothing happened. He examined the card, turned it upside down, and tried again. Nothing.

'Jesus fuck,' he muttered, contemplating having to ride down to reception to sort this shit out.

He wiped the card on his sleeve, tried again, and this time heard a click.

'At last,' he said, grinning as he pushed open the door. The smile faded when he saw his room for the night. It wasn't so much a room as a closet. Under the tiny window the single bed was pushed up tight against the radiator, the wardrobe was a rail with a couple of wire coat-hangers on it, and the bathroom door slid aside rather than opening regular style. Reminded unpleasantly of prison, American Troy swung his bags on the bed and decided to go out right away. Jacking off could wait.

He took the stairs, encountering no one on his way down. The reception desk was now deserted and the hotel completely silent. He noticed there was a painting of a waterfall, a mural he guessed you'd call it, decorating the back wall of the dining room. In the bay window was a single table with two chairs, on one of which sat a well-fed black cat licking something off of the table cloth. American Troy scowled at it: it was unhygienic, allowing animals where people ate.

He went out into the street. It was early evening and fairly quiet and the air was fresh and cool. He got his bearings, heading down the street in the direction of the pizza joint he'd passed on his way in. He was thinking about tonight's movie. Would it be McQueen or would it be the Coen Brothers? As he walked, his mind wandered. He began to mutter lines from one of his favourite movies: 'You don't understand the play you gifted me,' and, 'But what's in it for anyone? There's no manouvre.' Yeah, the trip to the woods – it was unforgettable. He pulled a face.

'Nah,' said American Troy to himself. He wasn't in the mood for drama. Maybe he'd watch a documentary instead, something educational. The Big Shilling was always going on at him to educate himself. Well, maybe he would.

He suddenly realised he had become the object of attention. Across the road, on the street corner, were a couple of hookers, and one of them was heading his way. Who knew Geneva's red light district would be so bland? No pimps hanging back, no ruined crack whores, no needles in the gutter, just a boring, respectable-looking neighbourhood and this big-ass black momma waddling over to check him out. She called to him in French.

'No thanks, sweetheart,' he told her as cool as you like.

'American?'

'As the day is long,' he said. That was how he thought of himself, even though he was part Brit and had spent a chunk of time in London, England: American as the day is long.

Now that the working girl was getting closer to him, ambling across the wide deserted street one hand on her swaying hip, he got a better look at her in the street lights and experienced a sudden repulsion. Her eyes were those of a crazy person, and he really didn't want to look too closely at the rest of her, at the sagging dugs and the stretch marks on those phat naked thighs. It must have shown in his face, this repulsion, for the crazy whore was suddenly cussing him out in African-accented French and waving her hands about, creating. He almost apologised, but another part of him took over, and he began yelling back at her, black or fucking not.

'Did you stop taking your meds, sister? You really shouldn't do that. You need to get some exercise, you're a slob. Who's looking after the grandkids? God-damned gilf.'

The unpleasant episode put him off his pizza. He stalked right past the restaurant, the smell of herbs, cheese and hot tomato sauce making him feel slightly nauseous. He was still within earshot of the two whores who sounded like they were hating on him for being American, the bitches. He looked back. The second whore hitched up her skirt and waved something at him.

'That's real nice,' said Troy to himself. 'A pre-op.'

It was a couple of streets before he was calm enough to even think about eating. He went into a crappy little bar and ordered a premium Italian beer. Seated at a table, his mind went to places he didn't care to go: to the little slut who'd cried rape and almost got him put away, to the disgust the merest thought of the actual physical act now produced in him, and, of course, to the Big Shilling, whom American Troy suspected knew all about his sexual hang-ups (though how, he did not know). Gradually the beer calmed him, and an empty stomach compelled him to go to the counter and order a ham and cheese toasted sandwich. He washed it down with another Peroni, and felt better, so much better that he decided to get a couple to drink back in the room. He relaxed and watched sportsball on TV for a while.

He returned to the hotel by the same route. It would have been humiliating to make a detour. Not that it mattered: the two hookers were gone.

'Goddamn animals,' he muttered, although part of him could now admire their feistiness. He could even laugh about it, a little. Man, she was ugly. He shuddered.

Back in his room with a couple of beers he fired up the laptop and, after some prevarication, finally ended up watching a documentary about these three dudes - brothers, triplets - who'd been separated at birth and sent to live with different families. They'd met up later in life, and it turned out they had all sorts of things in common, even though they'd had no contact at all. For instance, they'd all wrestled in school, they had the same favourite colours, brand of cigarette, beer, and what not, and not only that but their expressions, their gestures were all exactly the same as well. Also, each of them had suffered from depression, and some of them (he was a little confused as to which brother was which by now) had spent time in institutions. It was kinda fascinating.

But what had started out as heart-warming now turned darker. One of the dudes took his own life, and the other two found out the adoption agency was hiding dark secrets about their past. That was when American Troy thought he'd stopped watching. Yeah, because by now, he was pretty drunk. Surprising really, as he'd only had a couple of beers. He remembered visiting the bathroom and banging into the door, and getting undressed and getting tangled up in the clothes. Next thing he knew, he was in bed and the light was out. When he opened his eyes the bed stopped pitching. His body was hot and itchy, and he was feeling disquieted. It was unsettling to think that Nature was so powerful. He thought of the mountains, and countryside he had driven through that afternoon, and was glad he was back in the city.

Tuesday morning, and American Troy came down to breakfast to find the Big Shilling seated at the cat's table in the window.

'Here he is,' said the Big Shilling, 'here's my boy at last. Sleep well, did you? I slept like a log, like a log, I tell you. Man, that bed is comfortable. I've never stayed in a better room, never in my life have I stayed in a better room. Tuck in, tuck in. Help yourself to an egg, and I'll pour you some of this delicious coffee.'

American Troy looked doubtfully at the breakfast buffet. He'd slept badly in the narrow bed in the airless attic room. His eyes were sore and his stomach ached, and he was pretty certain he'd been bitten by something in the night. Scratching his arms, he regarded the unappetising selection of processed meat and curling cheese. The boiled eggs turned out to be as cold as the cold meats and the inferior croissants stale, and when he poured himself a glass of OJ he found that it had been watered. What a lousy dump! He looked around, hoping to see a staff member so that he could complain, but the dining room was as deserted as the reception desk. He drank the juice. He was thirsty and his mouth tasted foul even though he'd brushed his teeth and rinsed with mouthwash.

'You're not eating?' said Shilling, feigning surprise.

'I'll eat later,' he said as he sat down fastidiously at the tiny table by the dusty window. Shilling's plate was empty apart from crumbs and egg shells and crumpled paper napkins, but at least the tablecloth seemed clean.

'At McDonalds,' said Shilling.

'At McDonalds,' said American Troy. 'There's one a couple of blocks from here.'

'I know. That's why I chose this joint for you.'

Shilling winked at him and slid a fold of bank notes across the tablecloth with his forefinger. Troy took the cash, being careful to hide his pleasure at doing so.

'A thousand Swiss francs,' said Shilling, 'on account. On account of the fact I want you to smarten yourself up, eh, get yourself a haircut, a sharp suit, a new pair of shoes.'

'What's the occasion?'

'You'll see. This evening we meet at seven o'clock in the bar of the Hotel Mercurius, have drinks and dinner, and then we'll take it from there.'

Troy could no longer keep a straight face. He grinned at his mentor.

'You see?' said Shilling. 'You see? Watch and learn, my young friend, watch and learn.'

A small part of Troy wanted to apologise for being such a douche about the motorbike, but that small part was shouted down by another voice inside him, a loud, swaggering voice that said, laughing: no fucking way. He picked up his cup and tasted the coffee instead.

'Jesus,' he said. 'Worse than jail.'

'Something wrong with that coffee? You don't like it? Give it here, give it me. You're spoilt, eh, that's what you are, you're spoilt. If you'd grown up where I grew up you'd never refuse food and drink, never mind what it tastes like, hey?'

And with that the Big Shilling scooped up the egg shells from his plate, crushed them with his powerful fingers and dropped them into his mouth. Then he noisily crunched them up between his teeth and washed them down with Troy's coffee.

'You're something else, boss, you really are,' said Troy, glad that they were the only guests in the dining room: it was like feeding time at the zoo here. Pig like that in the prison chow hall and you'd straight away get a metal tray upside your head.

The Big Shilling, now that he'd swallowed the egg shells, was smiling lazily.

'I'm a Bimshire boy, that's what I am, eh? And if there's one thing a Bimshire boy is, it's a survivor. We're all survivors, us Bimshire boys. Out in the bush when I was on the run I've eaten worms and grubs and ants and termites, and drunk water from waterholes that were filled with crocodiles and buffalo shit. Oh yeah, I've eaten things that would turn your stomach, that would turn your stomach, eh?'

Troy pulled a face. His stomach had already turned. What the fuck was a Bimshire boy? That was a new one.

'I think I'll go up to the room,' he said, placing his hands on the arms of the chair.

'You think you'll do that, do you? Need a dump, do you? Got guts ache? Well, maybe you should lay off the grog for a few days. The dose makes the poison, as the wise man said. How the hell you survived in the joint I do not know. Well, don't be long. Before you drop off that hire car you can run me back to the Hotel Mercurius.'

'You're at the Hotel Mercurius?'

'What's the problem, my boy? No point both of us slumming it, eh? Besides, the money you're making, you can't afford a flash hotel. If you're paying five hundred francs a night plus drinks plus tips plus dinner, your hundred large isn't going to last very long, is it, hey? Not with the dollar being so weak.'

'I guess not,' said American Troy, ironically, thinking – but the dollar isn't weak at all.

The Big Shilling laughed at him. American Troy didn't care for it, but he said nothing – he needed the bathroom. Not for the first time with the Big Shilling, he had the impression that he was missing something, but couldn't for the life of him think what. But at least he finally had some cash.

It was snowing when American Troy caught the

train back into town after dropping off the hire car at Geneva airport. The sight of the falling snow lifted his spirits. He decided he'd have brunch at McDonalds. He was becoming something of a connoisseur of the variations in McDonalds European menus. He hoped the Swiss restaurants stocked the chocolate milk he'd got a taste for in Amsterdam. Or maybe he'd get a beer like they served at McDonalds in Paris. The prospect cheered him further.

'A Royale with extra bacon,' he said to himself, smirking.

He loved Tarantino. He loved all movies, but he loved Tarantino's the best, even more than the Coen brothers'. That's what he'd buy today with his Swiss francs, a black suit, a white shirt and a black tie, just like the ones Travolta wore in Pulp Fiction. Tarantino was cool in a geeky, autistic kind of way, but no one would ever be as cool as Travolta. American Troy put on his sunglasses. Even though it was snowing outside, he wore shades all the way to Geneva-Cornavin, the main station.

And so, at seven o'clock that evening, American Troy strode into the bar of the exclusive Hotel Mercurius wearing the brand new black suit, white shirt and skinny black tie that he'd purchased at the Globus department store. He was rocking a new hair style as well, and felt as sharp as a knife. He knew the Big Shilling was already there – he could hear his loud voice and raucous laughter from the far side of the lobby. Now he saw him, standing at the bar next to a couple of girls, and almost did a double take.

The Big Shilling had changed. He'd grown a couple of inches in stature, for one thing, and his faded ginger hair had been dyed brown, and there was a big diamond ring on the pinkie of his left hand. He was holding an empty martini glass and telling the pianist to play something, anything, by John Barry. The piano guy was looking kind of put out and so too was the mixologist behind the bar. Troy smirked: it was the Big Shilling Effect. BS put people's backs up, and he just didn't give a damn.

When he saw American Troy standing on the threshold in his new threads, the Big Shilling raised the glass to him and said, 'Looking the part, my boy, looking the part. Do you like my tuxedo? What do you reckon, do you like it, eh? It was made for me by the same geezer who makes them for James Bond, the exact same geezer who makes them for Daniel. Come here, my boy, come here and have a drink. Vodka martini, hey, you'll have vodka martini like me and the ladies. American Troy, meet Marianne and Marina. They're my present for you, my boy, my present for a job well done. They're going to drain you dry, so they tell me, eh ladies, you're going to drain the life out of him, hey?'

American Troy wasn't really listening. His ears were ringing and he felt a little nervy, but even so he couldn't help feasting his eyes on the two hookers, Marianne who was a voluptuous dirty blonde, and Marina who was lithe and athletic and aloof.

'Hi,' he said to them both, glad that he sounded game. But he felt unpleasantly apprehensive as well, and determined to hide the fact. The pianist began to play the theme from 'Born Free.'

'A martini,' cried the Big Shilling, 'a martini for our young friend!'

It was the beginning of one of the most memorable evenings of American Troy's young life. It was memorable because it was the first time he'd had full sex – and with not one girl but two. It was memorable because the Big Shilling spent most of the first part of the night telling everyone they met he had lifts in his shoes. And it was memorable because at the casino during the second part of the night, after they'd eaten dinner and Marianne and Marina had entertained American Troy, the Big Shilling bet and lost three quarters of a million dollars at the roulette table. It was memorable too in other ways, but American Troy did his best not to think about that.

'Easy come, easy go,' said the Big Shilling as they drank the complimentary bottle of vintage Tattinger delivered to their table with the commiserations of the management. 'What goes around comes around. Another day, another dollar.'

'I can't believe you just did that,' said American Troy, weakly. He was drunk and slurring.

'Seeing is believing.'

'Seven hundred and fifty grand!'

The Big Shilling wasn't even fazed. 'Peanuts,' he said, 'small change.'

Loose-necked, Troy tried to focus on him. 'You had a phone call? You had a phone call?'

BS had said there would be a phone call, a phone call from the Turk. He'd said that back in Antwerp.

The Big Shilling quaffed champagne. He'd drunk as much as Troy had but appeared to be entirely unaffected.

'I had a phone call, I had a phone call, eh? Tell me, how do you fancy getting on a plane in the morning and flying to Sofia, Bulgaria? Do you fancy that? I fancy that. I think that's what we'll do, eh? Go to Bulgaria, and initiate things further. See a man about a dog.'

The Big Shilling snapped his fingers at the waiter and yelled in French, 'Another bottle of champagne, if you please!'

'No more,' said Troy, 'no more for me. I don't want any more.'

'What's wrong with you, kid? Why are you squirming? Something wrong with your bottle?'

Troy sat still. He hadn't realised he'd been fidgeting. He was hot and sweaty and he didn't want to think about it.

'Nothing wrong with me, nothing,' he said, aggressively.

Initiate things further? What did that even mean?

The Big Shilling laughed at him. 'That's okay then.'

'You always laugh at me. Why? Why? Am I missing the joke?'

But American Troy didn't hang around for an answer. He lurched suddenly to his feet and staggered off in the direction of the toilets.

Was he bleeding? He thought he might be bleeding.

CHAPTER THREE

The following morning around about eleven, American Troy was woken by some kind of commotion. For a few seconds he didn't know where he was, then he remembered: he was in the smaller of the two bedrooms in the Big Shilling's suite at the five star Hotel Mercurius, Geneva.

He sat up in bed to get a handle on what was going on the other side of the bedroom door, and wished he hadn't. His head spun, and he felt so nauseous he thought was going to throw up. He lay down again, sweating, and closed his eyes, the room listing first one way, then the other. He didn't like the room, or the hotel. The Louis XVI décor reminded him of high tea at grandma's house in north London, of sugary cream cakes and pink icing.

'Oh man,' he said.

Now he thought about it, when they'd returned to the hotel from the casino there had been some kind of altercation in the glittering, mirrored lobby, although the details remained for the moment somewhat sketchy. At the edge of consciousness, just out of reach, there were other things, bad things, outrageous things, that Troy couldn't quite put his finger on either. He wrinkled his clammy forehead.

'Oh man,' he said, moaning. 'Fuck this shit.'

A door slammed and he heard the Big Shilling laughing. Then the bedroom door burst open.

'Out of bed, my boy, it's time to go,' Shilling shouted. 'I've been asked to leave, I've been asked to leave, very politely but firmly in the Swiss manner, to pack my bags and get out of here and never darken their doors again.' Shilling laughed raucously and ripped open the curtains. 'Stop groaning, kid, and get your sorry arse out of that pit and into the shower.'

Troy sat up in bed again, squinting horribly against the glaring daylight.

'They threw us out?'

'Ah, what can you do,' said Shilling, shrugging his shoulders, 'what can you do, eh? The assistant manager was here, the house detective, two or three security men, a couple of burly kitchen porters. I'd've fought every last one of the bastards, taken them on all at once, but what would have happened, hey? I'd've been down the road in a black maria, and the cops would want to know exactly what the Big Shilling was doing living it large at the Hotel Mercurius. No, no, no, I've bigger fish to fry.'

Shilling hadn't finished talking, or rather shouting, but American Troy had done listening. He flung back the covers and raced into the bathroom where, unable to raise the toilet lid in time, he was spectacularly sick in the bathtub.

Tearful and retching and seated on the cool marble floor, he heard Shilling tell him, 'You're disgusting, boy, a disgusting drunk, make sure you clean that up. Don't you dare leave that for the maid to find, don't you dare leave it.'

'I'll clean it up, all right?'

'You'd better, boy. Don't you dare leave it. I'm warning you. If you leave it, I'll drown you in that bathtub, drown you, you skunk.'

'Enough, Jesus.'

'Maybe I should leave you here, maybe I should do that, eh? Leave you here with your puke. Maybe you're just a waste of space, boy, eh? Maybe you're surplus to requirements.'

'All right then, leave me.'

'Maybe I will, maybe I will at that.'

The foulness welled up again and Troy hurriedly stuck his head over the side of the bath and puked again and again and again.

When it was over and he had recovered somewhat he cleaned the bath. It was complicated. He ran the cold tap and that got rid of some of the filth, but by no means all of it. In the end he was forced to employ the small plastic trash can. He took off the lid and removed the liner and scooped up the solids and deposited them in the toilet.

Three quarters of an hour later, a ghost-like American Troy, showered but dressed in last night's clothes and underwear, left the Paracelsus suite along with a relaxed Big Shilling. In the wide hallway, the house detective and two security men with walkie-talkies patiently awaited their departure. There was a chambermaid waiting there as well, a diminutive Filipina with a cart. The Big Shilling shook everyone's hand in turn, saying how much he'd enjoyed his stay and how he'd recommend the hotel to all his friends and that there were no hard feelings, no hard feelings at all.

He and American Troy, who was green around the gills and bleary eyed and feeling empty inside, were approaching the elevator when Shilling suddenly turned back and insisted, with some gallantry and charm, that the chambermaid accept as a gift his diamond ring, on account of the state of the bathroom. She kept refusing and Shilling told her then in that case he wasn't leaving, and it was only when the detective gave her the nod that she took the ring, her glowing face a mixture of girlish delight and acute embarrassment.

'Can we go now?' asked American Troy who was both angry and embarrassed.

'Of course,' said the Big Shilling, brightly.

In the palatial lobby, the security detail escorted American Troy and the Big Shilling out to the waiting cab, and as Shilling told the cabbie to take them to Troy's hotel, the Reichenbach, Troy glanced back up the steps at the golden statue of Hermes and suddenly remembered the night before when they'd returned to the hotel, the Big Shilling running around the fountain chasing the night manager. Why, he could not recall.

He got into the cab gratefully and sank into the seat, a hand shielding his eyes. It was a cold, cloudless morning and the glaring sun had barely any warmth. To American Troy the world seemed intrusive, noises too loud, things too real. He closed his eyes, grateful that Shilling wasn't presently yapping, and for a few minutes managed to fall into a doze. As he dozed, other memories of the night before returned to him, unpleasant memories that caused his face to heat up and almost made him groan with self-pity and shame. He took a deep breath and sat up straight, trying not to think of Marina and Marianne, but of course he could think of nothing else. He felt nauseous, both physically and – what was this? - morally. That had to be a first, didn't it? But come to think of it, no, no it wasn't. American Troy shifted in his seat. He felt dirty, wanted to change his clothes, particularly his boxers. Again he was forced to sit up straight, determined that he wasn't going to puke again. Soon, they got caught in traffic, and the Big Shilling, without fuss, cracked open a half bottle of cognac and pressed it on American Troy who by now was wearing sunglasses and belching repeatedly into his fist. The cab crawled along, stopping and starting. The motion was making Troy feel even worse.

'No.'

'It'll set up for the day, my boy, take a slug of this and you'll be as right as rain, hey?'

'I couldn't.'

'You can. Drink it. Do it, go on, or I'll stop the cab and you can walk.'

Troy drank the brandy and was surprised, if not exactly delighted, when a few moments later he began to feel slightly better.

The Big Shilling said, 'You know what? That's a good idea, I think I'll join you. Nothing like a heart-starter the morning after a big night out, eh?'

'How come you're not hungover? You drank more than I did.'

'Will power,' BS explained. 'Will power, unity, and harmonious development. Even if 'it' becomes drunk, 'I' do not become drunk."

'Fuck,' said American Troy, moaning. What did that even mean? Why did he speak in riddles?

'If you can't do the time,' said Shilling, archly. 'If you can't do the time, eh? Hey?'

Then he announced there had been a change of plan. They weren't flying to Bulgaria from Geneva, but from Zurich airport.

'Don't worry, my boy, don't worry about a thing, I've booked the tickets myself, I booked them my-self while you were stinking in your pit, and had our boarding passes printed as well.'

'I would've done it, if you'd asked me,' said American Troy, peeved.

'You were in no state to do it, no state at all, eh? You were as drunk as a skunk, drunk as a stinking, reeking, useless skunk.'

Angered, Troy put his hands over his ears and closed his eyes. 'Enough already.'

The Big Shilling laughed at him.

'You'll get no sympathy from me, eh? If you can't do the time, don't do the crime, that's what they say, hey? If you can't do the time, don't do the crime. You shouldn't drink if you don't have the stomach for it. Did I ever tell you about my buddy, Garth? No? I thought I did. Now Garth, he could drink. Man, could Garth hold his liquor. Dead now, stabbed, or shot, I forget which. No, I tell a lie. I tell a lie. Garth died in the throes of passion. That's right, so he did, eh. Poor old Garth. A woman got him in the end, eh.'

American Troy bristled. Was he insinuating something? Did this mean Shilling knew he'd been a virgin up until last night? Further shameful recollections came to mind, of interruptions when he thought he was alone in the Amsterdam apartment, and Shilling one time bursting into his bedroom. But he was mouthing off about something else now, so maybe Troy had imagined it. He turned to look at the little guy, wishing to Christ he'd shut the fuck up. It was a vain hope. On and on it went, the Big Shilling monologue, his endless confabulations. Now that Troy looked at him, he was like a force of nature that morning, brimming over with vitality, a compact body of highly-concentrated energy. American Troy curled up in the corner of the seat and wearily covered his ears with his coat collar. The Big Shilling eventually got the message.

'Not interested, eh?'

He shut up, for two seconds, then started quizzing

the cab driver about what he termed 'the taxi game' in Geneva. For instance, who were the best tippers? American Troy groaned and was glad that they were approaching the street with his hotel.

'It's over there,' he said. 'Up there, on the other side.'

'The man's a professional,' objected the Big Shilling. 'Don't insult him. This is his town, he knows where your poxy hotel is. And don't be long. We have a train to catch.'

'I'll be as long as I need to be.'

'Sure, take your time. Take your time but hurry up. And get changed. Get out of that suit, it stinks. And change your underwear as well, eh.'

Muttering to himself, American Troy got out of the cab as soon as it stopped moving and slammed the door on the Big Shilling's mocking laughter.

It was an early evening flight, departing at 1820.

American Troy spent much of the day dozing, on trains, in cabs, and accepting nips of cognac from the Big Shilling who seemed entirely unaffected not only by their night on the town, but also the loss of most of their money. Yes, Troy had eventually remembered what had happened at the roulette wheel, and when he did his heart rate accelerated and his face burned at the memory of it. All their money, all of it, gone! And not in stages, not in multiple bets, in one fucking go, one single stupid gigantic fucking bet! The guy was a fucking lunatic.

The idea that he should cut his losses and split

crossed Troy's mind, but only briefly. What would he do on his lonesome? Not much, that was the answer. Looked like he was stuck.

In the air-side bar at Zurich airport, after they'd checked in and passed without difficulty through security, the lunatic showed Troy the new passport that matched his change in hair colour. It was an Irish passport in the name of Robert Irwin. American Troy was travelling on British papers, the ones he'd been using since they'd left Antwerp.

'It's not one of your Uncle Nathan's,' Shilling explained, speaking much more quietly than he had all day. 'I had it stashed in Geneva, along with my James Bond dinner jacket and one or two other things, like hair dye, and a pair of patent leather shoes.'

'The ones with the short-ass lifts,' American Troy heard himself say.

He simply couldn't help himself. How many fights had he gotten himself into with his smart mouth? It was the money, the loss of the goddamned money that made him say it. Fortunately, the Big Shilling appeared not to have heard, and the little flutter of fear American Troy had experienced after speaking abated.

'I have stashes all over the world, eh, so I can change identity as often as I like,' the Big Shilling was saying, 'the way normies change their ringtones.'

Surrounded as they were by normies of various kinds glomming on their phones, the simile was kind of amusing, and American Troy, in a small way, began to pay attention to what the Big Shilling was saying. This was why he was with the man, right? To learn the ways of the international outlaw, even if the ways of this particular outlaw were more often than not unfathomable. Shilling looked him in the eye, and pointed a stubby finger at him.

'I want you to pull yourself together, eh? No more getting drunk, going gambling, and chasing whores.'

Troy was about to blow up at this blatant misrepresentation of the facts, but he managed to control himself. Instead, he merely nodded and held Shilling's eye.

'Okay.'

'That's good, eh, that's real good, looking me in the eye like that,' said the Big Shilling, almost whispering. 'That's what I want you to do when we meet the Turk. Look him in the eye when you speak to him, and smile. Be very polite to him, very polite, he's an important man, in his own world he is a very important man. There will be two meetings, two meetings most likely. The first will be social. He'll congratulate us on the successful operation, and since he hasn't met you before he'll ask about your family, your interests, what sports you're into, shit like that, eh?'

'He'll ask about my family, and sports?'

American Troy felt deflated. What was this? The Boy Scouts? They were supposed to be international outlaws, for Christ's sake.

'That's right,' Shilling continued in the same quiet

tone, 'it's the way these Turks do business, eh? Before they get down to the real business, they ask about family, get to know you, size you up. The first meeting is social, the second will be business. He may not want you at the second meeting, but I want you at the second meeting, so I'll tell him, eh, that you are my apprentice, and you're not going to learn the business unless you're allowed to sit at the top table with the senior men, hey?'

'Learn the business.'

'That's right.'

'Is that what I'm doing?'

'You tell me, kid. You tell me. What are you doing? What are you doing, eh? This isn't what you expected? This isn't in the script they sent you, eh?'

American Troy held Shilling's gaze but found no clues there. He didn't know what to say, so he said the first thing that came into his head.

'This guy's a Muslim, right?'

'This guy? This guy? Never refer to him as 'this guy,' never, hey? His name is Ahmet, and you will address him as Ahmet Bey.'

'Ahmet Bey.'

'That's right, it's very polite. You're just a punk kid and he's a gentleman of some standing, and the Turks respect their elders, eh? They respect their elders, unlike some people I could name. In return he won't call you Troy, eh, he'll call you Mr Troy, Mr Troy.'

'Mr Troy?'

'Yes, it's the way the Turks speak, hey? And I'm

way ahead of you, eh? You're thinking, should I tell Ahmet Bey I'm a Jew, and my old man's serving thirty years in the hole for a five hundred million dollar Ponzi scheme, eh? Well no, it's probably best not to do that. Ahmet Bey has a real downer on Hebrews. Tell him instead, eh, about your step-father the motorcycle nut, only don't call him step-dad, call him dad.'

'That way I can talk about motorbikes,' said Troy with a touch of sarcasm.

'Exactly. Exactly that. Now you're getting the idea, hey?'

'One thing.'

'What's that?'

'You remember. I'm not a Jew. I'm Italian-American.'

The Big Shilling appeared surprised. 'I thought you were a Brit.'

'I'm not a Brit, I'm an American.'

'So your dad and your Uncle Nathan aren't Jewish.'

'You know they're not.'

'I do?'

'That's right. I told you. They pretend they're Jewish, but they're not, they're of Italian heritage.'

The Big Shilling himself was pretending to look puzzled. 'Remind me again why they'd do that.'

Controlling his temper with difficulty, American Troy said, 'You know why. I told you why.'

'What about your mom. Is she Jewish?'

'No, she's not Jewish either.'

'Is she British?'

'She used to be British, before she moved to the States when she was a kid.'

'Crypto-Jewish,' declared the Big Shilling.

American Troy didn't like the sound of that word, or the way that Shilling had said it, with relish, kind of. It was Troy's opinion that the Big Shilling, like most old school white guys, was a racist, usually on the quiet, but not so quiet this time. Troy was summoning up the effort to confront him on this, but the effort to do so was slow in coming, what with the hangover and him feeling so tired.

'Fuck this,' he murmured.

'Ah!' cried Shilling, suddenly. 'I remember now. You did tell me. They're Eye-talians.'

'Italian, not Eye-talian.'

'Italian, right. You sure?'

'Yeah.'

'You sure you're mom's Italian?'

'Yes.'

'She's not Egyptian, your mom?'

'Nope,' said Troy, who could see where this was going. 'She's not an Egyptian mummy.'

'Sharp,' said Shilling, 'mummy's boy is smart.'

'I'm no mummy's boy. The fuck are you saying?'

'Take it easy, Sparky, take it easy, eh? And keep your voice down, you're annoying the normies with your potty mouth.'

American Troy took a big gulp of air and tried to calm down. He said, 'What is it with you and Egypt? You're always talking about Egypt, but you never say why.'

It was indeed true that the Big Shilling had a thing about Egypt. In Amsterdam, he'd insisted American Troy accompany him to an exhibition at some museum to look at mummies and strange artefacts depicting animal-headed gods. It had bored Troy, bored him, and at the same time, unsettled him, for reasons he didn't care to understand. Ancient Egypt was real weird.

'Egypt? You want to know about Egypt?'

'Not really.'

'Then I won't tell you.'

And so, of course, American Troy did immediately want to know about Egypt.

'Oh man, you're the limit.'

'The lament of eternity,' said his inscrutable mentor.

'Why can't you just be straight with me? Why can't you just tell me what you want I should know?'

The Big Shilling looked at him across the little circular table in the air-side bar at Zurich airport, and topped up their glasses with a new half-bottle which he uncapped, surreptitiously, beneath the table. They were drinking brandy, like they had been for much of the day, and for a moment American Troy thought nothing of it, that the insufferable assassin was topping up their glasses with a new half-bottle. But then it struck him: where had the bottle come from (BS hadn't bought anything at the perfumed duty-free), and how had he got it through security? Troy picked up his glass and toasted the senior man, only half-ironically.

'See?' said the Big Shilling.

'Kinda.'

'It's all good, man.'

There was a beat before the kid picked up the reference: they were back to the Jewish thing.

'You do remember,' he said. 'It's all good man: Saul Goodman.'

'Oh I remember all right. Another one of your stupid TV movie shows.'

'Yeah, well that's not where Nathan got it from. It's from a Sly Ritchie movie. Doug the Ted, he wasn't Jewish either.'

'You and your movies, eh? You and your movies.'

'What? What's wrong with movies?'

'Turn off the TV. Turn off the TV.'

'That's it? You want me to turn off the TV?'

'Turn off the TV. Turn off the internet. Turn off everything.'

'The world's changed.'

'Nothing changes, kid. Everything stays the same. You, for instance. You never change, eh? The thing about you that never changes is that you're always changing.'

American Troy had the uncomfortable feeling that the Big Shilling was about to bring up the subject of sex, and so he was glad, kind of, when BS returned to the subject of Troy's mother.

'Tell me about her.'

'What for?'

'Tell me about her,' said the Big Shilling, forcefully.

There was an announcement: any further passengers for London Heathrow should make their way immediately to the gate, which gave Troy a few moments to collect himself.

'What's to tell? She's my mom. She's kinda feisty, you know?'

'She's got a smart mouth.'

'Sometimes, yeah.'

'Your step-dad, he's a doormat, is he? She walks all over him? Or does he black her eye for her now and then? Is that what he does, hey?'

Troy stared at the diminutive assassin. How the hell did he know that?

'Well?'

Troy nodded.

'What was she like as a kid? What did she like to do?'

'What? Christ, I don't know. She's was athletic, a runner, yeah, and er . . . gymnastics. And horse-riding. Yeah, her old man bought her a horse.'

'Her old man, what did he do?'

'I told you. He was a thief, a house-breaker but high class.'

'What happened to him?'

'I told you. Some guy shot him.'

'Right, a home-owner, some normie with a gun. He killed your grandpa.'

'You do remember. Then they moved to the city. My mom was sixteen. They moved into an apartment in the same building as my dad.'

'First love, eh? First love.'

American Troy kept a straight face. The Big Shilling regarded him with a half-smile.

'Your dad, the conman, the unsuccessful conman.'

'Yeah,' said Troy, dolefully. 'The one and only.'

'You don't get along with your dad, but you do get along with your step-dad, right?'

'I guess.'

'Don't guess, kid: decide.'

'Yeah, we get along.'

'The outlaw motorcycle gang-member.'

'When he was a kid, yeah,' said Troy, feeling he was on safer ground now. 'He did a three stretch and it straightened him out. He got clean, went straight.'

'Stopped dealing drugs, started dealing motor-bikes, and guns.'

'That's right, I told you. There's a range out back. I've been shooting guns since junior high.'

'Finish your drink, kid,' the Big Shilling told him. 'This is us.'

American Troy glanced at the departures board: Sofia – Gate 12.

'What's the hurry?' Troy asked. 'Tell me about your family. Tell me about your old man and your mom.'

'My old man?' said Shilling, standing. 'He was a conchie.'

'What's that?' asked Troy, getting up as well. 'Like a beachcomber, back in Bimshire, collecting shells and shit?'

'A conchie? You know what a conchie is. A conchie is a man with a conscience.'

'A conscience?'

'Yeah, he had a conscience. He was a conscientious objector. He objected to the war, eh, to killing, refused to serve in His Majesty's forces. What could you expect, though, eh? The man was a commie, completely gaga.'

'You don't take after him then,' said American Troy without thinking.

The Big Shilling laughed indulgently. He pointed a finger at Troy, saying, 'You, you.'

It was a relatively short flight from Zurich, Switzerland to Sofia, the capital of Bulgaria, and since the aircraft wasn't crowded, the kid was able to sit apart from his mentor. It was a relief not to have to deal with him for a while. He even managed to get an hour's sleep. The plane was on its final approach to land and the seatbelt sign had just come on when the Big Shilling leaned across the aisle and told American Troy they'd be meeting his namesake.

'South African Troy, have I ever mentioned him, eh?'

'I think you might have done,' said American Troy, sarcastically.

This time, for some reason known only to himself, the Big Shilling didn't let it go. 'Watch your step, boy. One more crack like that and you'll find yourself flat on your back, picking pieces of broken teeth out of your mouth.'

Automatically, American Troy lowered his gaze, and hated himself when he realised what he'd done. Looking down was for bitches. Angrily, he looked the Big Shilling right in the eye, and said, 'You must have told me a thousand freaking times how you and he smuggled cigarettes and hash across the Mediterranean Ocean to Spain.'

'That's right, you remembered,' said the Big Shilling, with feigned amusement. 'Great days, great days. Well, South African Troy's shacked up with a Bulgarian girl, and he'll be meeting us at the airport with a car and some supplies.'

The Big Shilling and American Troy didn't speak much after that, not until they'd cleared passport control without any problems and collected their bags. South African Troy was waiting for them among the throng of touts ('Taxi, sir, very good price?') and travel reps, land-side.

He was dressed in the black trousers and white shirt with epaulettes of an off-duty pilot. He greeted the Big Shilling with a curt nod of the head, and ignored American Troy entirely. Not that Troy minded too much. His head still ached and the clamour of the arrivals hall was making him wince. It reminded him somehow of leaving county jail for the big house. He trailed after the other two, seeing his namesake but not taking any interest in him, all the way to the wall of glass and the automatic doors. All around, the signs were in Russian script and not a single person was speaking English, which only served to alienate him further. Outside, there were taxis and buses with their engines running and the night air was cold and stank of diesel fumes, but it was kind of refreshing nonetheless after the canned air of the airplane. They crossed the busy approach road and entered a sparsely-lit car park. Troy began to feel better.

It turned out that the car South African Troy had brought to meet them was a Mercedes G Wagon, and the supplies were warm clothes, a couple of Glock 17s, an AK-47 and a Mossberg shotgun.

'Jesus,' said American Troy when he saw the armoury hidden under a blanket in the back of the truck. Even though he turned grinning at them, the older men ignored him. Put out, Troy straightened his face.

South African Troy wasn't much taller than Troy himself, who was five seven, but the South African was as wide as he was high, and his wrists were as thick as Troy's thighs. Troy tried to follow the conversation Shilling and South African Troy were now having, standing by the Mercedes with the doors open wide, but the slang and the South African's accent were so impenetrable that he only understood one word in four. He got the strangest impression that his namesake was at once very strong but also kind of defeated. But then he suffered a violent sneezing fit, the result of breathing the canned air on the plane, and the insight was immediately forgotten. By the time he'd recovered, South African Troy had disappeared and the Big Shilling had changed into a padded coat and heavy boots.

'Cold where we're going, eh,' he said, 'up in the mountains.'

'Not a problem,' said Troy, getting into the passenger seat of the big G Wagon. 'I don't feel the cold.'

The Big Shilling laughed. 'Real hard case,' he said, 'a real hard case: I don't feel the cold. But that's good. That is good. Hard case is what we need, it's exactly what we need from now on. There'll be a lot of hard cases at the dog fight.'

'Dog fight?'

'Dog fight. You trying to sound cool about it?'

'Me? I am cool.'

'Sure you are, kid, you're stone cold, you're Mike TV.'

'Neat ride.'

'You approve do you? You approve of my G Wagon, hey?'

'It'll do.'

'It'll do the kid says. It'll do.'

'What's this?'

'What does it look like?'

'Like a map.'

'Can you read a map?'

'I can read a map,' said American Troy, feeling a little stupid.

They'd dumped their phones in Zurich, the Big Shilling having first of all wiped their memory, and travelled to Bulgaria on false papers. No one knew they were here, they couldn't be traced: no phones, no satnav.

'Old school,' he said.

'The old ways are the best,' pronounced the Big Shilling. 'Direct us to the motorway.'

On relatively good roads in the powerful Mercedes

the journey time was less than an hour. When he wasn't looking at the map, American Troy closed his eyes and pretended to sleep, but really he was thinking about the guns on the seat behind him. He wanted to reach round and pick them up and examine them one by one. Once they were on the freeway, the Big Shilling turned on the radio, found a station playing traditional folk music and hummed along with the strange tunes. It was irritating, and was probably meant to be, but American Troy would not give the little man the satisfaction of complaining. He sucked it up instead, and fantasized about blowing the Big Shilling's head off with the Mossberg, which was strangely calming. American Troy sat there, smirking to himself and quietly fuming at the folk tunes.

Their destination was a hotel near Kostenets, a spa town about 70 kilometres from Sofia, at the foot of the Rila mountains. American Troy had the impression that they had never left Switzerland. The hotel had the same steeply pitched roof as the buildings he'd seen in Geneva and Zurich, and there was an icy dry wind blowing off the mountains that irritated the sinuses. They were expected. In the lobby of the hotel, which was panelled with wood and decorated with the mounted heads of grey wolves, brown bears and mountain goats, one of Ahmet Bey's men greeted them respectfully and said that Ahmet Bey would be pleased if they would join him for dinner. It was by now late, and Troy was hungry. He wondered what sort of food they served here. He was pretty sure it wouldn't be hamburger. Next to reception were photos of saunas, plunge pools and treatment rooms. The smiling receptionist, an attractive blonde, gave Ahmet Bey's man the keys.

'Please tell Mr Ahmet that we will join him directly,' said the Big Shilling, accepting the keys in turn.

American Troy's room was right next to Shilling's on the top floor, but the place was nothing like the Hotel Reichenbach or the Mercurius. No, this place was like a cross between a hunting lodge and a high-end spa, no doubt owned by the local mob, thought Troy. He was feeling excited. He had an idea what the job was going to be. He had the idea that the target was going to be the Russian, the top man himself. There was a knock at the door and Shilling let himself in. He carried a gun.

'Here, kid, a present for you.'

'Nice.'

'You ready?'

'I'm always ready.'

They rode down together in the old-style elevator – it had concertina doors - both of them wearing the Glocks in holsters on their belts.

'We're not going to shoot our way out of here, are we?' Troy asked.

'Just for show, my boy, just for show. Around here, everyone carries a piece. Relax.'

'I am relaxed.'

'You sure?'

'Sure I'm sure.'

The Big Shilling nodded. 'Just so long as you're sure. No TV for you tonight, and no internet either.'

'Real life, you mean?'

The Big Shilling laughed appreciatively before imparting a few last minute words of instruction.

'Remember yourself. Keep your wits about you at all times. Things may not be what they appear to be. Keep your wits about you but don't make a show of it, eh?'

'Okay.'

When they entered the dim, overheated pine-panelled dining room that stank of cigarettes, it was almost midnight and Ahmet Bey's table was the only one still occupied. The Turk turned out to be singularly unimpressive. If American Troy hadn't known better, he might have taken Ahmet Bey to be the head waiter, resting his aching feet after another interminable day of split shifts and short tips. He was a worn-out little dude with a paunch, a salt and pepper moustache, and a pitted nose that was two sizes too big for his face. But Troy followed the Big Shilling's instructions to the letter: he kept his wits about him, held eye contact, smiled, and was impeccably polite.

'Merhaba, Ahmet Bey,' he said as per Shilling's prompting.

'Merhaba, my American friend.'

Ahmet Bey spoke some English, but he mainly communicated through an interpreter who hovered deferentially beside him and never made eye contact with anyone. American Troy decided this was a blatant ploy, and that the Turk's English was much better than he let on.

Once the introductions were over, they sat down, and dishes of food appeared from the kitchen almost immediately. Troy was still feeling the effects of last night's hangover and took only the smallest of portions from each offering, the Big Shilling having warned him that it would be taken amiss if he left anything on his plate. Troy was relieved to discover that no alcohol was to be served, and throughout the meal he drank the local sparkling mineral water which he found agreed with his delicate stomach.

He made his only faux pas when coffee was brought and he refused a cup. The Big Shilling glared at him and Troy quickly changed his mind. Ahmet Bey beamed, and lit his fourth cigarette of the meal.

'You like dog fight?' the Turk asked him.

Troy wondered what was the best reply. 'I am looking forward to experiencing it, sir.'

'Tonight you will see dog fight dog, dog fight wolfs, dog fight bear,' said Ahmet Bey, raising his cup of strong black coffee in salute.

Troy did the same with his cup and took a sip of coffee. It was so strong it was like smoking a cheap Havana. His heart accelerated and sweat dribbled between his shoulder blades, but suddenly, looking round the smoky room, he decided he'd never been as happy as he was now. So this was real life, was it? Real life at the top table with the senior men. Yep, this is where he belonged, no doubt about it.

He turned, and smirked at the Big Shilling, who nodded sagely, his eyes animal-like and depthless.

CHAPTER FOUR

On the bus that was taking them, the Turks and a whole lot of others to the dog fight, American Troy, eager for congratulations, asked the Big Shilling how he'd performed at dinner. By now it was after two in the morning.

'You did swell, my boy, you did just swell,' said the Big Shilling, laughing.

'What are you laughing at?'

Shilling threw back his head and laughed some more.

'Tell me, you bastard.'

'All right, I'll tell you, eh. When you excused your-self very politely, eh, and went to the can, eh, after you'd asked him if he was the owner of the hotel, Ahmet Bey said to me that you were a good boy and a talented motorcycle rider who's won a dozen races, but that he could not understand why you hadn't mentioned the fact your real father was in jail in America, and wouldn't get out until he's 77 years' old. He thought that very strange, and a little bit disappointing.'

'You mean he knew?'

'Of course he knew. It wouldn't surprise me, eh, if he hasn't seen your juvie record, and knows about how you tried to burn down that kid Boozer's house after he called you a faggot.'

'You bastard, you knew he knew all along,' said Troy.

Shilling just laughed. It was a grating laugh, and very, very loud, the laugh of a man who didn't care what other men thought of him.

'My boy, you've a lot to learn, you have got a lot to learn, hey?'

'Fuck you, man. I'm not your boy.'

'Hey, just remember who you're talking to. It's, fuck you, boss, remember? Fuck you, boss,' said the Big Shilling and laughed even more raucously than before.

American Troy spent the rest of the journey with folded arms, staring sourly at the darkened window beside him, listening to the Big Shilling laughing and joking with the Turks and the other passengers, most of whom seemed to be Bulgarian. All he'd wanted was a little praise. He reckoned he'd done okay at the dinner. In fact, looking back, he knew he'd done okay. Shilling was just messing with him.

Ahmet Bey didn't own the hotel. It was owned by Hylic Malamikov, the philanthropist and financier. Troy had heard of Malamikov, who hadn't? The Turk explained that the billionaire had bought the hotel off of the communists, and that it was the first privately owned hotel in Bulgaria. Then Shilling had chipped in when Troy had said he'd thought the place was owned by the mob: what makes you think the communist party isn't the mob? When the comment was translated, Ahmet Bey had laughed, but not unkindly.

Right after that the Turk had asked about Troy's time in prison, not county, but the pen. Had American Troy joined a gang, such as the Aryan Brotherhood? No, he had not, he'd done his time as an independent. He'd explained that he despised the AB and all racists. Ahmet Bey had nodded. Maybe that was when he'd expected Troy to tell him about his old man. As Italian-Americans he'd probably expected Troy to tell him he'd been taken under the wing of a mafia shot-caller. But what did it matter, anyway?

The bus slowed down and took a right off the highway.

'Nearly there,' said the Big Shilling. 'Nearly there.'

The bus took another turn, to the left, and the ride deteriorated as the driver accelerated along a dirt road. Someone began to sing. Other voices joined in and the men began to clap rhythmically. The song sounded like the ones Shilling had been playing in the G Wagon. Troy didn't care for it. It made him feel alienated, an American far from home, amongst strangers. He was glad when one of the men called for quiet and the singing stopped.

'Listen,' said the Big Shilling.

'What for? I can't hear anything.'

'Shut up and listen.'

'What?'

'There.'

Now he heard it, American Troy's annoyance evaporated. They'd arrived at the venue for the dog fight, an abandoned moonlit farmstead in the foothills of the Balkan mountains. Even before the bus had come to a stop at the end of the rutted farm track, American Troy could hear wolves howling, and the hairs on the back of his neck stood on end, an expectant grin spreading across his face that he only half-succeeded in concealing. It felt good to be alive, it felt good to be here, even if it was far from the city. The men were singing and clapping again, now that they'd heard the voices of the wolves. He looked around at the eager piratical faces.

Everyone got off the bus. Troy was pleased to be out in the fresh air again, for the bus had become unpleasantly filled with smoke from the cigarettes just about everyone seemed to use. Ahmet Bey and his entourage appeared beside them, and flashlights were produced to guide the party towards the venue. The muddy, rock-strewn path wound downhill behind the farmhouse, and at the bottom of the slope behind a high stone wall was a recently constructed metal-clad barn. As they got closer, the noise of the howling wolves and barking dogs reached a crescendo, and American Troy's heart rate accelerated. He was reminded of an old Bond film, with that guy Connery not Roger Moore, a gypsy encampment, girls fighting. 'From Russia,' that was it. Now, men dressed in high boots and brightly-coloured shirts hauled open the barn doors, revealing the dimly-lit interior. American Troy and the Big Shilling followed Ahmet Bey inside.

They weren't the first to arrive. For a moment, Troy was startled to find himself confronted by a senior Bulgarian police officer in dress uniform, complete with medals. The grizzled cop broke into a massive smile and threw his arms wide. The guy reeked of garlic, liquor and cigarettes.

'Welcome, welcome, friends,' he boomed, 'please, please to come in.'

It took American Troy a few minutes to get his bearings. The crowd at the dog fight, just like a prison yard, was evidently divided along ethnic lines. The local Bulgarians had taken up their place on the right of the fighting cage. In front of the cage was a smaller but still numerous Russian contingent whose leader appeared to be a blond giant who held in one hand a litre bottle of vodka and in the other an enormous wad of bank notes. Ahmet Bey's party was greeted by a small group of fellow Turks who occupied the space on the left of the fighting cage.

There were two other things American Troy noted: that there were no women present, and that practically everyone was armed. The mountain Bulgars mainly carried shotguns slung over the shoulder, muzzle to the ground. The Russians toted AKs. The Turks, like American Troy and the Big

Shilling, wore pistols, apart from two big guys Troy took to be Ahmet Bey's chief bodyguards – from out of nowhere they'd produced a pair of M16s which they held at the port.

Troy stifled a sneeze. He sniffed mightily, and with his nasal passages now clear he caught an unpleasant whiff of the zoo: animal urine, and faeces, and damp fur. In spite of himself, an atavistic chill thrilled his body. It was an unexpected, disquieting feeling, exciting but unpleasant at the same time. The Big Shilling nodded to him the way a doting father might, knowing the excitement he was feeling. American Troy took a breath, got a grip on himself. He didn't want to look like a noob amongst all these hard cases.

But for the next half hour, American Troy experienced little more than growing weariness. There was much noise, much drinking, and many bets were laid, but nothing happened of any real interest to the kid. Even the Big Shilling, who'd returned from a chat with Ahmet Bey, was looking like maybe he'd rather be in bed sleeping. Then finally at long last, the barking which had died down rose to a pitch again, and a dog and a wolf were released into the cage from sliding iron doors. The Russians, the Bulgars and the Turks crowded in to watch, and Troy hardly had a glimpse of the fight which ended suddenly with a terrible whimper from the dog. The second bout was similarly a let-down. At the end of it, the Big Shilling thumped American Troy on the shoulder with the bottle of cognac, and indicated that he should follow him. Troy took the bottle out of Shilling's hand and drank. He wasn't drunk, he was feeling all right, trooping along behind Shilling.

Now this was more like it. No more grubbing about in the cheap seats!

He'd barely registered the gallery, because he'd been standing directly in front and beneath it. He followed the cat-like Big Shilling heavily up the ringing metal stairs. Gunmen and guards parted to allow them through, and they sat down on a row of wooden benches directly behind Ahmet Bey and the big blond Russian and their respective entourages.

'Ahmet Bey's Kangal is up next,' whispered the Big Shilling loudly in his ear, 'fighting the big Russian bloke's bear.'

'What's a Kangal?' asked Troy, taking another nip of brandy.

'It's a sheep dog, an Anatolian sheep dog.'

'A sheep dog?' asked Troy, taking another bite off the bottle. 'Against a bear?'

'Hey. Take it easy on the sauce,' the Big Shilling advised him.

Troy shrugged and handed over the cognac. 'I ain't drunk,' he said.

It didn't sound like a fair fight to American Troy. But then he had never seen a Kangal before, one of the largest shepherd dogs in the world, and there was not one dog but two.

The Kangals entered the arena first. From his

new vantage point, like sitting in the circle in one of those old time movie theatres, American Troy could see everything. The two dogs were magnificent, proud and fierce, aroused and ready for battle. Then the second iron door slid open and the bear lumbered into the arena to rousing cheers from the Russians. When the bear saw the dogs it stood on its hind legs, ten feet tall, and roared, and Troy was on his feet roaring as well along with everyone else.

He'd never seen anything like this, wild animals fighting for their lives, furious, wonderful, blood and spittle and fur flying, the red wide-open mouths, the sharp white teeth and flashing claws. This was real life all right, not the movies or the half-measure that satisfied normies. This was the way he felt cornering his Kawasaki at a hundred miles an hour in the wet, or beating some punk with a baseball bat who'd called him a bitch. This was how he would live his life, American Troy, or die trying, red in tooth and claw, like a fucking hero, not just some guy! He grabbed the Big Shilling and they stood there, swaying together, leaning first this way and then that to get the best view.

The bout went on for eight long minutes. The bear killed the smaller of the two dogs with a bite to the neck barely half way into the fight, but the second Kangal was indefatigable. Although terribly wounded it would not give in, and the bear, bitten and mauled, and trailing a hind leg that the first dog had ravaged, suddenly seemed to deflate, its energy spent, and the dog went in for the kill, tearing off the bear's nose before ripping at its throat, worrying the dying beast until it too keeled over, utterly exhausted, and died.

Troy was suddenly exhausted too. Utterly empty, he slumped down in his seat, overwhelmed by what he'd experienced, and, he had to admit, drunk.

Later, when he was in bed at Malamikov's hotel, trying to get to sleep, he remembered seeing the big blond Russian handing over a bundle of banknotes to Ahmet Bey's interpreter, and he remembered getting back on the bus as well and how the first light of dawn was showing in the eastern sky, but the journey itself back to the hotel was a blur, as though time had telescoped, and once Ahmet Bey had said his good nights and gone off to bed, American Troy unsteadily did the same, leaving the Big Shilling in the car park drinking raki with the exultant Turks and firing the Mossberg and the AK47 into the early morning sky. American Troy finally fell asleep.

He dreamt of the Big Shilling, back in Bimshire as a boy. The boy was out in the countryside, naked, smooth-skinned, red-haired. The boy entered the woods and began to morph into a strange creature, a faun with goat's legs and little horns that grew out of the hair on his head, a faun with staring eyes and a sinister, otherworldly smile.

American Troy woke with a start, but almost immediately fell asleep again.

The following afternoon at three o'clock, American Troy, irritable and hungover, arrived promptly at the hotel meeting room. As usual he was playing wingman to the ace big shot, and, also as usual, he was flying on automatic pilot. He followed the Big Shilling inside, sat down at the table, and waited.

The Big Shilling said little. He was sometimes like this, appearing to be moody and brooding, as though he were plotting and scheming. Troy closed his eyes and lounged in the chair. His lunch hadn't agreed with him, and he promised himself some real food sometime soon, a genuine American hamburger with fries and a milkshake. His stomach spoke in anticipation, and he scowled, shifting in his seat. He hated this backward country, and looked forward to leaving it as soon as possible. His disgust focused on the waitress who had served them lunch. Slattern: that was the word for her. Her dirty fingernails had repelled him. Like an animal. You were waiting table in what was supposed to be an upscale hotel and you couldn't be bothered to clean your fingernails? He tried to think about the dog fight and how that had made him feel, but he couldn't recapture the experience, which annoyed him further. Inevitably, into his mind came memories of humiliation, particularly the most recent humiliation, in the hotel in Geneva, memories he became entangled with, that burned him up inside like they were a match and he was a gas-soaked rag, and that he couldn't shake free from.

'What's wrong with you?'

'Nothing's wrong with me.'

'Then sit still, eh.'

'Yeah.'

Time dragged.

It was after three forty-five when the Turk finally arrived, accompanied by his obsequious interpreter. The two bodyguards, minus those M16s, stationed themselves outside the meeting room door. Shilling got smartly to his feet, so reluctantly Troy did as well.

'Please,' said the Turk, indicating they should sit.

They sat, and so did the Turk. The interpreter stood beside him, hands folded behind his back, head humbly bowed. American Troy had to drag his eyes away from the interpreter, hating the schmuck for acting so beta.

'Mr Shilling,' said the Turk, 'please to kill the Russian exile, for me.'

American Troy was a little surprised the Turk had got straight to the point, with no prevarication or preamble. The Big Shilling was nodding, a half-smile on his face. He leaned forward and tapped the table top with the tips of his fingers before twisting his little hand over to show the Turk his empty palm.

'Ahmet Bey, I have given this matter a lot of thought, a lot of thought, eh,' he said. 'But Cyprus is an island. Terminating the Russian exile would be extremely difficult, eh, but not impossible, but making a clean getaway, that would be more than difficult, it would be almost impossible.'

Ahmet Bey stared mournfully at the Big Shilling for some time, then spoke rapidly in Turkish to the interpreter.

'Here I can help you,' quoted the interpreter, his eyes averted, 'the border between the Turkish north and the Greek south is entirely porous. My people cross it all the time. There is no difficulty at all. Once you are on Turkish soil, my private jet is at your disposal. Twelve hours after completing this work, you can be anywhere in the world.'

'Ahmet Bey,' said the Big Shilling, looking from the interpreter back to the Turk, 'I thank you sincerely, eh, it was my thinking that you would offer me your kind assistance, hey? But I think by now you know my methods, my modus operandi. I organise every part of the job myself, every part of it. We speak plainly, you and I, eh, Ahmet Bey? So you know I am not being disrespectful, not in any way at all, my friend, by declining this offer of assistance.'

The Turk's eyes were hooded, but he nodded, eventually. He said in hesitant English, 'It is my thought you will say this.'

'You see,' said Shilling to American Troy, 'you see, Ahmet Bey and I understand each other, eh? We know each other well, and we speak plainly, eh. This is the best kind of business relationship, the best kind. I am honoured to do business with a gentleman of Mr Ahmet's calibre.'

And so for the next hour, the Big Shilling and Ahmet Bey discussed the problems inherent in the assassination of the Russian exile. American Troy began to feel better, enjoying being part of the planning. He even made a couple of suggestions that were in no way stupid or naïve. The Turk produced a map of the Akamas, the Cypriot national park where the Russian had built a house. Shilling and Troy examined aerial photographs of the locale, and Ahmet Bey played them video of the house and its surroundings. According to the Turk, the Russian exile had not left the house since the killing of Aias Pneumaticos, and neither had his wife or his two children.

'Fear,' said Ahmet Bey. 'He is feared.'

'Fearful,' said the Big Shilling, 'he is full of fear.'

'Full of fear, yes.'

'But difficult, very difficult,' said the Big Shilling. He rubbed his fingers and a thumb together, the universal symbol of cash money, and frowned. 'I am thinking that this would have to be my last job, Mr Ahmet, my last job of all. The Russian exile is connected, eh. He has brothers, cousins, very powerful men in Moscow. If I take him out I would have to disappear, disappear off the face of the Earth, and to do that I would need a lot of money, a lot of money. No, to take out the Russian exile, it would cost, it would cost big shilling, big, big shilling. You're looking at twenty million US.'

'Excuse please,' said the Turk, abruptly.

He swiftly left the room with the interpreter hurrying after him, and a guard closed the door behind them.

'Shit,' said Troy, whistling, 'he didn't like that, did he?'

The Big Shilling was unperturbed. 'He's just gone

for a sly ciggie, eh, for a little burn, top up the nicotine in his bloodstream. He knows what he's doing, old Ahmet, he will've mapped out these negotiations down to the smallest detail, the smallest detail, hey?'

'Are you really thinking of taking the contract?'

The Big Shilling grunted. 'Haven't decided yet, have I? I wasn't bullshitting him, eh, this job is a fucking nightmare. If the guy lived in mainland Europe or the States, no problem, no problem at all, I'd take it straight away, but an island, an island is bad news to escape from, eh?'

'And you meant it about retiring?' asked American Troy, who had only half-listened to what Shilling had said. The thought that he might be about to lose his mentor kind of dismayed him.

'Sure I did. That Russki used to be bosom buddies with old Vlad himself, back in Petersburg, eh?'

'Vladimir Putin,' said American Troy, with an automatic sneer.

'None other, and old Vlad doesn't mess about, eh, he doesn't care about due process, and human rights legislation, and the rule of law, any of that shit. Step on Vlad's corns, eh, and he's likely to send you a bullet dipped in plutonium, a bullet dipped in plutonium.'

American Troy wasn't sure, but he thought the Big Shilling meant polonium, and that other Russian exile, he hadn't been shot but poisoned. What was his name? The guy died of radiation sickness, in a London hospital. It was on the tip of his tongue.

American Troy was still trying to remember Alexander Litvinenko's name when Ahmet Bey returned with the interpreter, who was carrying a tea tray. American Troy regarded the guy with disdain, this fag carrying a tea tray like someone's grandma. Where was the waitress?

'Jesus,' he said, under his breath.

Drinking the tea and sampling the baklava, sticky sweet pastries loaded with honey and nuts, took a good twenty minutes, during which time business was suspended if not forgotten. American Troy grew restive. The baklava was making him a little nauseous and he had to force himself to eat it. At least the tea was palatable. He almost smirked. Jesus, who would have thought being an outlaw would involve so much fagging around?

'Have I news for you,' said Ahmet Bey when they had all finally finished eating. 'Mr Shilling, a price on your head: the Russian, price on head, a half million US dollar.'

The Big Shilling appeared at first unfazed. He pushed away his tea cup and plate. 'Half a million, eh, half a million?'

'Is insult,' said the Turk, his face darkening. 'Is big insult. Pneumaticos one million, Mr Big Shilling half million. This not good, oh no.'

Shilling placed his hands on the table and got slowly to his feet.

'The dirty, fucking conniving, back-stabbing bastard,' he began, his voice growing louder as he worked himself up into a rage, 'half a million? Half a fucking million? The Big Shilling's worth only half a lousy, fucking million, eh? Well, I'll show him, eh, I will show him. Ahmet Bey, I hereby take your contract, I hereby take your contract. I'll kill that lousy, fucking conniving, back-stabbing bastard, and I'll kill him good, hey? I'll kill that fucker, and that fucker will know he's been killed.'

'Ten millions,' said the Turk.

'I am the best. No one is better than the Big Shilling. No, I want twenty.'

'Eleven.'

'No no no. Eighteen. I won't go lower than eighteen.'

'Twelve, no more. Twelve.'

In the end they settled on sixteen, plus expenses, and a quarter of a million for American Troy. Ahmet Bey and the Big Shilling shook on it.

'Believing is seeing,' the Big Shilling told the Turk.

'Yes, yes, of course.'

'The Russian exile? Ahmet Bey, the son of a bitch is already dead.'

CHAPTER FIVE

A few weeks later, on a wet, grey morning at the end of May, the Big Shilling woke from a troubled sleep and remembered the death throes of the bear in the Balkan mountains.

It wasn't in Shilling's nature to be depressed or indulge in negativity, but that morning he woke feeling old and tired and dispirited. It did not help that it was the morning of his sixtieth birthday. The thought of the dying bear, how it had seemed to have given up the fight and run out of steam, had now and then played on his mind ever since he and American Troy had left Bulgaria for London, England. He did not believe in omens, but that bear would not leave him alone. He even dreamed about it. He lay listless in bed for a long time before summoning the strength to get up.

The Big Shilling dragged open the bedroom curtains in the service apartment American Troy had rented. Rain hammered down from a slate grey sky, and in the street below huddled pedestrians carrying umbrellas streamed across the junction outside the tube station. Shilling found himself yearning for the sunshine, warmth and open skies of the Caribbean, having completely forgotten the upcoming trip to the Levant. Remembering the rundown brothel his mother had kept on the outskirts of Bridgetown depressed his mood further. Redlegs, that's what they'd been called, the descendants of Irish slaves Cromwell had shipped out to Barbados, white trash, despised, and poorer than the poorest Bimshire blacks.

Sixty.

He was now older than his father had been when he'd died, unloved and unlamented as far as the Big Shilling was concerned. He still carried the scars, both mental and physical, that the old swine had inflicted.

'What is this?' he said suddenly, when he realised he what was happening.

He burst out laughing, he laughed long and hard, and anyone hearing that cracked cackle would surely have feared for the Big Shilling's sanity. He laughed so hard his eyes leaked and tears ran down his cheeks.

'Ha ha ha ha ha! Oh dear, ha ha ha ha ha!'

The truth was, the Big Shilling had had so many identities over the years, it was sometimes difficult to remember who he actually was. And in any case, the past did not matter, nothing mattered, not some bear, or what your old man may or may not have done to you. You created your own reality, you stepped over the past, you imagined the best, and the power would come to you! Believing was seeing, wasn't it? Of course it was! The secret of life: imagine what you desire to the point of self-persuasion.

'I am,' he affirmed aloud, 'I am,' and he experienced the familiar expansion, the elevation of consciousness, everything more vivid.

How many times! Would he never learn?

And so for the next ten minutes, the Big Shilling performed a punishing routine of calisthenics - press-ups, star jumps, sit-ups, and burpees - that pushed all thought of failure and past shame from his mind. He did not even allow himself to catch his breath. As soon as he was done, he marched smiling into the bathroom, turned the setting to ice cold and got under the shower. Three minutes later he was feeling wonderfully clean and invigorated, and as he dried himself and shaved, he had a big lupine grin on his face. No, the bear meant one thing, one thing only: the Russian was already dead.

It was eight o'clock when Shilling entered the living room to find American Troy fixing coffee in the galley kitchen. They breakfasted together the two of them most mornings, the Big Shilling eating his habitual hard-boiled eggs and fresh fruit, American Troy munching his way through a big bowl of factory-made, globally-advertised, over-priced cereal. And, as though they were family in some old time TV show, it had become their habit at breakfast to discuss the day's schedule. That morning, American Troy was due to see his Uncle Nathan and pick up no less than five passports and matching driver's licences.

'What about you, boss?' asked American Troy.

'I'm meeting Frankie the Fish for lunch. Then I've got a couple of meetings in the pm.'

The first of the meetings was with Lena. The angry Albanian, after Shilling had spent several days briefing him (with bullshit, mainly), had flown to Spain to play in a poker tournament, and little Lena was all alone. The second meeting was with the Blees, and if there was time he might even meet up with the idiot Tryphon as well. Troy was smirking at him.

'Frankie the Fish?'

'Frankie the Fish.'

'Does everyone you know in London have a dumb nickname? 'Sly Man' George, Morris 'The Saint' Nickle, 'Time-Haunted' Peter, Neville the Hermit.' Troy laughed.

The Big Shilling didn't answer right away. He smiled slyly. Troy's errand, and that little crack about Neville the Hermit - it was Neville the Hermeticist, and he didn't live in London - had given him an idea. Out of devilment, he cast himself in the role of AT, and imagined a self-aggrandising scenario played out in Uncle Nathan's underground lair.

'Well?' said American Troy, oblivious. 'Do they?'

'Pretty much, my boy, pretty much, but there's nothing dumb about Frankie the Fish, eh? And you'd better remember that, eh, since most likely you and he will be working together out on the island.'

American Troy looked up from his bowl of skimmed milk and vitamin-fortified cereal. 'Finally,' he said, 'finally you're telling me something.'

'Don't start that again,' the Big Shilling told him, playfully, 'don't start whining about how I never tell you anything. I tell you plenty. If you're too dumb to pick up on it, well, that's your loss, kid. This is need to know, strictly need to know, hey?'

'I know, I know, you keep telling me, everything is strictly need to know.'

'Do you need to know?'

'Yeah, I need to know.'

'You think so?'

'Yeah.'

The Big Shilling pointed at American Troy with an egg-smeared spoon. 'And keep your mouth tight shut when you see your goddamned uncle, hey?'

'Don't worry about it, I can handle myself. Jesus.'

'You're sure you can keep your mouth shut when you see him?'

'I told you already.'

'You angry at me? The kid's angry at me.'

'I'm not angry.'

'And don't break the speed limit on that Yamaha. The last thing we need is the cops pulling you over and finding out your licence is fake, eh?'

'It isn't fake,' said Troy, sighing. 'How many times do I have to tell you? Nathan's shit is not fake.'

'Yeah yeah,' said the Big Shilling, acting out the

scenario once more as he spoke. 'Nathan's shit isn't fake. Man, this coffee is good. Is it Lavazza? Lavazza make the best coffee. When we head off to the sun, make sure we pack some Lavazza, eh?'

'Right.'

'I mean it.'

'Lavazza, okay, I got it.'

'And make sure the comms are sorted.'

'They are sorted.'

'Double check.'

'Christ, all right already.'

American Troy thought Shilling was about to needle him about over-confidence, and how underestimating law enforcement could get you ten years inside, and was glad when he just sat there grinning at him.

'What?'

'Nothing,' said the Big Shilling. 'Be sure to give Nathan my best regards, won't you?'

American Troy lay down the spoon and pushed the cereal bowl aside. He was still waiting for some crack about his antecedents' ethnicity, and was relieved when none was forthcoming.

'I'm out of here.'

'Have a great day, junior.'

American Troy's Uncle Nathan worked out of a basement in an alley off a side street near Hatton Garden, the centre of the London diamond trade. Uncle Nathan was, amongst other things, a highly successful fence, handling stolen goods for some of the most prolific jewel thieves in Europe, not only the angry Albanian poker player, but also the infamous Pink Panther gang. But diamonds and jewels weren't his only business. Uncle Nathan had a lucrative side-line in identity documents - driver's licences, passports and the like. And as American Troy had told the Big Shilling more than once, Uncle Nathan's documents were not fake at all, at least not entirely.

This is how Troy's Uncle Nathan carried out the scam: his people found schmoes - drug addicts, derelicts and drunks in the main – who, for a couple of hundred nicker, would apply for a passport or other document using their own name, but accompanied by photographs provided by Uncle Nathan. The photographs, along with the application forms, were all countersigned by persons of good standing in the community - clergymen, lawyers, local government officers - who'd also been corrupted by Uncle Nathan. Uncle Nathan even provided a next-day service. And he had other people who bought up fast-track slots at the Passport Office and applied for the fake passports in person. For a side hustle, it was big business.

Of course, it all cost. American Troy had a theory that the reason the Big Shilling affected to dislike Uncle Nathan was because Uncle Nathan was as greedy for cash as the Big Shilling was himself. The difference was, Uncle Nathan didn't piss it up the wall and gamble it away the way the Big Shilling did. He invested it, in real estate, and cutting-edge technology stock.

Somehow, Uncle Nathan's shrewd investments rankled with American Troy as well. If he had to choose, he told himself weirdly, he'd choose the Big Shilling's attitude to money over that of his blood relative. Uncle Nathan reminded Troy too much of his own father, and Shilling's jibe at breakfast about whining had cut him to the quick, for American Troy's abiding memory of his father was of his kvetching about his treatment at the hands of the system that had sentenced him to half a lifetime in jail.

And so when American Troy met his Uncle Nathan in the basement near Hatton Garden he was in an altogether truculent mood.

'What's wrong with you?' Uncle Nathan demanded. 'Is there something the matter with my work? Tell me, is there something wrong with the documents?'

'There's nothing wrong with the documents.'

'Then why so angry? Always so angry when you come to see your Uncle Nathan.'

'Traffic,' explained American Troy, laconically, as he briskly counted out the cash. 'Eighteen grand,' he said, 'as agreed.'

'Eighteen? Eighteen? Shilling takes the bread from your cousins' mouths.'

'Twenty was too much, Uncle Nathan. Twenty is express service, we don't need express service.'

'Not in a hurry, is that it? It's a job with long planning, a big job needing five persons this time.'

'The job is none of your business.'

Uncle Nathan was a small well-fed man with watery eyes, the result he liked to say of using a jeweller's glass for so many years. On his head was a kippah, and he was wearing a handmade Savile Row suit and silk tie, with a monogrammed handkerchief in the top pocket. Now he plucked out the handkerchief and used it to blot his red-rimmed eyes.

'None of your business? He says this to his mother's brother? He's been in London for three weeks and still he hasn't come to visit his aunt and grandmother who dote on him.'

'For Christ's sakes, Nathan, enough already!'

'Why don't you come? You're ashamed of us, is that it? You'd rather spend time with that South African psycho than with your own flesh and blood?'

American Troy laughed. 'South African psycho? You know nothing about the guy. Number one, he's not even South African, he was born in Barbados.'

'I know everything about the guy, everything about him. He's an animal, a human animal. You're wasting your life with him, an intelligent boy like you! You should be in business, you should be a lawyer, with a brain like yours. But no, you want to play at being a wise guy.'

American Troy regarded his uncle with contempt. 'You keep taking his money though, don't you?'

Uncle Nathan finished counting the bundled cash and quickly locked it away in the floor safe under the desk. He was agitated now and wiped beads of sweat from his brow with nervous fingers as he effortfully stood up.

He said, almost tearfully, 'Your grandmother, your sweet innocent grandmother asked me this very morning, is Troy smoking his cigar? Is Troy smoking the Big Shilling's cigar? Your own grandmother asked me that this very morning. What was I to say?'

For a moment, Troy was nonplussed, and when the words did come, they were accompanied by a rage that surprised both his Uncle Nathan and Troy himself.

'I'm not a fucking faggot, and neither is he! You lying bastard, grandma would never talk like that. She doesn't even know who the Big Shilling is. You disgust me, Nathan, you're lower than a goddamned snake's belly.'

'You talk to me like that? You talk to me like that? Let me tell you about the man you share an apartment with, let me tell you.'

'Shut the fuck up, Nathan. Say one more word about Shilling and God help me, I'll fuck you up.'

Uncle Nathan stared at his nephew in consternation. His wet mouth opened and closed a few times silently and then he subsided into the swivel chair behind his crowded desk, covered his face and tried not to weep.

But American Troy wasn't finished, not by a long chalk. Ignoring the older man's snuffling protestations, he delivered a speech in praise of the Big Shilling. He didn't know where the speech came from, American Troy, but he spoke it like he was on the stage of one of the theatres in London's famous West End. Uncle Nathan, cowed and red-eyed, listened open-mouthed.

'You're possessed,' said Uncle Nathan, weakly, when Troy was finished and making to leave. 'You're possessed by an evil spirit.'

'Spare me, Nathan, just spare me,' said American Troy, yanking open the door.

An hour later, at 12.30, the cause of all this familial upset negotiated the worn-smooth stone steps at Gordon's, a basement wine bar near the river Thames in central London.

Frankie the Fish had just arrived. The Big Shilling knew this because he'd been staking out the place for the previous forty minutes, hidden by a billboard advertising the anniversary celebrations of the Great Fire of London. Shilling also knew something of Frankie the Fish's own domestic travails. Frankie the Fish was down on his luck, he was broke and grubbing about for work. The story was his wife had left him for another man and taken their daughter, whom Frankie loved more than anything in the world, to live overseas.

Not that you'd have known it, seeing Frankie the Fish that Monday lunchtime in May. He was suntanned and relaxed, and dressed in an expensive blue blazer and a colourful cravat. The two men ordered food and glasses of Gavi white wine. Carrying plates of bread and cheese and cold meats and pickles, they secured a table in one of the busy wine bar's many candle-lit nooks and corners.

'I hear you've been teaching CQB out in Cyprus, eh?' said the Big Shilling once they'd got settled.

'Was,' said Frankie the Fish. 'All finished now.'

He had the type of affected English accent that usually put the Big Shilling's back up, but for some reason neither of them could fathom, Frankie and Shilling got along like fast friends. Frankie was wise enough to realise that if the Big Shilling knew about his teaching job in Cyprus, he probably also knew about the divorce and family breakdown. That's what his face was saying, anyway.

'Still got that boat of yours?' the Big Shilling asked him.

'The Melissa? Yes, still got her, kind of. She's in dock, in Rhodes, and she'll be staying there until I get enough cash together to pay the repair bill.'

'What would you say to a retainer of ten grand?' asked the Big Shilling.

'I'd say, how do you do?'

'No further questions, hey?'

'My dear old thing, as I'm sure you already know, your faithful friend is in no position whatsoever to turn down paying work.'

'This job pays well, it pays very well, but it could be hairy, eh? And it's all got to happen in double quick time.'

Frankie the Fish shrugged. 'That's all right. If I don't get Melissa back from the wicked witch then I'm not sure I want to live to see next year, never mind old age and retirement.'

Melissa was the name of Frankie the Fish's daughter as well as his yacht.

The Big Shilling said, 'You make your own luck, Frankie, and don't you forget it.'

'Here's to luck then.'

'No, here's to believing.'

'If you like,' said Frankie.

The two men clinked glasses, the deal done, then got down to specifics.

'I want you to rent a house in Latchi,' said the Big Shilling, naming the fishing village on the north-west coast. 'We'll need cars, motorbikes, a couple of safe houses, and guns, and plenty of other kit as well. Here, I've made a list, and I need it all by yesterday.'

Frankie the Fish nodded. 'No problemo, no problemo at all. The Cypriots are the most entrepreneurial people I've ever met. Everything's for sale, including the island itself, Russians and Chinese swarming all over the shop. Buy a property for a few hundred thousand and they'll throw in a Cypriot passport, free, gratis and for nothing.'

In a roundabout way, Frankie was fishing for information, and Shilling wondered what Frankie had heard on the grapevine about the Aias Pneumaticos assassination.

'It's a Russian, eh,' said Shilling.

'My dear old thing, I thought it probably might be.'

'We're still on?'

'Of course we are, I've said, haven't I? My word is my bond and all that malarkey. You're thinking we'll sail away into the sunset after the deed is done?'

'Maybe,' said Shilling, 'maybe.'

'Tricky,' said Frankie the Fish.

It was indeed tricky, which was why the Big Shilling had other irons in the fire. He took out the mobile phone he'd taken from his stash in Knightsbridge and slipped it across the table.

'Don't let me down, Francis, don't you dare let me down.'

After his convivial luncheon with Frankie the Fish, the Big Shilling strolled up to the Strand where he caught a cab. Strolling wasn't his normal style of locomotion but he adopted it in order to give himself chance to see if he had a shadow. He did. In fact, he reckoned there were two shadows, watchers from the Security Service, MI5, most likely. As the cabbie negotiated the heavy traffic at Trafalgar Square, the Big Shilling spotted a motor-scooter. Fifteen minutes later, in west London, the same scooter was up the street as he paid off the cab. But the Big Shilling was not in any way perturbed. He knew full well the service apartment was being watched as well. He jogged down the stone steps and knocked on the door of the basement bedsit. The door opened almost immediately. The Albanian girl, Lena, had been eagerly awaiting his arrival.

'Happy birthday!' she cried, and took his hand to lead him inside.

'Got it all planned out, have you?' he said as she knelt down before him on the cushion she had prepared.

He was in two minds. Their previous assignations had taken place in darkness, and while this pokey basement flat, even with the lights on, wasn't exactly brightly lit, there was no doubt that she would see his scars.

'I want to give back to you,' said Lena, breathing heavily.

The Big Shilling had more often than not been parsimonious with his vital energy. Perhaps it was growing up in a brothel that had caused it, the constant procession of men in the grip of blind lust. He didn't know. He felt the girl's warm mouth work on him, her hands too. He'd never allowed her to touch him before. While their couplings had resulted in satiation for her, he himself had never ejaculated. She thought he perhaps couldn't, or only with great difficulty, due to his advanced age, and he'd certainly never bothered to explain. He felt her pause. Then she gave a little gasp.

'What is this? Poor baby! Who did this to you?'

'I did it,' he almost said, but didn't.

Instead, he helped her to her feet, pulled down her yoga pants along with her thong, and bent her over the back of the two-seat sofa. When he left her twenty minutes later, the Albanian girl was a quivering, breathless wreck.

'But is your birthday,' she managed to say. 'I make you?'

'Sap my vital energy? On my birthday? No thank you,' he said, getting ready to leave.

The Big Shilling laughed happily at her bemused expression and waved her farewell.

Feeling on top of the world, and no longer interested if he was being tailed or not, he took the tube to St Pancras International and caught a train to St Albans, Hertfordshire, northwest of London.

There the Big Shilling took a stroll around the historic city where the eponymous St Alban was martyred in the third century. At a newsagent's, he bought a couple of Kinder eggs. Standing beside a rubbish bin by the busy road, the stink of petrol fumes in his nose, he ate the chocolates and opened the small plastic containers inside which were little toys in need of assembling. He crushed the toys in his fist and dumped them, but he kept the containers, playing with them in the palm of his hand as he walked. He was thinking about martyrdom, and about how church Christianity had weakened the West, how it had sapped the animal vitality of Europeans and turned them into slaves. Looking about him, here, and in London, he saw only weakness and avarice and abject conformity. Even the MI5 man tailing him looked like a big girl's blouse.

The Kingdom of Heaven is within, he said to himself, as he crossed the road, but why did so few realise? Egypt, Egypt, the land of Al-Kemi, the land that was Christian thousands of years before Christ. It had all been lost, lost so far as the common man was concerned, lost, but not quite: some initiates still knew the key to success in this life, and immortality in the next.

'I am,' he murmured, 'I am that I am,' and he remembered waiting outside the wine bar and imagining American Troy lauding him to his Uncle Nathan.

The Big Shilling exhaled, and relaxed his body, visualising the death of the Russian exile, believing it, knowing that soon he would see it, plainly, just as he now saw and heard and smelled the city of St Albans, along with its somnolent people and unceasing traffic.

Happily, he checked the time. It was getting late and he had an appointment to keep.

Near the abbey which bears the saint's name, the Big Shilling met an elderly English couple in the beer garden of an ancient public house. Amiable old age pensioners they might have been, but there was nothing saintly about Brian and Betty Blee. Shilling well knew that both of them had been deep in devilment since the Piranha brothers had lorded it over the London underworld in the 1960s.

'So you're interested?' the Big Shilling asked them, scanning their unreliable, venal faces.

'Course we're bleeding interested,' said Betty Blee. 'Let's get cracking, I say.'

'Another pint of Spitfire?' asked her corpulent, red-faced husband, pointing to Shilling's empty glass.

'Cheers, Bri.'

'Nice one.'

While Bri was busy at the bar, the Big Shilling had a little chat with Betty.

'You can't frighten me,' said Betty when he had finished, but her bluster lacked all conviction, and she knew it.

'I can and I do,' Shilling told her, grinning. 'Let me down and I'll butcher you and that fat fool you call a husband, eh? I'll cut you into little pieces and feed you to the sharks.'

Bet's walnut face blanched.

'Here we go,' said Brian, returning with the drinks a few moments later, a big grin on his stupid, flabby face. 'Nice little session, eh?'

'Cheers, Bri, my son.'

' . . . What?' said Brian, upon finally realising something was amiss.

'It's nothing,' said his wife, angrily.

'Oh, right,' said Brian and nosed into his pint, careful not to eyeball the little man.

'How many are you?' the Big Shilling asked him.

'Come again?'

'You heard me, Bri. How many are you?'

'There's the two of us,' said Blee, ignorantly. 'Just me and Bet. Eh, Bet?'

Betty Blee scowled and said nothing.

The Big Shilling said, 'There are five functions in man, discounting the two higher functions. The five functions are thinking, feeling and moving, plus the instinctive function and the sexual function.'

'That's right,' said Brian Blee, gormlessly.

His wife was regarding the little man with as much

93

comprehension as if he'd been speaking Aramaic.

'So,' the Big Shilling went on, 'how many are you, hey? At least five, right? At least five, and many more. Consider, for instance, the Gadarene swine, eh.'

The reference dimly chimed in Betty Blee's Roman Catholic memory.

'Our Lord,' she began, 'he cast out a demon, from out of the mad man of Gadarea.'

'Not one demon,' the Big Shilling corrected her, 'many demons. Do you remember, Bet, what the mad man said?'

'Yeah, he said his name was Legion,' said Betty Blee, 'for we are many.'

'Exactly that, eh, exactly that. We are many, we are many. And the purpose of our lives is to become one, to become a unity, for we have many I's, many, many I's.'

Betty Blee was nodding, regarding the Big Shilling strangely. Her husband was nodding as well, imitating her, as though he understood, although he didn't. He belched unexpectedly.

'Pardon,' he said, sniggering.

'Dirty pig,' said Betty.

'Pearls before swine, Betty, pearls before swine,' said the Big Shilling. 'In the words of St Clement, self-knowledge is the beginning of all wisdom. Am I right? Of course I'm right.'

He produced a brown envelope, inside which was a mobile phone and a single sheet of instructions.

'Take this, Betty,' he said, before naming the

widow of a notorious Irish gangster. 'You two are acquainted, I take it, eh?'

'Oh yes,' said Betty Blee. 'We go way back, way back.'

'Diamond,' said Brian Blee.

'She'll provide you with the camper van.'

'Sorted,' said Brian Blee.

'Shut your trap, you,' said his wife. 'You're a bleeding embarrassment, that's what you are.'

'Strewth,' said her husband, and winked at BS.

Altogether, it had turned out to be a most enjoyable birthday, and so, when the Big Shilling arrived back at the service apartment in Paddington that evening, still under surveillance and secretly planning his trip to Beirut, Lebanon, he told American Troy to take a few days off and see something of historic England.

'It's the anniversary of the Great Fire of London,' he said, '1666. Go and see the exhibition, educate yourself. From the ashes, a new city arose. They're building a floating model of the seventeenth-century city on the River Thames, hey? They're going to set it on fire, as a commemoration.'

American Troy, whose pasty face had been as foul as the English weather, broke into a smile at the thought of a vacation and made him seem much younger than his years. He looked up from the obsolete ThinkPad laptop he'd been fiddling with.

'I'd rather check out the British speedway tracks.'

The Big Shilling regarded him indulgently. 'Whatever you like, kid, whatever you like, but I thought you had a thing for fires. Why don't you take Tryphon with you? He's mad about bikes.'

'He's a dumb-ass.'

'He has his uses. You got the documents?'

'I got them. No problems.'

The Big Shilling picked up one of the mobile phones American Troy had laid out on the kitchen table.

'It stinks in here. What have been doing all afternoon? Jacking off, I'll bet. You're a profligate, my boy, that's what you are, a profligate.'

The kid wouldn't look at him, had coloured a little, pretending to be interested in the ThinkPad. Shilling let it go.

'Will this thing work in Beirut?'

American Troy looked at the mobile, then looked the Big Shilling in the eye. 'Beirut?'

'Beirut, Lebanon. Well? You don't know where that is, do you?'

'No.'

'You're a know-nothing, a real know-nothing. It's near the island, of Cyprus, on the coast of what you think of as the Mediterranean Ocean.'

'Right, there. It'll work.'

'Double check.'

'It'll work.'

'What about you?'

'What about me?'

'Will you work, out there in Cyprus?'

The kid put on his game face. 'Yeah.'

'Well we shall see, shan't we?'

'No, I'm solid.'

Shilling let it go, nodded at the laptop instead. 'Comms all set and ready to go, eh?'

'They certainly are.'

And Troy began to talk about Linux and Tails and Tor, and why he'd bought ten year-old ThinkPads, and only stopped when the Big Shilling yawned elaborately. Shilling grinned, and winked at him.

'Nothing changes, eh? I'm for my bed. Early night tonight – I've got work to do. Book me a cab, kid: I need to be at Heathrow at oh-seven thirty tomorrow morning. Nathan all right?'

'I straightened him out,' said American Troy.

'Knew you would, my boy, I knew you would.'

CHAPTER SIX

W hen the Big Shilling cleared passport control at Beirut international airport on the afternoon of June the first and deselected flight mode, the mobile phone he was carrying accessed Lebanese telecom provider Alfa, and pinged. The Big Shilling read the text while waiting at the baggage carousel with his fellow passengers from the London Heathrow flight. It appeared that Omar the Sailor had gone home to buy mules. This wasn't some secret code that only the Big Shilling and the man he had come to Lebanon to meet could understand. No, Omar the Sailor had indeed gone back to his village near the border with Syria to buy pack animals.

'It was terrible, an ambush on Mount Hermon,' explained Omar the Sailor's youngest son, Antoine, once they were seated in the big Nissan Patrol Antoine had driven to the airport.

'Anyone hurt?'

'Only mules,' said Antoine. 'They were our best

mules though. They know the routes so well they walk them alone, no one need guide them.'

The Big Shilling knew all about pack mule smuggling, but he was content to sit back, enjoy the sunshine, and let Antoine talk.

Back in the '80s, when the port of Naquoura, Lebanon was under Israeli occupation, he and Omar the Sailor's father used to buy cigarettes from Jewish traders there, thus avoiding Lebanese government taxes. They'd smuggle the smokes all over Lebanon, using trucks and cars, and into Syria by mule. Mules were the best, indeed only, transport in the mountains that formed a natural border between Syria and Lebanon.

'One hundred US dollars to carry canned food, bread and flour,' explained Antoine in his fluent French, 'two hundred dollars per mule if the cargo is weapons and ammunition.'

'And in the other direction?'

Antoine considered his answer for a moment. They were driving south-east through the outskirts of Beirut and the air con was on its highest setting, for the afternoon temperature outside the car was thirty-eight degrees Celsius. Antoine overtook a dawdling cart that was stacked high with watermelon, and said:

'Refugees - the old, the very young and the sick. Wounded fighters too, and of course people who want to go somewhere a little cooler.'

Antoine glanced at the Big Shilling to see if he understood. Shilling understood: somewhere cooler was Germany or Holland or Britain or Sweden, the go-to destinations for human beings Western liberals designated economic migrants or asylum seekers.

'My grandfather is looking forward very much to seeing you,' Antoine added.

'Is he, eh? And I'm looking forward very much to seeing the old rogue again as well, hey? In good health, is he?'

The Big Shilling's French was a little rusty, but he had a facility for languages, and with just a little practice it was coming back to him already.

'He's an old man,' said Antoine, with the lack of sensitivity one expected from a boy who was not yet twenty, 'seventy years' old. I keep asking him to give up smoking, his chest is bad, but he refuses.'

The Big Shilling smiled ruefully – grandpa's only a decade older than me, he thought.

'How much does Omar pay for a decent mule these days?' he asked, and for the next half hour they talked about mules, about their nature and their foibles, about the best routes across the mountains, and about when the snows would come this year, and how it was imperative to work day and night until the passes were closed for the winter.

But at no point did the Big Shilling mention Cyprus, or the new boat Omar the Sailor had bought to transport people from the Levant into Europe. No, he left that discussion till the following morning, after the feast of roast lamb at the house of Omar's father in the village of Cheeba, south-west of Mount

Hermon, the peak that soars seven thousand feet above sea level.

'I have ears everywhere,' said the Big Shilling, when Omar demanded to know how the hell he knew about his new boat. 'However stealthy you are, word always leaks out.'

Omar grunted, and puffed on his third cigarette of the morning. He wasn't pleased, and his hangover didn't help any, for there had been some serious drinking the night before. The breeze ruffled his thinning grey hair.

They were seated under an arbour of grape vines, drinking coffee and eating yoghurt and figs with honey. After the heat of Beirut, it was pleasantly cool in the mountains, and the Big Shilling had been glad of the blanket Omar's mother had thoughtfully left folded on his bed. He added a little more honey to the yoghurt, feeling relaxed and thoroughly at home in the village of smugglers.

For a time they spoke about Omar the Sailor's daughter who was about to start her PhD at the Sorbonne in Paris, France, and about Antoine's brother who was far too enamoured of smuggling to take studying for his accountancy exams seriously. When Omar the Sailor excused himself and went coughed and spat into the dirt before lighting another cigarette, the Big Shilling brought the conversation back to Cyprus.

'The Greek side, not the Turkish.'

'You are mad,' said Omar, hunched in his chair. 'The Turks I can work with, they know the value of money. The Cypriots are different. Sometimes you can pay them off but most of the time the maritime police are a real headache, and then there is the British to consider as well.'

'But with your new boat,' said the Big Shilling.

A sly look came over Omar's seamed, brown face. 'A moment of madness,' he said, 'a moment of madness to pay so much money for such a craft.'

That wasn't what the Big Shilling had heard. He'd heard that after Omar's scheme to smuggle a big group of Lebanese from Indonesia to Australia had floundered - the Indonesian police swooped and arrested everyone, and impounded Omar the Sailor's biggest ship - to save face, Omar had paid for all the Lebanese to come home again, and promised each one of them that he would get them to Germany instead. That was why he'd bought the stealth boat, and paid an astonishing sum for it as well.

'I'm willing to pay big shilling, eh?' said the Big Shilling. 'You come in close to the SBA, because no one will expect us there, and I'll pay you big shilling.'

Omar threw up his hands. 'Close to the British bases! You haven't changed, you haven't changed a bit, man, you always were insane!'

The Big Shilling waited a beat before speaking.

'That's twice you've called me mad,' he said, smiling dangerously. 'The first time I let it go. I'm a guest here and you are hungover. The second time, I draw your attention to what you have said.'

Omar the Sailor held up a hand that trembled a little. 'There will be no third time.'

'Then we shall say nothing more about it, old friend, nothing more about it. In fact, I have already forgotten about it, it is completely forgotten, eh?'

The Big Shilling looked away and heard Omar the Sailor swallow audibly, just as the Big Shilling had expected he would. The nervous gulp: the Big Shilling had that effect on people, even hardened smugglers like Omar.

The Big Shilling stayed in Cheeba as a guest of Omar the Sailor's father for three days. He walked in the stony fields with the old man and watched him as he chain-smoked and tended his olives and his vines, but he did not offer to help. His hatred of farming had diminished over the years, but he had vowed as a young man never again to work the land, and it was a vow that he had kept. The old man's spine might have been bent and his body betraying him, but his essence, that inner strength wrought from a life of struggle and suffering, was undimmed, and, in the shade of an olive tree the Big Shilling speculated about the outcome of the old man's forthcoming interview with Amit, the devourer of souls. Such thoughts were natural here, in the shadow of the majestic mountain that spoke of eternity and the immortal. Particularly so, when during the feast, an uncanny bright light had been seen in the night sky. Young Antoine called it a ufo, but his grandfather had firmly disagreed: the jinni have always been with us, he said, they are not spacemen and do not need spaceships. The Big

Shilling, who was a student of the uncanny and had made an investigation into the so-called ufo phenomenon, agreed wholeheartedly with this verdict.

In the afternoons, when the house was hot and quiet, Shilling lay on the bed in his simple room and kept in touch with the world, for the village had that spring been connected to fast broadband. He checked for messages from Ahmet Bey and read the Russian and Cypriot newspapers, and sent and answered emails from American Troy and Frankie the Fish. Troy had curtailed his motorbike holiday to conduct the Greek gangster, Tryphon, along with the Albanian couple, to London Gatwick airport where he'd seen them board a flight to Paphos, Cyprus. And Frankie the Fish had paid his debts in Rhodes and was about to set sail on the Melissa for Latchi on the north-west coast of Cyprus where he had rented a villa. Weapons, safe houses, vehicles – Frankie had seen to it all in double quick time.

Yes, it was all coming together nicely, so nicely in fact that the Big Shilling began to worry at his plans to see if there was anything he had overlooked. He regarded things as objectively as he could. He knew that the contract was risky, but risk-taking was part of his nature. The biggest problem, so far as he could see, was the certain involvement of other intelligence services besides the British. He wasn't naïve enough to believe that Ahmet Bey was acting in this matter without the approval of the Turkish state, implicit or otherwise. And then there were the Russians, and the Israelis to consider as well.

But the wheels had begun to turn in any case, so there was no backing out now. He was a man of his word, and he had said he would kill the Russian exile and so that is what he would do. Once more, as he lay on the bed, the Big Shilling felt that welling up of power and certainty that he knew so well, and which seemed to come from a source outside of him. He was invincible, the fates were on his side, he could achieve anything, anything at all, if he set his mind to it. After visualising once more the death of the Russian exile, he fell into a satisfying doze, a wolfish grin on his weathered, freckled face.

That evening, after a dinner of beef shawarma with tahini sauce, he and Omar agreed a series of codes and fall-back lines of communication. They also discussed the merits of the different Cypriot beaches. The Big Shilling had half a mind to tell Omar the Sailor to take him the following night by stealth boat to Lady's Mile, the long, shallow-shelving bathing beach west of Limassol in southern Cyprus, but he discounted the idea as rash, and the following morning, the fifth of June, Omar the Sailor drove him back to Beirut to catch a flight to Larnaca.

'Don't let me down, Omar,' said the Big Shilling as they parted.

'Have I ever let you down?'

'If you let me down you know what I will do.'

'I know what you would do,' said Omar the Sailor, thinking of his daughter in Paris, and his sons. 'I won't let you down.'

'It's all good, man.'

'Yes,' said Omar the Sailor.

The flight was uneventful. The Big Shilling charmed a young Cypriot couple by entertaining their fractious toddler with magic tricks. Where is the coin? Is it in this hand, or is it in that hand? Is it up my nose? No, it was in your ear all the time! Next, he drank red wine from a plastic tumbler and chatted with an Englishman about golf and property prices. One of the air hostesses was so taken with him that she brought him another miniature bottle of wine, gratis, and shook his hand for longer than was necessary, giving him that look as he left the plane. He knew that smile and that look, and sometimes despised it. Did she sense something beneath the surface of his bonhomie, something fundamental that attracted her to him, automatically, like a moth to a flame? He knew she did, he knew she did, eh.

From Larnaca airport, the Big Shilling hired a taxi to take him to Nicosia, the Cypriot capital. He had a meeting scheduled for seven thirty that very evening. The taxi driver was a Tottenham Cypriot and spoke English with a north London accent. He was friendly and wanted to chat so the Big Shilling wove him a tale about visiting Cyprus to look at some properties. Inevitably, the taxi driver had friends and relatives in real estate. Affably, the Big Shilling accepted a couple of business cards and tipped the cabbie well.

After dropping his bag at the hotel, the Big Shilling went shopping. He had a long list of items to purchase. Some things, like knives, he carried away himself, the larger items, like a tent, he arranged to have delivered to his hotel. By the time he'd finished his chores he was hot and sweating, and once back at the hotel he sank a cold beer at the bar.

'Man, that's good. Boy, did I need that. It's Keo, is it? Man, that beer is good.'

The girl behind the bar regarded him doubtfully.

From the window of his room he could see the giant floodlit flags on the Turkish side of the border, and minarets, and a United Nations watch tower as well. He nodded once, deep in thought about the task ahead, and went into the bathroom. He took a quick shower, changed his clothes and, feeling relaxed and energetic, sauntered over to the café where he was due to meet the Zimbabwean.

In preparation for this aspect of the operation, the Big Shilling had learnt some Shona, one of the native languages of Zimbabwe, but when the land mine clearance operative arrived for their meeting, the Big Shilling decided to speak to him only in English. The Zimbabwean, whose name was Joshua, was in his late twenties but his face was that of much older man: mine clearance work did that to a person. He was a little jumpy as well, but the Big Shilling put that down to the matter they were discussing and not the result of Joshua's work. Seated at a rickety wooden table on the terrace, they shared a large bottle of Keo, the way the Cypriots did – the chilled beer would get warm if you attempted to drink a whole bottle yourself. Gradually, the Zimbab-wean relaxed. It was the alcohol, and the Big Shilling's winning charm, of course. Now, when Joshua smiled, he looked like a ten year-old boy.

'Finished your beer? It's the best beer, Keo, eh. Shall we go then, Joshua?'

'We go now.'

'That's right.'

Joshua drove them south from Nicosia in a bat-tered Peugeot 205 that he had borrowed for the evening. The Big Shilling knew exactly how much black Africans like Joshua were paid for their dan-gerous work, and he also knew how much the white men who ran the mine clearance charities were paid. It was a disgrace, eh, but it was the way of the world, and in any case if Joshua were properly paid then he would most likely not have been willing to clear a path through a minefield for a man like the Big Shilling.

'Show me where you think we can make a crossing, Joshua, eh,' said the Big Shilling, 'and I will give you five hundred euro.'

'Fi'e hunnerd?'

'Yes, cash in hand, tonight. Here, I'll give it you now, hey? No problem. Show me the place and how you can clear a path for me. If you decide it is too dangerous for you to do it, then you keep the five hundred, eh, and we part company as friends.'

Joshua looked at him suspiciously.

'I mean it, my friend, you can back out at any time. I give you my word, you won't see me again and there will be no come back, eh?'

When he decided that the Big Shilling was telling the truth, Joshua began to feel happy. It was his sister in London who had arranged the meeting with this strange little man, and Joshua had sometimes regretted agreeing to it, but now he was feeling cheerful and confident. It will work out fine, no worries, my friend, and the promise of five thousand euro when he got the white man across to the Turkish side caused him once more to start imagining what he could do back home with such a fabulous sum. He would be rich like Mugabe!

The place that Joshua had chosen to breach the minefield was a strip of no-man's land only sixty metres wide. In some places the territory that separated the Greeks and the Turks was several kilometres deep but here it was a short walk, and there were no guard towers or United Nations patrols. Joshua himself had marked some of the mines here, but the work had stopped, as it so often did when the Turks and the Greeks argued and could not agree going forward. He thought it would take him only a couple of hours to mark out a path. Enthusiastically, he showed the Big Shilling a potential route.

They spent twenty minutes there, talking quietly in the hot darkness about how it would be, the Big Shilling smiling every time Joshua smiled and Joshua smiling every time the Big Shilling smiled, and then, with five hundred euro carelessly folded in his back pocket, Joshua drove the Big Shilling back to Nicosia. Before the white man got out of the car, he shook Joshua's dusty hand.

'Thank you, my friend!' said Joshua.

'No, thank you, my friend,' said Shilling. 'And remember, you can back out at any time, no hard feelings, eh,' again, that portentous Big Shilling beat: 'but on one condition.'

Joshua looked in alarm at the white man's face which had suddenly darkened.

'You keep stumm,' the Big Shilling went on, casually producing one of the knives he'd purchased earlier, 'you keep your mouth shut, or your sister in London will get a visit from me she will never forget. I'll slice her up, eh? I'll cut strips off her, but carefully, so that she doesn't die.'

The black man watched in wide-eyed horror as the Big Shilling mimed cutting strips of human flesh.

'No,' said Joshua, terrified, 'no. Please.'

'Too late,' the monstrous little man told him, 'far too late.'

Joshua began to quaver. Shilling opened the passenger door.

'Enjoy the rest of your evening, eh?'

At the hotel, he discovered that the tent and some of the other supplies had already been delivered. They were stacked behind the reception desk in the luggage store. He made a quick phone call to the Turkish side of the island and arranged with the Irish widow woman to come and collect the camping equipment at 7.15 the following morning. More than satisfied, the Big Shilling went up to his room where he stripped and took another shower. When he came out of the bathroom, a towel wrapped around his waist, he stood under the air conditioning unit and luxuriated in the cold blast. As he got into bed, his phone pinged. It was a text from Betty Blee. She and her husband Brian had landed at Paphos airport in western Cyprus and were now on their way to the apartment on the edge of the Akamas National Park.

It was all coming together nicely. The Blees should come and collect the van in Nicosia. He sent the text, a big smile on his face.

Shortly after that, the Big Shilling turned out the lights, lay on the bed, and visualised the future that he would cause to come to pass.

CHAPTER SEVEN

J ust before lunchtime on the morning of June the sixth, after running errands with the diminutive Irish woman that were no concern the kid, the Big Shilling arrived at the house in Latchi with American Troy who had driven a hire car to Nicosia to collect him. It was a hot, sunny day without a cloud in the sky. In the garden sparrows were twittering.

American Troy was glad to arrive back at the house. It was a new build, clean and fresh, and with powerful air conditioning in every room. He was suffering from the heat and humidity. It was worse than summer in Chicago, only there weren't McDonalds restaurants on every block, and everyone you met was white. American Troy had seen only one black man the entire time he'd been in Cyprus, and everywhere he looked there was yet another Greek Orthodox Church or roadside shrine. For some reason he couldn't fathom, this lack of diversity along with the symbols of a Christian nation only added to his discomfort. Not for the first time, he wished he was back in rainy, cosmopolitan London, or Amsterdam, or even Geneva. Coming to Cyprus was like going back in time.

'Buy yourself some flip-flops,' the Big Shilling said, for about the hundredth time.

'Jesus, I'll buy some of the damn things if it will shut you the fuck up.'

'You can't wear those damn things in this heat.'

'At least Nikes keep my feet clean. Have you seen these people? Goddamn animals, they all have filthy feet.'

'Listen to me, kid, are you listening, eh? Adapt to the local colour, that's what you have to do, adapt to the local colour, hey? You'll attract attention wearing those stupid plimsolls, eh?'

Plimsolls? What the fuck were plimsolls?

They were inside the house by now, and even the forty seconds or so it had taken them to get out of the car, collect Shilling's bags, and come in the front door had resulted in American Troy breaking out in a sweat.

'Jesus, that's better,' he said. 'What are you doing! Don't turn it off.'

The Big Shilling turned off the air con which had been running for the two hours Troy had been out of the house.

'You need to acclimatise, my boy, you won't be indoors in air conditioned rooms the whole time, hey? We have to get you outside, get that pale hide of yours exposed to the elements, eh, get you out of your comfort zone, hey? There's nothing wrong with a bit of dirt. It won't hurt you, eh?'

Now the Big Shilling kicked off the sandals he was wearing, turned around and showed American Troy the sole of his left foot. Troy pulled a face.

'Jesus, man, that's disgusting, you really need to wash your feet.'

'That isn't dirt, my boy, that is callous. I'm calloused, eh. I ran around bare-foot right from the time I could walk. You, you're too soft, you've lived indoors your whole life, hey? I worry about you, I worry about you, I really do. If you're frightened of getting a bit of dust between your toes, what are you going to be like when there's blood on your hands and on your face and in your mouth, hey?'

American Troy looked at the Big Shilling more closely. 'You mean I'm going to pull the trigger?'

The Big Shilling hefted his two bags. 'Who knows what is going to happen, eh? But I tell you this, if I find you skulking indoors all day and jacking off, you'll be on the first plane out, you understand me, boy? The first plane out.'

'All right, all right, I'll buy some goddamned flip-flops.'

'The internet's up and running, you say?'

'I told you.'

'Because that'll be the first job - communications. That coffee table you've got your dirty shoes on, that will be comms central, hey? I'll bring my laptop down, and my phones, and we'll lay it all out there, hey? You too. Get a move on, eh? Take your time, but hurry up, hey? That's the order of the day.'

After the Big Shilling had moved into the master bedroom with its en suite bathroom and balcony overlooking the Mediterranean Sea, he and American Troy set up the communications centre on the coffee table in the living room, and ate lunch. Without too much cajoling, American Troy agreed to try some of the local food that the letting agent had put in the fridge.

'You like hummus, hey, and taramasalata?' said the Big Shilling. 'This is the first time I've seen you eat real food, food that hasn't been processed, hey?'

'These flat breads are okay,' American Troy allowed.

'Taste like bread, eh, these pittas? Not like those buns they give you in your burger bar, eh, full of sugar. That's why you can eat junk and still be hungry a few minutes later, because it's full of processed white sugar, eh? You've grown up eating crap, my boy, eating processed crap.'

'At least processed crap doesn't give me guts ache.'

'You've been drinking the local water, hey? Not a good idea. See the kitchen tap, at the bottom there, hey, the little knob, that's drinking water. Don't use the main tap to drink from.'

'Christ, you said it was safe to drink the goddamned Cyprus water.'

'So it is, hey, so it is. So long as you drink the drinking water and not the regular stuff. There's a bottle of soda water in the fridge, eh, that'll calm your stomach.'

And so it went on, all afternoon, the Big Shilling helping American Troy acclimatise to Mediterranean mores and conditions. As he talked, the Big Shilling was aware of playing a role. He felt like an actor on the stage, and wondered when the kid would realise he was watching a performance. He worried about the kid, he really did. It was like having a somnambulist for an apprentice. Well, he'd just have to wake him up somehow. Yes, one way or another American Troy was going to wake up, even if it killed him in the process. For a moment, the Big Shilling imagined the kid post mortem, and saw nothing but a cloud of gas dispersing.

The house was only a hundred yards from the sea, and to the east, next to the beach, there were bars and restaurants lining the road that led to the harbour where the glass-bottomed tourist boats plied their trade. Late afternoon, the Big Shilling took American Troy to buy flip-flops and swimming trunks, bottles of water and sun cream. American Troy was still complaining.

'I've got a pair of shorts, what do I need trunks for?'

'You're going to learn to swim, my boy, that's why. I'm going to teach you to swim, eh?'

'I don't need to learn to swim. I hate the water, I hate the sea.'

'I don't give a flying duck what you hate, you're learning to swim and that's that. If we exfiltrate by boat, then you need to be able to swim out to it. If the boat capsizes, you need to be able to swim back to it, eh? Because then I won't be wasting my time saving your sorry ass from drowning, you understand me?'

Troy cursed under his breath. He knew when he was beat. He allowed the Big Shilling to buy him flip-flops and swim shorts, and they spent the afternoon at the beach.

True to his sometime maxim of not attracting attention, the Big Shilling swam in a t-shirt. American Troy knew why. He may not have seen the soles of Shilling's feet before, but he had seen the scars on his back. It reminded him of one of those old British movies where some dude gets flogged on the deck of a sailing ship for taking a swipe at the second-in-command. American Troy couldn't be certain who'd flogged the Big Shilling but he had the strangest idea it was the little guy's old man.

The Big Shilling carried other scars too, on his legs, neck and arms, but these did not seem so out of place on the beach that afternoon, for there were British servicemen enjoying a day by the sea with their families, and American Troy had noticed this one guy with Liverpool FC tattoos whose back was pitted with shrapnel scarring, and another who had bullet wounds in his thighs and calves.

It was in part being in the presence of men who had gone to war that made American Troy throw himself wholeheartedly into learning to swim. He'd been to the pool as a kid of course, but the chemicals they put in the water made his eyelids swell, and as a result he'd never really got the hang of swimming, but here in the warm sea, buoyed up by brine, he soon learned how to tread water, and before long could just about manage the breast stroke.

'That's great work, eh, great work,' said the Big Shilling, bobbing about nearby. 'You were having me on when you said you couldn't swim, hey?'

'Just need some practice,' American Troy said, bitterly resenting being coached in public.

'Every morning we'll swim, eh? Every morning and evening, we'll swim. We'll get you some goggles, eh. That will give you confidence to put your head under.'

They came out of the water together, the Big Shilling and his apprentice, but American Troy was soon left behind. The Big Shilling strode up the beach bare-footed. Troy nearly fell over in the sucking shingle, and he had to slip his feet into the flip-flops before he could negotiate the burning hot sand.

American Troy sought out the shade of the sun umbrella and dried off, feeling angry and humiliated. The Big Shilling stood out in the broiling sun scanning the horizon. He was searching for sign of the Melissa, but the only boats they'd seen all afternoon were the glass-bottomed craft taking tourists round the headland to the west.

Troy lay down on his side and checked out some of the Cypriot girls a few sunbeds along. They weren't his type he decided. Their skin was nice and brown, but they were nowhere near good looking enough. The girls with the British soldiers were much more to his taste - milfs, amateurs, pawgs - but he had to be circumspect about checking them out: the big guy with the tats and the scars kept staring at him, like a fucking animal. Troy lay on his back. He was hot, way too hot. Even the breeze off the goddamn sea was hot. Eventually, his bad temper subsided, and he lay there uncomfortably, hammered into submission by the heat.

It was early evening when they got back to the house. Troy went up to shower and change. He rinsed out his new swim shorts in the sink and examined his shoulders for sunburn. He was going to have to be careful. Even though he'd applied factor thirty sun cream his shoulders were pink and tender. The Big Shilling had slathered himself in factor fifty. For a guy who'd grown up in Barbados his skin was whiter than white. American Troy reckoned the Big Shilling had Irish blood. Yeah, his skin colour was the same as Johnny Rotten's circa 1976. And Irish ancestry would account for his love of the blarney. Man, could he talk. Troy had never met anyone who could talk like the Big Shilling. Not even his own father, the master confidence trickster, could talk the way the Big Shilling could talk.

He could hear him now, speaking into the phone in the living room downstairs. It sounded like bad news.

'It couldn't last,' said the Big Shilling when American Troy came downstairs. 'It couldn't last, eh? You knew it couldn't last, didn't you?'

'When did I say that?'

'You didn't have to say it, it's in your demeanour.'

The Big Shilling was drinking bottled water from the ice box, seated on the couch in front of the comms centre.

'What's up?'

'What's up? I'll tell you what's up. That was the Turk, news from Moscow. The word is, Putin is about to announce a pardon for the Russian exile.'

'Shit, so that means he'll go back to Russia.'

'It means he might go back to Russia.'

'And we can't hit him there.'

'Worse than an island, Russia, eh,' said the Big Shilling. 'I've operated on five continents but I've never taken a contract in old Rusland, and I never will, hey? It's impossible to work there, impossible, even for a man of my prowess, even for the Big Shilling.'

'Fuck.'

'No,' said the Big Shilling, 'not fuck in any way, shape or form. Fuck your fucks, eh, fuck them. It's time to get down to work, boy, no more lounging round in the sun. We still have time to pull this off, eh, we still have time if we get our fingers out, extract our digits. Believing is seeing, remember? From now on, no mistakes, everything has to be done right first time, every time, hey?'

'What mistakes? There haven't been any mistakes.'

'No mistakes?'

'What mistakes?'

'You tell me.'

American Troy shook his head in frustration. 'We

can't do anything until Frankie the Fish gets here.'

'You've briefed Tryphon and the Albanians?'

'I told you I've been over to Paphos to see them, I told you in the car.'

'So you did, so you did. Well, I'm off for a shower. We'll leave at ten to seven.'

'Where are we going?'

'To meet Frankie. Didn't I tell you? He dropped anchor an hour ago. The Melissa is here, anchored off-shore, eh? We'll have a sundowner on the boat and then dinner. What? Maybe if you hadn't been checking out the talent you'd have noticed.'

'My bad,' said Troy.

'It's not a fucking joke, boy,' said the Big Shilling, loping up the stairs. 'No mistakes, no mistakes from now on.'

'Right.'

That guy, thought American Troy, and his need to fucking know.

Frankie the Fish was waiting for them when they got to the harbour a little after seven o'clock. It was cooler now, and American Troy was getting used to walking in flip-flops, or so he thought. The restaurants on the quay were already filling up, and the music and the lights lifted Troy's spirits.

'You walk like an American,' the Big Shilling observed. 'Even in flip-flops you walk like an American.'

'I am an American. How else can I walk?'

'Like an individual. Nothing you have is your own,

American Troy, it's all copied, even your walk. You walk like an American, hey?'

'Can't you leave me alone, just for five minutes?'

'You want me to leave you alone?'

'Yeah, I want you to leave me alone. Is this him?'

'Frankie the Fish? Looks like him, but who knows? Maybe he's someone else.'

Troy sighed and said nothing. Did all of that mean anything? Or did it mean nothing at all? He didn't know and right now didn't much care.

Frankie the Fish was shooting the breeze with the guys who rented out speedboats. From what Troy could make out, Frankie the Fish spoke fluent Greek. He was a funny-looking guy, floppy fair hair, blood-shot blue eyes, bandy legs. His front teeth were too big for his mouth, and he appeared to be lacking a chin. American Troy thought Frankie the Fish wouldn't have looked out of place in one of those English costume dramas about country houses and Oxford University.

The Big Shilling introduced them.

'Delighted,' said Frankie the Fish.

'Hey Frankie,' said American Troy.

'Brandy sour suit you?'

'Sure, why not?'

'Why not, indeed?'

In one hand Frankie was holding a string shopping bag filled with bottles, in the other a frayed blue rope attached to a ring on a dinghy with a little outboard motor.

The dinghy hardly looked big enough for one man,

never mind three, but they managed to squeeze aboard somehow. Frankie the Fish entrusted his shopping to Troy, started up the motor, and guided the little craft out into the harbour. Troy squirmed and silently fumed. He hated the confined space, and being in close proximity to men wearing few clothes. His discomfort did not go unnoticed.

'You all right there, shipmate?' asked Frankie the Fish.

'Yeah,' snapped Troy.

'He doesn't like the water,' the Big Shilling observed as the dinghy left the harbour and the swell suddenly increased. 'He can't swim, you see.'

'Some of the best sailors can't swim.'

'Fuck this,' said Troy, squirming and fuming.

The Big Shilling laughed at him, then began to tell Frankie the Fish the best way to make a brandy sour.

Troy was doing his best not to get soaked by the sea slopping over the side of the dinghy. They were sitting alarmingly low in the water. As they approached the Melissa, American Troy felt even more dismayed. Was this the boat they were going to make their escape on after wacking the Russian? Jesus Christ, he was surprised it could even float, never mind sail. It looked like it belonged on the beach in a breaker's yard. Troy muttered under his breath, wishing he was elsewhere, wishing he'd never got caught up in this lousy business.

'You say something?' the Big Shilling demanded.

'Me? Say something? I didn't say anything, I didn't say anything at all.'

'You sure? I thought you spoke.'

American Troy filled his lungs.

'Why do you needle me? Why do you always have to needle me?' American Troy appealed to Frankie: 'Why does he needle people? You know him. Why does he always have to needle people?'

'Ha ha ha,' said Frankie the Fish, as though American Troy was making a joke. 'Nearly there now.'

The Big Shilling laughed, and his laughter transmogrified into an impression of a pantomime pirate that would have been deeply irritating had Frankie not sought Troy's assistance as they came along side. Mercifully, Shilling shut up.

Getting aboard the yacht was relatively easy, three steps up an aluminium ladder, but there was hardly more room aft than there had been in the dinghy. Frankie took the shopping bag from him, and American Troy found a place to sit by what he supposed was the tiller, and tried to look more nonchalant than he felt. The yacht bobbed up and down unpleasantly, and as Frankie mixed the drinks, he and the Big Shilling chatted. Troy tried to follow the conversation, but it was like the time they'd met South African Troy at the airport in Sofia, Bulgaria. The Big Shilling and Frankie the Fish were definitely speaking English but Troy could understand only half of what was said. He found Frankie's upper class British accent particularly off-putting. It made him feel like a hick, but there was one thing he couldn't fault and that was the brandy sours Frankie fixed.

'You didn't tell me I'd be working with an RSP,' said

Frankie to the Big Shilling at one point.

'You talking about me?' demanded Troy, suddenly belligerent now he had a couple of drinks under his belt. 'What's an RSP?'

'A snip-cock,' said Shilling with a wicked grin. 'A Red Sea Pedestrian.'

American Troy was on his feet, ready to smash his glass into Frankie the Fish's stupid, inbred British face. 'You son of a bitch,' he said, 'no one speaks to me like that.'

But of course they were winding him up. It turned out that Frankie the Fish's wife was Jewish, which made his daughter Melissa Jewish as well.

'Bastards,' said American Troy, subsiding into his seat. 'And for the record, I am not a Hebe.'

'All right, old boy, you're not a Hebe,' said Frankie the Fish.

'He's not a Hebe,' said the Big Shilling.

'I'm not a Hebe,' said American Troy, starting to laugh. 'I'm a wop, and don't know one forget it.'

They all laughed, they laughed a lot out there on the bobbing yacht as the sun went down, what with all those brandy sours they kept putting away. American Troy laughed so much he had tears in his eyes, although later he couldn't exactly recall what had been so funny.

The quick trip back to shore in the dinghy was a breeze compared to the journey out, and they were greeted like royalty at the restaurant beside the maritime police station. Frankie the Fish seemed to know everyone and everyone seemed overjoyed to see him. American Troy could see now why the Big Shilling had insisted Frankie was the man they needed as a fixer on the island. Troy even laughed when his miniature hamburger arrived and it turned out that Frankie had ordered it off of the kids' menu.

Listen and learn, he told himself, when the two older men spoke more quietly together about the matter in hand, listen and learn. That's what you're here for, to listen and learn. That's what American Troy told himself, but it didn't prevent him from chipping in from time to time and cheeking them. Troy just couldn't help himself.

He was drunk and happy, and Cyprus now seemed to him to be the most amazing place on earth. There was a sudden commotion, and the sound of smashing glass. A waiter had tripped over one of the cats that infested the fish restaurant and dropped a loaded tray, but Troy didn't even start.

Then the Big Shilling said, 'Hey, wise guy, smart mouth, come here, come here,' urging Troy to move closer. He moved, no longer troubled by proximity to other men. In fact, for a moment or two, the Big Shilling wasn't there at all, and Troy couldn't see a thing. He had to raise his chin and refocus before the Big Shilling reappeared. Blind drunk, Christ, I'm blind drunk. Troy had heard the phrase but this was the first time he'd actually experienced it.

'You see,' the Big Shilling was telling him, 'you see, a crime is a lot like a movie, a lot like a movie, eh. First of all, you have the producer, in this case

Ahmet Bey. The producer decides he wants to make a certain kind of picture, eh, in this case it's about an assassination, an assassination. The producer says, let's make a movie about an assassination. Are you listening to me, boy?'

American Troy's head bobbed about liquidly. 'Sure I'm listening. Listen and learn, right? Jesus, I'm listening.'

'So listen, and learn. The second stage is the screenwriting stage. The producer needs a screenwriter. He came to me and asked me to write the script. I am the screenwriter, and I use my wonderful, inner creative powers to write the script, eh? In my script, the assassination succeeds, and the assassin escapes with the prize, he escapes with the prize and thus realises the producer's vision for a successful assassination movie.'

American Troy reached across the table, plucked the bottle from the bucket of melted ice, and sloshed wine into his glass.

'Go on,' he slurred when the Big Shilling glared at him, 'assasha ... assassination sucks ... succeeds.'

'Listen to me. Are you listening to me? It's all about vision, of visualising the outcome, hey, the successful outcome of the crime. The question I ask myself is: what would I see? What would I see, eh, when I succeed? What would I see? What would I say? How would I act? And once I've answered those questions, I write the scene, eh, the scene of fulfilment.'

Troy put down his wine glass carefully, but even so

he heard it thump against the table. What the Big Shilling was saying suddenly seemed to him to be of fundamental importance, and Troy resolved to concentrate harder on what was being said.

'Right, scene of fur-filment.'

'Fulfilment.'

'What I said.'

'What comes next?' the Big Shilling asked him. 'Producer, screenwriter ...'

'Actors. No, director.'

'And who is the director?'

'You are.'

'I am.

'What is the director? No, shut up, shut up, keep your mouth shut, boy. You don't know the answer, eh, so I will tell you. The director is my ability, honed to a razor's edge through years of effort and hard work, to control my attention, to control my attention and become completely absorbed in that single scene, the scene of fulfilment.'

'Right,' said American Troy, raising the wine glass to his parched lips, 'that's right.'

'That's right, kid,' said the Big Shilling, strange-eyed, 'have another drink.'

CHAPTER EIGHT

The restaurant was closing by the time the three conspirators had rounded off their meal with coffee and Cyprus brandy.

'Go back to the house and check on the news,' the Big Shilling told American Troy.

'Huh?'

'Get your head off the table, and go back to the house and check on the news.'

American Troy lifted his head off the table. The restaurant spun.

'You all right, old boy?'

'He'd better not be drunk, eh? Not on company time.'

Holding onto the table and the back of a chair, Troy climbed swaying to his feet. He stood there, his head wobbling on his neck. He shuffled his flip-flops clear of the chair legs, straightened his back and let go of the table. He stood there for a moment unaided, then, trying not to slur his words, he told them he'd see them later.

The Big Shilling and Frankie the Fish watched the American kid as he stumbled across the car park in front of the police station.

'He's all right,' said the Big Shilling, ironically. 'He comes from a long line of shysters, shylocks and schlemiels, but he's all right, eh?'

'If I had to make a prediction,' ventured Frankie the Fish, 'I'd say he's the kind of chap who'd be running back to get you, if you'd been winged and the bullets were flying, that is. He's the kind of chap you'd want in your section, spirited.'

'Yeah,' said Shilling, 'he'd fight anyone, any place, any time, any size. Just like me, eh? Just like the Big Shilling. We'll see. We will see, in the fullness of time.'

'So there'll be two of you, will there, when we rendezvous?'

The Big Shilling regarded Frankie with cold, slightly unfocused eyes and did not respond.

Instead, he said, 'The kid's step-dad was a gun nut, and a biker. That's where he gets his love of firearms from, eh, and his love of motorcycles. He's spent a lot of time on the range but he's got no military training, and he's never been in a gun fight.'

'Perhaps I could help rectify that particular deficiency,' said Frankie, swirling the last of the brandy in his glass.

'I'll bring along a couple of other guys, eh, and we'll make a party of it.'

Frankie swallowed the last of the brandy and wiped his lips with a paper napkin. The table was littered with the remains of their meal. Frankie ate a chip that he spied sticking out from under a fish head, and called for the bill.

'I've got a selection of Cypriot army uniforms, and boots, up at the farm. Any idea of sizes? I'll sling them in the back of the Land Rover when I pick it up in the morning.'

The Big Shilling thought about it, then described the build of the male model Tryphon and of the Albanian card sharp. He knew their shoe sizes.

'My dear old thing,' said Frankie with a smile, 'I forgot to mention it. I've managed to get hold of an absolute beauty of a .303 for you, plus sniper scope and fifty rounds. I'm sure we'll be able to find a quiet spot for you to give it a try out.'

'What about the rest of your shopping list, hey? Any problems?'

'None whatsoever, old chum, none whatsoever. If there's one thing you can rely on in Cyprus, it's a ready supply of arms and ammunition. Chap's are practically giving it away. Ah, thank you very much indeed, my wanker,' he added in Greek, as the waiter brought them the bill.

'Malaka mou,' he explained to the Big Shilling, 'it means 'my wanker'. Everyone says it these days, even kids to their grandmamas.' Frankie laughed and finished the last of his coffee.

'Malaka,' said Shilling, trying out the word for size, 'malaka. I'll remember that.' He unpeeled two 50 euro notes and gave them to Frankie who tucked them under a cup and saucer before sorting through some change.

They were both more than a little drunk, the Big Shilling and Frankie the Fish, and they too stumbled a little as they got up, shook hands effusively with a waiter, and the proprietor, and a second waiter, and made their way unsteadily down the steps to the car park.

'Did you leave a tip?' Shilling asked Frankie.

'A Cypriot tip.'

'Not much of a tip then, eh.'

'It's what they expect, it's what I usually leave. No point in drawing attention to oneself.'

Saying that, Frankie the Fish turned to the darkened balcony of the police station where two cops were sitting smoking cigarettes, and engaged them in a long and rather loud conversation.

The Big Shilling concealed himself in the shadows cast by the beach changing booths, and looked up at the maritime police patrol vessel which had been winched out of the water and into the car park for repairs. One less patrol boat, that had to be good news. He could hear the cops calling Frankie their wanker. Suddenly, the Big Shilling was more alert. His Greek was poor but he could make out the gist of what Frankie and the cops were saying. It appeared to be quite innocent, but the Big Shilling was nevertheless reminded of Frankie the Fish's connections to the secret world of special operations and the intelligence agencies. The sooner this job was over the better, thought the Big Shilling, the sooner it is over the better.

'I am,' he said to himself, swaying slightly with his hands in his pockets. 'I am – drunk.'

Now that Frankie the Fish's banter with the cops was finished, he and Shilling meandered across the car park and stood looking at the sea.

'Motorbike,' said Frankie, 'oh yes, I almost forgot, the motorbike. Does me laddo still get to see it first?'

'No time for that,' said the Big Shilling. 'Just as long as it can shift and there's two seats, hey?'

'500cc Yamaha, two seats, two helmets, which is more than you can say for this clown.'

The clown he was referring to was a Cypriot kid on a trail bike, racing past the police station without lights, without helmet, and without silencer.

When the ear-splitting noise had abated as the kid roared out of town, Frankie said as though to himself, 'They take the silencers off so you can hear them coming.'

The Big Shilling began to regale Frankie with a tale about motor-biking in the Australian outback but Frankie had heard him tell it before, and interrupted.

'Where to, my dear old thing?' he said. 'After the rendezvous, I mean. That's what I meant to ask you. And how many passengers will we be welcoming aboard?'

The Big Shilling looked at the Britisher. He didn't like to be interrupted, he didn't like it at all. Now he wondered if Frankie the Fish was as drunk as he appeared.

'I'm thinking about fuel and provisions, you see,' said Frankie, oblivious, kicking at a pebble with a canvas deck shoe. 'No point in carrying more weight than necessary.'

'All right,' said the Big Shilling, belligerently, 'I'll tell you, Frankie old friend, I'll tell you, eh. The Greek and the Albanian, they're a present from me to the cops, from the Big Shilling to the Cypriot public prosecutor, hey? Why? Loss of face. I mean, loss of face, eh? I'm going to give the cops, and the politicians, those two guys on a plate. That's what I'm going to do, eh, that's the Big Shilling's plan. I'm going to serve those two guys up to them so they can save face, so they can save face, eh? There's no point in humiliating them, is there, eh? No point at all.'

'All right, all right, there's no need for unpleasantness.'

'Bollocks,' said the Big Shilling, toe to toe with the other man, 'bollocks to your unpleasantness, you posh English prick, eh? Hey? You'll be waiting there, you'll be waiting there for me, for us, for however many bodies I turn up with, right? Right. And if I tell you to take me, us, them, to Croatia, then we go to Croatia. If I say Bulgaria, then Bulgaria it is. Sicily, then Sicily.'

'I get the idea,' said Frankie, moving away.

'Where are you going when I'm speaking to you, eh?'

'Back to the boat, old bean. Time to catch some shut eye. I think you could do with a bit of rest as well, if you don't mind my saying.'

'Time for another drink, time for one more, eh?'

'I don't think so, got to be up bright and early to go up to the farm.'

'All right,' said the Big Shilling moving closer to Frankie. 'You get off then. You get off, old chum.'

For a moment, the two men stared each other out. Then the Big Shilling winked, shook Frankie's hand, and told him he'd see him in the morning.

Shilling walked unsteadily back to the house, past the bars and the night clubs which were filling up now that the restaurants had closed. The pavements were crowded, and so was the roadway where the pavement ended, but no one got in the Big Shilling's way, not when they saw the murderous look on the face of the truculent little actor.

Back at the house, the Big Shilling kept up the routine, pretending to be drunker and angrier than he was. He wanted to see how American Troy reacted, but Troy himself could hardly keep his eyes open.

'No news,' he repeated, slurring the words. 'Nothing new, nix. I'm going to bed now, I got to go to bed now.'

'No,' said the Big Shilling, holding the fridge door open. 'We'll have a nightcap, eh? You'll have a final drink with the Big Shilling before you go up to bed, eh? Of course you will.'

'I can't drink a thing more.'

'Of course you can, of course you can. I'll pour you a small one.'

'Just a small one.'

'What's happening in Russia?'

'Nothing.'

'You sure?'

It was as though the kid hadn't heard. He said, drunkenly, 'What's my angle?'

'Angle? What is this? The method method?'

'I mean, if I have an angle, I can feel a lot better.'

'Have another drink, that'll make you feel better.'

'Nah, I have to go to bed.'

'It's only wine,' said the Big Shilling, 'there's only white wine.'

'It's Keo wine,' said American Troy, laughing.

'Keo make beer.'

'They make wine as well,' said Troy, laughing a little more loudly.

'What are you laughing at?'

'I'm laughing because it is funny.'

'I'm not laughing.'

Troy stopped laughing. Through the fug of alcohol he had finally recognised the Big Shilling's foul temper.

'I have to go to bed,' he said in conciliatory voice.

The Big Shilling stopped glaring at him and examined the label of the bottle of Aphrodite white wine instead. Sure enough, he saw that it was made by Keo.

'No nightcap then,' said the Big Shilling, crossing to the sink and sluicing the whole bottle down the plughole with a blast of hot water from the tap.

'Maybe he was winding you up.'

'No,' said the Big Shilling, 'no.'

'When Frankie said Keo's profits go to the church and the communists, maybe he was j-joking.'

'He wasn't j-joking,' said the Big Shilling, 'it's true. I don't know who I despise more, eh, Christians or communists.'

'You said they were the same.'

'They are the same, they are the same, but even so, eh, I don't know which I despise the most, Christians or communists.'

'Christians,' said Troy.

'You only say that because all you Hebes are communists. Where are you going?'

'To crash.'

'Problem is,' said the Big Shilling as though to himself, 'I like Keo beer, I like the taste. That Leon is just fizzy water, fizzy water, hey?'

'Night, boss.'

'Goodnight yourself. Get to bed, get to bed and sleep it off.'

After American Troy had gone to bed, the Big Shilling slammed the fridge door, poured himself a glass of iced water, and sat on the couch. The kid hadn't shut off the laptop. Shilling checked the open tabs: various news websites, an advertisement for a camwhore, and a Hollywood gangster movie – what else? He touched play, and saw a gangster taking some other gangster into the woods to waste him, that old trope, eh? One after another he closed the tabs, and when the computer was done shutting down, he slammed the lid closed.

He thought about the Lee Enfield sniper rifle that Frankie the Fish had procured for him, and imagined shooting the Russian exile in the head with it. He imagined the Russian exile standing on the sun terrace of his big house in the Akamas, the big house with the Russian flag on it, of him standing there surrounded by his wife and kids and henchmen, and his head exploding, bursting red like a watermelon.

That was what was going to happen. That was what he visualised, and believed, as though it had already happened.

But suddenly it wasn't enough. It wasn't in any way satisfying enough. Shilling hunched his shoulders and clenched his fists. He was drunk, he knew he was, but anyway, everything proceeded, as it always did.

This was the man, this Russian exile, who had put out a contract of half a million US, half a million, a derisory sum, an insulting sum, on his head, on the head of the Big Shilling. No, this man had something better coming than a clean shot through the brain, he had something worse coming than that. No one crossed the Big Shilling and got away with it, no one. No.

The Big Shilling imagined the Russian exile on his knees begging for his life. He imagined the Russian exile kneeling there as he, the Big Shilling, executed the Russian's wife, the Russian's children. Yes, that was what he would do. Forget the sniper rifle, forget the long shot, the clean kill in the Akamas, forget the escape by trail bike across the rocky, dirt roads of the Akamas, forget all that, eh. Yes.

No, there would be horror, there would be terror. He would terrorise this Russian fucker, terrorise everyone, terrorise the whole of Cyprus, the world. That is what he would do, the Big Shilling.

When the One became Two, then Seth, the Opponent, was born!

'That which is falling ought to be pushed,' said Shilling, his voice a cracked murmur, 'that which is crawling ought to be crushed.'

The incantation pleased him, so much so that he repeated it, again and again.

He was on his feet now, unsteady, fists clenched, his face hard, wishing there was a mirror on the wall of the open-plan living room so that he could see his own murderous expression.

'Half a million,' he muttered, crapulently, 'half a fucking million?'

Fists thrust in the pockets of his shorts, the Big Shilling lurched across the room to the downstairs toilet, and urgently emptied his bladder.

'Don't they know who I am?' he demanded, leaning heavily against the wall. 'Don't they realise who it is they are dealing with? I am the Lord, and vengeance will be mine!'

He cackled with laughter.

CHAPTER NINE

'There's no menu,' said American Troy when he came back from the bar with an earthenware jug of village wine. He cleared his throat and coughed. He was seriously dehydrated. Even after sinking glass after glass of water he was still seriously dehydrated.

'What did I tell you, eh? You get what you're given here, and you'll like it.'

Troy sat down at the table under the vines and shakily poured them each a glass of wine. The Big Shilling was preoccupied, staring out to sea. The breeze ruffled his dyed brown hair.

It was the following lunchtime, and American Troy and the Big Shilling were eating out at The Eagle's Nest, an open-air restaurant on top of a flat hill in the Akamas national park in south-west Cyprus.

American Troy sipped the wine gratefully, hoping it would have a similar effect that the brandy had

had in Geneva. He was hungover and feeling a little nauseous. The journey to the restaurant hadn't helped much. The Land Rover that Frankie the Fish had delivered to the house that morning had no air con and its front springs were shot, so American Troy had arrived at The Eagle's Nest dripping sweat and feeling sick. He'd slept badly the night before and upon waking had discovered his legs were covered with mosquito bites. Now he was thinking about the bites, they began to itch. He resisted the urge to scratch them.

Why was he drinking so much? He could barely remember a time when he wasn't either drunk or hungover. There was only the here and the now, his acid stomach and a thick head, the foul taste of last night's booze in his parched mouth.

He looked around the joint to distract himself. At least there was a nice breeze up here on the hilltop by the sea, and the vines overhead provided protection from the fierce sun. A dusty cat was begging scraps from the plates of a Chinese couple, and there were sparrows hopping about, pecking at crumbs on the stone floor and on the table tops. It looked unsanitary to American Troy, allowing animals where humans were eating. He would have much preferred to have been in one of the many clean, air-conditioned restaurants that they'd passed on the way to the Akamas. Also, the wine wasn't anywhere near chilled enough.

'I'll go get some ice,' he told the Big Shilling, but the Big Shilling ignored him.

Shilling was looking down at the fenced planta-tion of citrus trees at the bottom of the hill. They were in dire need of water. Whoever had planted them was neglecting them. Further along he could see bananas and avocados, green and flourishing. And beyond those fields he could just make out a corner of the wall of the Russian exile's compound, peeping out between the brown slopes of the hills.

'Can you believe it?' asked American Troy when he returned from the bar. 'They're out of ice.'

The Big Shilling ignored him. 'Come and sit over here, eh, and have a look up there.'

American Troy did as he was told. He sat down next to the Big Shilling and looked along the escarp-ment.

'I see it,' he said. 'Is that it?'

'A little slice of old Russia, eh, transplanted to a small sandy island in the eastern Mediterranean. What else do you see?'

'Rocks, dirt, and trees.'

'Anything else?'

'The island. There's an island off-shore.'

'Yeah, it's uninhabited. In ancient times they used to perform human sacrifices there, eh.'

American Troy smirked. It seemed like a good omen.

'What don't you see?' the Big Shilling asked him, curtly.

'Jesus, man, why don't you just tell me? What don't I see? A Maccy D's, polar bears, the Sears Tower.'

'Quit whining, kid.'

'Jesus,' mumbled American Troy.

'Houses,' said the Big Shilling, 'houses, eh? Except one, the Russian exile's place.'

'It's a national park,' said American Troy. 'No construction.'

'Exactly, exactly. Now you've got it, now you've got it, hey? Except, this is Cyprus, and if someone wants to build in the Akamas he builds in the Akamas. Only one problem: electricity, electricity, eh? The local city council won't hook you up, not unless you pay the mayor a fat bribe.'

'And that's what the Russian did,' said American Troy.

'That is what he did. Some people hate him for building a house in the national park, but a lot of people love him for it, eh, the local people here, eh, because they want to build houses here as well, and gas stations, and bars, and restaurants, and supermarkets. They want to make the national park look like the rest of Cyprus, the rest of the 'developed' world, an eyesore, an eyesore, eh?'

'Right,' said American Troy, doubtfully.

'What else do you see?'

Troy turned away from the view, because there was nothing else to see, and surveyed the lunch crowd instead.

'Greek families, a couple of Chinese with a kid feeding a dirty cat, and a yuge table of Brits, old guys and gals celebrating a birthday, or some such shit.'

The Big Shilling was looking at Troy questioningly, but fortunately for the kid at that moment a waiter appeared bearing food who was followed by a waitress with plates and cutlery. There was a village salad in a metal bowl, a platter of chips, and two platters of meat, one of chicken and the other pork.

'Pork?' queried American Troy. 'I hate pork.'

'You get what you get here, eh,' said the Big Shilling, dismissing the waiter who was hovering doubtfully.

'The chicken looks okay though.'

The Big Shilling sighed. 'It's all okay, kid, you think they want to poison you? This is a restaurant run by a nice Cypriot family, mom and pop and grandma and the kids, eh? They don't want to kill you, they want you to come back next week and bring your family and friends.'

'Pork doesn't agree with me.'

'It doesn't agree with your religion, hey?'

American Troy took a breath, and said, 'I don't have a religion. I told you I don't know how many goddamn times.'

'All right, all right, it doesn't agree with your ethnicity then.'

'I don't have an ethnicity, I'm an American. It's just pork. I've eaten pork in the past and it doesn't agree with me.'

'Have some salad,' said the Big Shilling, breaking up the feta cheese with his fingers and mixing up the tomatoes, lettuce, olives and shredded cabbage the way the Cypriots did it.

'I'll just get the chicken and the French fries,' said

Troy, pulling a face.

'They're not French fries, they're chips, eh, made out of Cyprus potatoes, the finest potatoes in the whole world.'

'For a guy who claims to hate farming, you sure as hell know your potatoes.'

'You know why they're the finest potatoes in the whole world, eh? Because they're grown in the best soil, the very best soil. The Irish grew potatoes in the worst soil, that's why they got potato blight, eh? The soil was bad. That's why the Potato Famine happened, bad soil, very bad soil, eh?'

American Troy nodded, wondering if there was a subtext he was supposed to pick up on, or was Shilling merely admitting he had Irish ancestry. The Big Shilling had been in a strange mood all morning. Troy cut off a piece of chicken and put it in his mouth speculatively. He chewed. It wasn't half bad, not bad at all. All he needed now was some ketchup, but he didn't signal to the waiter. After the fiasco with the ice he decided it was a waste of time.

The Big Shilling ate heartily, as he always did. He ate heartily, and noisily, the way he always did. That afternoon he ate enough for two men, and both of them twice the size he was.

'You need fuel, eh,' he kept explaining to American Troy, 'you need a store of energy for the job in hand.'

Troy ate sparingly and feasted on the wine instead. He ate sparingly because of his acid stomach, and because of the annoying animal-like noises the Big Shilling made while masticating, which put him off his own food. The wine gave him a mellow buzz that eased his hangover and made the masticating noises seem less intrusive. Indeed, the wine jug appeared to be bottomless. Then, as he recharged his glass for the umpteenth time, he realised the jug held a litre, almost two pints. It was village wine, and not particularly strong, and Troy was experiencing a pleasant fuzziness.

'The Brits drink it,' the Big Shilling explained, his mouth half full of meat, 'the expats. You buy it in the supermarket for a couple of euros. It comes in a carton, eh, not a bottle, a carton.'

Again, American Troy had the idea that he was missing something, he just didn't know what. He looked over his shoulder.

The seniors at the long table were merrily chorusing 'Happy Birthday' for the second time. The beaming waitress had just delivered a cake and a big red-faced guy was using the cake-slice to conduct the singing. There was something about the scene that American Troy found deeply irritating. His face was burning up and his ears started to hum. Mumbling, he excused himself and went to the bathroom.

As he took a leak he read the sign requesting soiled toilet paper be placed in the bin provided rather than flushed. This disturbed him still further. Fastidiously, once he had finished, he folded a square of toilet tissue into four and used it to dry the tip of his penis. He dropped the paper into the bowl and flushed it. Exiting the stall, he used the gel he carried in his pocket to wash his hands. Now he felt sick and drunk, and not the nice kind of drunk. He wished he were someplace else. He wondered if he should make himself throw up, but the thought of sticking his fingers down his throat repelled him. Despondently, he traipsed back to the table.

'Get the bill,' the Big Shilling told him shortly afterwards. 'And lay off the wine, eh, you've had enough. We're leaving in five minutes.'

The Big Shilling crumpled a napkin, tossed it on the table, and went off to the toilets. There he found the red-faced Englishman who had been conducting the singing waiting for him.

'Brian,' said the Big Shilling.

'All right, mate, how's it going?' said Brian Blee.

They stood side by side at the twin urinals, and peed.

'Betty's been down the school, her grandson's only moving out here next month,' explained the cockney gangster. 'Saw his wife and their little girl. Strewth, you should see her, the mother, legs up to her armpits, tiny little denim shorts, fuck me. The little girl's talking to her pal, in English because it's an international school, like. It's only her birthday coming up. She's having a party, down the ice cream parlour in Paphos. I tell you though, them legs on her mother, cor, I haven't had wood like that in fucking years. Betty can hardly walk in a straight line, know what I mean?'

The Big Shilling ignored the leering red face.

'Which ice cream parlour?'

'We think we know. I followed the guards down there this morning, they was on a recce. It's near the bus station. There's two places. Not the small one, the big one.'

'Thanks, Bri, you're a diamond. Put this in the kitty, eh?'

'Don't mind if I do.'

In return for the wad of euros, the fat cockney handed the Big Shilling a mobile.

'Photos of the guards,' he said. 'Scroll through, there's loads of them. Tasty geezers, ain't they? That big house near to our place? The last ones before you get to the Akamas? The guards hang out there, by the pool.'

'Right.'

'We done?'

'Oh no, not yet, not by a long chalk.'

Brian Blee laughed, delightedly.

'You're a fucking legend, BS.'

'That I am.'

Brian Blee, chuckling to himself, left first. When he was gone, the Big Shilling washed his hands at the sink. There was a mirror on the wall and he stared at himself in it for ten long seconds, imagining the future, imagining success, visualising it, visualising the dying Russian.

American Troy found him a few minutes later, strolling through the kitchen garden at the rear of the restaurant.

'Did you leave a tip?'

'Sure I left a tip. I always tip.'

'A Cypriot tip, or an American tip?'

'I tipped fifteen per cent,' lied American Troy. In fact, he had queried the bill and pocketed most of the change, leaving hardly any tip at all.

But the Big Shilling appeared to be satisfied. He and American Troy walked along the path between the furrows, past a shed and a couple of parked pick-up trucks, and up an incline to a bluff. From there they could see the rocky shoreline and the waves breaking white on the beach. In a flurry of energy, the Big Shilling scrambled up onto a pock-marked brown boulder and stood there with his hands on his hips. From the side pocket of his cargo shorts he produced the telescopic sight Frankie the Fish had left in the back of the Land Rover along with the Lee Enfield rifle.

Like the rifle, the telescopic sight was World War Two vintage, but that didn't mean it wasn't service-able. American Troy, who had downed a double brandy at the bar and so wasn't feeling quite as ill as he had been, watched the Big Shilling as he scoped out the Russian exile's house. Three or four minutes passed before the Big Shilling came down off the rock, handed Troy the scope and told him to have a look.

'Reckon I could take him from here, hey?'

'I guess so,' said American Troy. 'If he comes outside and stands there for long enough. Think he would? It looks like there's a sun terrace in back of the house. There's a bunch of umbrellas and sun loungers, and shit.'

'What else do you see?'

'I see a flag, a yuge Russian flag.'

You couldn't miss the flag, the huge Russian flag. It flew from a flag staff on the roof of the Russian exile's house, and the flag staff must have been seventy feet tall. The flag itself was smaller than the Olympic-sized swimming pool in the well-watered garden of the house, but not by much.

'It's not like he's hiding, is it?' said American Troy, impressed. 'This guy's living it large, oh yeah.'

'It's an insult, that's what it is, eh?' said the Big Shilling, suddenly angry. 'He's an insolent man, this Russian exile, eh? If I was a Cypriot I'd come up here and tear down that Russian flag. I would rip it down, hey?'

'The guard dogs might stop you, and the razor wire, and the high fence, and the guards with the sub-machine guns.'

'They wouldn't have stopped me, eh, not the Big Shilling. Nothing stops me, nothing at all, I'm invincible, I am. Get down from there, kid. We're going back to the car, and then we're going to have a closer look.'

CHAPTER TEN

They returned to the Land Rover. In the back of it, the Big Shilling had stashed a cool bag. Now he unzipped the bag and handed American Troy a couple of bottles of iced water. Troy watched as the Big Shilling changed his flip-flops for a pair of walking boots.

'You'll be okay in those, eh?' said the Big Shilling, indicating the Nikes that he'd insisted American Troy wear for their trip to the Akamas. 'You can't ride a bike in flip-flops, hey?'

American Troy smirked. He could hardly wait to get back on two wheels. He took a few sips of water.

'Are we bringing the rifle?'

The Big Shilling paused, grinning at him like it was a dumb question, and threw a beach towel over the Lee Enfield rifle in the back of the Land Rover. They set off. Shilling didn't bother to lock the car. It was the Cypriot way. Only tourists locked their cars. In any case, the Land Rover looked entirely innocent. It was battered and dented and dusty, and the paint was sun-scorched and blistered. Frankie the Fish had borrowed it from a friend who ran safari tours, ferrying tourists through the Akamas gorge, pretending it was Africa and there were big cats to goggle at. No one would look at it twice.

Now that he wasn't having to think about his hangover or his stomach, American Troy was thinking about money. He hadn't left much of a tip at the restaurant because of the toilets, and the wine being too warm, and their having run out of ice. That's what he was telling himself. Having said that, he had intended to leave a bigger tip, to tip the way the Big Shilling tipped, whether the service had been good or bad. He remembered the Filipina girl at the Geneva hotel, the way she'd accepted that big diamond ring. That was class, man. That was the way he wanted to behave. He was thinking of his old man, and Uncle Nathan as well. But it was difficult. When there was cold hard cash in his hand he found himself doing something other than he'd intended.

'You don't think you should tip?' he mumbled, repeating the movie dialogue that was sounding in his head. 'I don't tip because other people tell me I ought to tip. Tipping is for girls.'

And that set him thinking about his share again. Not just of this job, but of the Rotterdam hit as well. The Big Shilling had finally paid him the hundred thousand in London, minus the thousand Swiss francs, minus another six thousand francs for Marina and Marianne, the two hookers, minus seven hundred euros living expenses, minus quite a few

152

other things as well. That's what he couldn't figure. It was like the Big Shilling was playing him for a fool, sending him this way, then that. Six grand for those two hookers, even though it was supposed to be BS's present! American Troy now told himself that the Big Shilling was like one of those Zen masters who taught you how to hear the sound of one hand clapping. He hoped that's the way it was anyway.

'Hey.'

Troy looked up. 'Huh?'

'What time are you planning to get out of bed today? You're walking round in your goddamned sleep. Wake up, eh, wake up, dipstick – the Russians might not all be lounging round the pool, hey?'

'Right,' Troy mumbled. He drank some water. He gave the Big Shilling the other bottle, and the Big Shilling drank some water as well.

It was hot. Now that they were away from the shady vines and the trees, it was very hot indeed. And dusty. A gecko stood open-mouthed on a brown rock. Overhead, a raptor soared in the endless blue sky. American Troy drank some more water. He was wearing the ball cap the Big Shilling had bought for him at Latchi. He wondered if he'd be billed for that as well.

'Quit guzzling,' said the Big Shilling, who was sporting a camouflaged cap with the logo of the safari company on the front. 'From now on, not a word, eh? Hand signals only.'

Troy nodded that he understood. He felt a thrill

of anticipation. What if there were guards outside the compound? What if they recognised him and the Big Shilling as the men who'd killed Aias Pneumaticos? American Troy wished they'd brought that old World War rifle with them. He followed the Big Shilling off the main path and scrambled up the rocky slope after him.

And if they had brought that old rifle with them, and if they'd already made good their arrangements for escape, the story might have ended a few minutes later, for when they crept to the top of the escarpment above them and peered over the top, much closer to the Russian exile's house now, less than five hundred yards distant, they saw the man himself standing on a balcony beneath the billowing Russian flag.

'It's him,' Troy spluttered. 'Jesus.'

The Big Shilling appeared to be amused, then annoyed because Troy had spoken, after they agreed hand signals only. Troy mimed his apologies, and when he looked again the Russian had gone. Deflated, he sat down on the reverse slope with his back to the house.

Unperturbed by the intervention of chance, the Big Shilling studied the house through the sniper scope. The first thing he noticed was the telescope on the balcony the Russian exile had just vacated. He didn't think it was for star-gazing, not on this side of the house. At night you'd sit facing the sea and look up at the stars and the moon, and maybe see a ufo. No, the telescope was for scanning the approach from the north.

Not that anyone approaching from the north would have an easy time of it. The only road was in plain view of the house, indeed it went right past the compound wall. And the wall was a good fourteen feet high. Even if you parked a Land Rover next to the wall, you'd still need a leg up to get your hands on top of that wall. And you'd need to be wearing heavy-duty gloves and be carrying a wire cutter, on account of the double roll of razor wire fastened to steel poles embedded in the top of the wall.

The Big Shilling adjusted his cap, and turned his attention to the eastern approaches, which was where the main gate was. Next to the gate was a big metal sign with a silhouette of a Doberman on it. There were a pair of real Dobermans on patrol behind the gate, and he could see a Rottweiler and a German Shepherd dozing in the shade beside a row of kennels. Clearly, the guy loved dogs, the Russian exile. The Big Shilling was fond of dogs as well, but he reckoned he'd be steering well clear of this particular pack.

Up there on the burning, dusty rocks, the swimming pool and the shaded garden looked infinitely inviting. He hoped he might see the Russian's wife, and his children, cooling off in the water, but he saw no one else at all.

The Big Shilling slithered down off the crest and gave the scope to American Troy who took his place up top. Shilling drank some water and wiped the dust from his eyes. It wasn't long before Troy was trying to attract his attention. The Big Shilling looked at him sceptically and deduced from his mime that there was a car with two guards heading their way.

The Big Shilling called Troy in and the two of them made their way across the slope, away from the path that led to the dusty, rock-strewn road. They slid down into a defile and waited in the cool shadows.

It was Shilling who heard the big 4x4 first. Then Troy saw it, a white Nissan Patrol, dust-streaked but in perfect order. The passenger door opened and a Russian in a white shirt used binoculars to scan the ridge. He took his time doing it as well, the way a professional would. They could hear the engine's fan working overtime. The Russian looked over his shoulder. Something had caught his attention. It was a motorbike, approaching from the north. The Russian said something to the driver, got back in his seat and slammed the door.

Half an hour later they were back at The Eagle's Nest car park, comparing stories. American Troy was sitting astride the Yamaha, sipping iced water and laughing.

'Told them to eff off,' Frankie the Fish was saying. 'Cheeky bastards, who do they think they are, demanding to know what I was doing? What do you think I'm doing, squire? I said, I'm riding my effing motorbike. If you don't like it you can eff off.'

'We saw him,' said Troy again. 'We saw him on the balcony.'

'Same time tomorrow?' said Frankie. 'You think he gets a spot of air the same time every day?'

'He's coming out,' said the Big Shilling, darkly. 'I saw it in his face.'

American Troy thought that was unlikely, on account of the Big Shilling not having been looking through the sniper scope at the time. He snorted in derision.

'You think I'm lying?' the Big Shilling asked him, calmly. 'You think I'm lying, eh, boy? I may be short-sighted and need glasses for reading but I spent years in the bush spotting game. I saw his face all right, eh? There's nothing wrong with me seeing into the distance. I saw his face, I tell you, and he's had enough of being cooped up there, hey? That man has no fear. What he has is bravado, hey? What he has is bravado. And that is what will do for him. If he was sensible he'd stay hidden away, but he isn't sensible, is he, the Russian exile, hey? He's going to come out, and I'm going to be waiting for him when he does.'

'Pity, though, you didn't have that old rifle,' said Troy.

'And what would have happened if I had? Have you thought about that, my boy? Have you thought about that? Do you think we would have made it back here to the car park before the Russians in that big 4x4? And even if we had, eh, even if we had, Frankie's still here. No, no, we weren't ready, we weren't ready. Just edit that part, edit out the intervention of chance. But next time, when he comes out, we will be ready, won't we, eh?'

'Do you want me to sail off into the sunset tonight?' Frankie asked.

'No, stick to the plan. You've sorted it?'

'Yes, for tomorrow.'

'Are you listening, eh?' the Big Shilling asked American Troy. 'Frankie's arranged a spot of shooting practice for you tomorrow, after you've got the hang of that Yamaha.'

'Awesome.'

'It'll be like nothing you've ever done before, eh, Frankie? CQB: close-quarter battle.'

'I'm ready,' said American Troy. 'Bring it on.'

'Oh to be young again,' said Frankie the Fish.

'You're saying I'm old, Frankie, eh? Is that what you're saying? That the Big Shilling is past it, eh, is only fit for the scrapheap?'

Frankie knew when he was being wound up. 'My dear old thing, that's exactly what I'm saying.'

'We'll see,' said the Big Shilling, 'we'll see who's past it, hey? Troy, ride that thing to Paphos and meet us by the bus station at eight o'clock. There's a big ice cream parlour I want you to check out. The Albanians and Tryphon will be there. You remember them, don't you, eh?'

'What does that even mean? Sure I remember them. I only saw them the other day.'

'You do? You did?'

'Yeah.'

The Big Shilling laughed.

'Frankie, here's the keys. You're driving this heap of junk. Old man Shilling's going to curl up on the back seat and get some rest.'

They didn't see any more Russian patrols on their way out of the Akamas national park. The Big Shilling lay on the back seat of the Land Rover like he'd said he would, but he wasn't asleep. He was spying. As they left the national park he spied the Russian guards by the pool in the house near the apartment that Brian and Betty Blee had rented. He saw Brian Blee as well, sitting naked save for a pair of Union Jack underpants in a deckchair on the balcony of the apartment. He had a folded newspaper balanced on his beer gut and appeared to be attempting a crossword puzzle, but the Big Shilling knew he was really recording who left the Akamas by the main road, and who entered it.

It took them nearly two hours to get to Paphos. There were roadworks, and it was rush hour. The Big Shilling listened to Frankie the Fish's commentary on the habits of Cypriot drivers.

'Look at this clown. Where does he think he's going? Thank you, squire, you didn't see me, did you? Pulling out without looking, without signalling, what a chump!'

And so it went on.

'Frankie?'

'My dear old thing, woken from your slumber, have you?'

'You know what I'd like, Frankie? I'd like an ice

cream. There's a place by the bus station I've heard does the best ice cream in Cyprus. That's where we'll go, eh?'

'But you don't want me to park outside, is that it?'

'You're way ahead of me, eh?'

'I'll park near the lighthouse. They've just completed a new pathway along the sea there, near the place with the mosaics. We can stroll along the prom and go and get you an ice cream.'

'Sounds perfect, old fruit.'

'Nothing like a promenade.'

'Frankie, did I ever tell you about the Angolan Drill, did I ever tell you, eh?'

'My dear old thing, you know I believe you did.'

But the Big Shilling wasn't listening, he was already talking, already telling Frankie the Fish all about the Angolan Drill.

'That bastard,' he was saying, viciously, 'that dirty bastard, he wasn't even in Angola when he claimed to have invented the Angolan Drill. No, I invented it, not him, that lying son of a bitch. He was still in Salisbury, in the army, when I'd been in Angola for almost six months, so how the hell could he have invented the Angolan Drill? Tell me that, Frankie. Frankie, tell me that, eh? That bastard!'

CHAPTER ELEVEN

You couldn't walk more than a few yards without being accosted by a tout. Paphos harbour as the sun was going down, during peak tourist season, Cypriot entrepreneurs trying to make enough money to see them through the winter. There were touts for restaurants and touts for bars, touts for boat trips and touts for the electric scooters that excited teenagers were zooming about on. The male touts were mainly Greeks, charming and handsome, the female touts were pretty foreign girls wearing too much make-up and too few clothes.

American Troy ignored the male touts but he kept allowing the female touts to deliver their spiels. Entrance only five euros, show the barman this flyer to receive your complimentary drink, it's a sports bar, live football, rugby, and cricket. Beckham's, the bar was called, though American Troy somehow doubted the profits went to Posh and Becks.

The streets around the harbour were packed with tourists, Russians, Britons, Chinese. American Troy even spotted a few blacks, and he lingered outside the hair-braiding salon gawping at the African girls for several minutes, feeling strangely reassured. Yeah, all things considered, he was feeling on top of the world. The motorcycle Frankie the Fish had procured for him had been recently serviced and tuned, and it went like the wind. His insect bites no longer itched, his head no longer ached, and on the way to Paphos harbour he'd stopped off at Maccy D's and treated himself to a cheeseburger and strawberry milkshake which appeared to have sorted out his stomach. He could still taste the burger and milkshake, and when he did it set him smirking. This was more like it. I'm living the dream.

He checked the time. It was just before eight, time to make his way back to the ice cream parlour next to the bus station.

He'd already cased the joint. It was a great big barn of a place with two entrances, a door to the kitchens in back, and two fire exits next to the rest rooms. He'd even made a foray down the alley at the side of the building. The kitchen door had been open and he'd heard women laughing, and chattering away in Greek.

When American Troy turned the corner near the bus station, he spotted Tryphon the Greek guy, along with the Albanian couple, waiting outside.

Tryphon was a lanky, dark-skinned twenty-five year old who looked like a lifeguard. He was smoking a cigarette and checking out the local talent, a shit-eating grin on his stupid face. The Albanian was older, about thirty, and to American Troy everything about him - the tattoos, the scars, the cruel, vigilant eyes - screamed state-raised. Yeah, a real pair of fucking animals, particularly the latter, who forever treated Troy with amused contempt.

American Troy had done some time himself, primarily in Mary Davis, the juvenile correctional home in Knox, Illinois, but also in county, and briefly at the big house, the same joint where his father was incarcerated, and he'd seen faces like the Albanian's every hour of every single day he'd served. In fact, the Albanian looked so untrustworthy, so blatantly criminal that American Troy was surprised the Big Shilling had hired him at all. But maybe that was part of the plan, thought American Troy with a sudden insight, maybe the Albanian was to be sacrificed like those kids on that island near the Russian exile's house, way back when.

American Troy's attention now turned to the Albanian's girlfriend, Lena. Troy had seen plenty of girls just like Lena before as well. Yeah, it was chicks like Lena who wrote love letters to serial killers, and got married in the joint to four-time losers who'd never make parole. Lovelorn Lena was hanging onto the Albanian's arm, and hanging on his every word as well by the look of it, her eyes as big and as trusting as a puppy-dog's. American Troy didn't doubt that the Albanian treated her like dirt, and he didn't doubt either that however badly she was treated Lena kept coming back for more. In a way he could understand it. Why settle for the humdrum life of a normie when you could have the excitement of living on the edge with your thug-life boyfriend?

Feeling ice-cold, American Troy leaned against a lamp post, and nodded imperceptibly when the Greek Tryphon caught his eye.

'Not now, sweetheart,' said American Troy to pre-empt one of the female touts from Beckham's sports bar who'd been about to approach him.

The girl swirled away and he admired her pert posterior and long brown bare legs. Next he knew, a fist had jabbed him under the ribs.

'Ooof!'

'Keep you mind on the job, hey? Keep your mind on the job.'

It was the Big Shilling, of course, grinning like it was all a joke, but American Troy could tell Shilling wasn't joking at all.

'You acting up?'

'No.'

'Well okay, just so long as you're not acting up. Not hurt, are you?'

Recovering himself, American Troy said, 'I already had a scout round.'

'You did, did you?' said the Big Shilling, himself glancing round, taking in the male model Tryphon and the Albanian couple across the road. 'You had a scout round, hey? Well, here's what we do. You and me will get on that bike of yours and go for a little ride, and Frankie here will take the kids inside for an ice cream. That all right, Frankie, eh? You'll get the kids some ice cream, and while they get some ice cream you'll get some footage of the place, hey?'

'Mum's the word, skipper,' said Frankie the Fish, wandering over to them.

American Troy and the Big Shilling watched Frankie cross the road and go and speak to the Greek gangster Tryphon and the Albanian couple. The Big Shilling was already edging away. Unlike North America and mainland Europe, in Cyprus there were few closed circuit video cameras monitoring public spaces, but the Big Shilling was always wary around large concentrations of people, wary that he would appear in the background of someone's selfie, pictured at the scene of a future crime. That also might have been why he was wearing yet another hat, this one a large trilby, that he'd bought from a street vendor near the castle that had once guarded the entrance to Paphos harbour.

'Where are we going?' asked American Troy.

Naturally, the Big Shilling didn't answer him. They were walking to the dead-end street the other side of the bus station where American Troy had left the motorbike, and the Big Shilling was telling him about the Killing House at the Special Air Service Regiment headquarters in Hereford, England.

'You mean Frankie the Fish is SAS?' asked American Troy, incredulous.

'What? You think all these SAS guys look like Arnie or Rambo, hey? Is that what you think? Oh, my boy, you've got a lot to learn, you've got a lot to learn, eh?'

'You're having me on, man, Frankie the goddamned Fish is not spec ops.'

'He's not SAS,' the Big Shilling averred, 'he's not SAS. No, he's not, but I never said he was, did I, eh? It was you who said he was SAS. He's not SAS, he's SBS, or was. He's not SBS now, eh, he's retired, freelance, he's his own man.'

When the Big Shilling did not elaborate, American Troy said, as he was meant to, 'All right, Jesus, what does SBS stand for?'

'SBS?' asked the Big Shilling, 'SBS stands for the Special Boat Squadron, Special Boat Squadron, that's what SBS stands for. It's the maritime equivalent of the SAS, the Special Air Service, the maritime equivalent, eh? Yeah, old Frankie used to be a Royal Marine, a Royal Marine commando, and they are some of the best soldiers in the world, eh, some of the best soldiers on land, sea or air in the world.'

'And there's one of these Killing Houses here on the island?'

'That there is, my boy, that there is,' said the Big Shilling. 'It's in one of the Sovereign Base Areas, at Akrotiri. You've heard of the SBAs, haven't you, eh? Cyprus used to be a British colony, back in the day, and when the British granted the Cypriots independence they kept base areas for military use.'

American Troy was glad when they reached the

bike and he could put his helmet on and not have to listen to the Big Shilling banging on about the SAS, the SBS, and the SBAs, but even with the helmet on, even with the noise the engine made when he fired it up, American Troy could still hear the Big Shilling talking, or rather shouting, about the British at Akrotiri.

'Take the road for Limassol,' the Big Shilling yelled, 'we're going to Lady's Mile.'

It took about an hour to get to the beach at Lady's Mile. Once they left the crowds and traffic of Paphos behind, the road joined a freeway which was in better condition than any Cyprus road American Troy had yet travelled on. But he didn't open the throttle, he kept within the speed limit, and rode like there was a cop car cruising along behind. Not that there was a cop car. The whole time American Troy had been on the island he was yet to see a Cypriot cop car.

But once the Big Shilling directed him off the freeway, down a road signposted Akrotiri, American Troy began to see cop cars everywhere. Not Cypriot cops, but British military police. When he saw a POLICE SLOW sign at the side of the road and British MPs up ahead, he thought they were about to be flagged down. He felt the Big Shilling's hand on his back, meaning, take it easy, so he took it easy, and they rode past the British cops without any trouble.

Next, the Big Shilling directed American Troy towards Happy Valley, that green oasis where the British in Cyprus have played rugby, cricket and football for almost two hundred years. Not that they could see very much of it in the dark. At the top of the hill was a military housing estate that looked distinctly out of place on this Mediterranean island, English-style houses in terraces with tiny well-tended gardens and little cars parked outside their front doors. There were lots of cyclists about too, British military guys taking advantage, now that the sun had gone down and the temperature had dropped, to get some exercise. Evidence of the British love affair with sport was making American Troy's lip curl. He loathed all sporting activity, had never seen the point of it, except for motorbike racing of course. He loved to ride, even with a passenger yapping behind him like the Big Shilling was.

They rode downhill towards the forested land beside Akrotiri air base. As they did so, the Big Shilling could see the lights on the giant aerials beside the RAF base that warned aircraft to steer clear. The aerials were everywhere, protected by barbed wire and electric fences, listening antennae used by the British state to eavesdrop on the Middle East. There were even more of the aerials than the Big Shilling remembered from his last visit to the beach at Lady's Mile.

Their presence gave him pause. He even shut up for a few seconds, before bursting out laughing.

The beach bar at Lady's Mile was closed, and there were few vehicles in the vast car park. American Troy stopped the bike, and they dismounted and drank some water.

'Why have we come here?' he asked, taking advantage of the fact that the Big Shilling could not drink and talk at one and the same time.

'I wanted to get you off the main roads and into the countryside,' explained the Big Shilling, pointing towards a chain link fence on the far side of the car park. 'Through there is the Killing House.'

American Troy looked but could see nothing apart from trees and brush. He waited for something to happen. It did, a few moments later, when a car engine was started and a pair of yellowish headlights lit up.

'Come on,' said the Big Shilling. 'This is my boy.'

They mounted up again, and American Troy aimed the bike towards the headlights. It turned out they belonged to a tiny car, a French Peugeot, model 205. In the driver's seat was a black African with a nervous smile who obviously wished he were somewhere else, like England for instance.

'We leave the bike here, eh?' explained the Big Shilling to American Troy.

They left the bike there, in the big car park at Lady's Mile, and the African landmine clearance operative whose name was Joshua drove them to the Green Line, south east of the capital Nicosia where he had cleared a path through the minefield and discreetly marked the way with strips of coloured nylon attached to wires driven into the earth. They stood close together, the three of them, beside the little car, the darkness warm and scented, cicadas speaking.

'Red on right,' explained the African, rolling his r's, 'yellow left. Yellow on left, red, right.'

The Big Shilling gave the agitated man a thousand euros, saying, 'You get the rest, eh, when we get across. For the next three days you wait by your phone, eh, you wait by your phone after you finish work, and when I call you, you come here to meet us, hey?'

The African smiled nervously. 'Of course,' he said, softly, 'of course, when you call, I come. I come when you call. And you have rest of money for me. When you come, you come with money.'

The Big Shilling was smiling as well. 'You give your sister half the money, hey? Half the money for your sister, eh, big surprise. And if you do not come, eh, I come looking for you, and give you a big surprise, okay?'

Suddenly, the African was round-eyed. The Big Shilling pulled him closer.

'Okay, boss, okay, no problem! No problem!'

'No problem at all, no problem at all, eh?' said the Big Shilling, removing the wicked-looking two-inch stabbing blade he'd been holding almost touching the African's right eye ball. 'Now, drive us back to Lady's Mile, eh, Joshua?'

American Troy regarded abject African with disgust. 'Pussy,' he mumbled. Then in a louder voice, he said, 'Oh yeah, oh yeah. This thing's finally starting to happen. Woo-who!'

'Shut up, you mutt,' said the Big Shilling.

CHAPTER TWELVE

That night, the Big Shilling couldn't sleep. And the reason he couldn't sleep was because he could not control his thoughts. Every time he imagined killing the Russian exile in the Paphos ice cream parlour, his attention wandered and it was sometimes several minutes before he noticed what had happened. He was tired, that was the trouble, but he refused to be beaten. He'd try again shortly. In the meantime he allowed his mind to do what it wanted to do, which was to drift. Everything flows, outside events and inside the head, oh yeah.

He sat alone downstairs in the living room of the rented house at Latchi, in front of the coffee table comms centre, smoking a cigar and occasionally sipping from a small glass of Cypriot brandy.

American Troy was in charge of information and

communications technology, and when they'd arrived back from their trip to the Green Line and Lady's Mile, the Big Shilling had quizzed him for half an hour before allowing him to go to bed. He'd quizzed American Troy partly out of devilment (back in London, the kid had wanted to tell him all the details), and partly because the sight of the SIGINT aerials at Akrotiri had caused him to worry just a little.

'Why,' the Big Shilling had asked, after first warning the kid not to be a smart ass, 'is Linux open source software better than regular?'

'Jesus, I already told you. Because you can check Linux code to make sure there're no bugs in it, sending all your data to the fucking feds.'

'What did I just tell you, boy, eh, about not being a smart ass? You liked it, didn't you, when I put the fear of God into that darkie, didn't you, hey? You liked seeing me hold a stabbing knife a quarter of an inch from his eye ball?'

American Troy glared at him for a couple of seconds before backing down. 'All right, for Christ's sake, ask your dumb questions and let me get a shower and go to fucking bed. I've had enough of you for one day.'

The Big Shilling regarded Troy with piercing eyes. The kid was scared, scared of crossing the mine field, that's what he reckoned. Shilling laughed pleasantly, defusing the tension.

'All right, that's better, a little deference, a little co-operation, the kid remembers who's in charge of this operation. 'Why are we using a flash drive on the laptops?'

'Like I told you already, the flash drive contains a secure operating system called Tails. Anyone booting up the laptop without the flash drive will find the laptop completely empty: zilch, zero, nada, nothing.'

The Big Shilling knew all about onion routing and Tor, and said so at some length, but he made American Troy describe to him how it worked and the reasons why they were using it. That took five or six long minutes.

'We're using it to stay anonymous, anonymous, you understand?' American Troy concluded, as though to a child with special needs.

'You're telling me that the American secret state was not in at the conception of Tor, eh? Is that what you're telling me?'

And the kid had had to admit that Tor may in some circumstances be compromised. 'Is that what you're worried about? Is this why you're shitting a brick? You mean the feds are on to us?'

'Calm yourself, my boy, calm yourself. No need to let your imagination run away with you, hey?'

American Troy gave him a sour smile.

'That darkie knows what he's doing,' said the Big Shilling, quietly.

As though he hadn't heard, American Troy said, 'Is that it? Are you satisfied now? Can I go to bed?'

'Not yet. There's one more thing, eh.'

Finally, the Big Shilling asked why, since he'd

given American Troy big shilling to buy laptops and phones, they were using ancient, reconditioned ThinkPads.

'It is yet another of my security devices,' American Troy explained. 'Laptops manufactured before 2008, as these are, have no built-in backdoor, whereby the feds can activate bugs to extract data from your hard drive.'

'Why, thank you, my boy.'

'Are we done?'

'We're done. Go and get cleaned up and go to bed, big day tomorrow.'

American Troy hadn't risen to the bait. He'd just stomped up the stairs without a word.

The Big Shilling took a sip of brandy, and began to think about the Killing House.

He'd visited the big ice cream parlour in Paphos, right after he and Frankie the Fish had walked along the new coastal footpath from the lighthouse. It was Frankie's job to make a mock-up of the place at the Killing House at Akrotiri. There, he and Frankie would drill American Troy, the Greek gangster Tryphon, and the Albanian in the fine art of close quarter battle.

That set him thinking about back-up plans. He loved back-up plans. It was back-up plans that made him so successful, that made him invincible. He had a back-up plan brewing. All that was needed was a little winding up. He sipped brandy, enjoying the mellow caramel taste.

Now that he was thinking constructively and not

pointlessly, the Big Shilling felt much better. As his optimism returned, so too did his bravado, which he had claimed in the car park in the Akamas to have identified in the demeanour of the target, the Russian exile.

One and the same, thought the Big Shilling, we're one and the same, you and I, my friend, for we both walk the razor's edge. The insight comforted him. Screenwriter, director, and now actor: the Big Shilling closed his eyes, and imagined himself the moment after he had killed the Russian exile in the Paphos ice cream parlour. This time his thoughts did not wander. He was there, his ears ringing from the gunfire, savouring the screams of the women, standing over the corpse of the Russian, smelling the blood and feeling the terror. The Big Shilling opened his eyes, a smile spreading across his face like the risen sun, triumphant.

After repeating a mantra of thanksgiving to the powers above, he decided he was ready for bed. He stubbed out the cigar in the saucer he'd been using as an ash tray, finished the brandy, and turned off the air conditioning and the lights. As he padded upstairs, the only noise was made by the living room ceiling fans.

Less than four hours later, at ten to eight, the Big Shilling and American Troy went to the beach to swim, and after a leisurely breakfast, the two outlaws monitored the news websites. For the first time, they discovered an update on Vladimir Putin and the Russian exile. It was expected that within the next forty-eight hours, the Russian exile would be pardoned. A statement made by the exile's brother in Moscow said that it was possible that he would return to Russia as soon as the pardon was signed.

'Does that mean he will return?' asked American Troy.

'It doesn't matter,' the Big Shilling told him. 'Bravado, eh, remember? Bravado. This man, the Russian exile, thinks his luck has changed, so he is exhibiting bravado. He thinks no one can kill him, hey? He thinks that he is immune from punishment, even from a man as powerful as Vladimir Putin. He insults me, when the thinks this, he insults me, hey? The Big Shilling, that's who he insults!'

American Troy was on the verge of making an insulting remark himself, and it was only with supreme self-control that he managed to keep his mouth shut. After their late night ICT quiz, Troy hadn't slept at all well. It had finally sunk in that if he wanted to get away after the hit, then he needed the Big Shilling. Without him, there was no way off the island. It grated, but that's the way things were. Troy scowled, and sighed. He was to do a lot of sighing that day.

It was a morning of waiting around. After lunch, which the Big Shilling insisted they eat on the blistering terrace, Shilling told Troy to iron their clothes. Not their ordinary clothes, but the military attire that Frankie the Fish had scored for them. American Troy was about to protest, but when he saw the look on Shilling's face he decided he'd better do as he was told.

'You're Cypriot army, and I'm British army, eh?' said the Big Shilling. 'Try that beret on for size. It suits you, eh? Yours is the brown camouflage shirt, mine are the desert combats. Make sure those creases are knife-edge sharp, eh? We don't want to make the MPs suspicious, hey? And we'll take along a change of clothes as well, eh, and our flip-flops.'

'We're going on to a British army base to use their special forces' Killing House,' said American Troy, laughing as he set up the ironing board in the kitchen. 'Christ, this is rubbing their noses in the dirt.'

Now the Big Shilling laughed as well, but not with American Troy, at him. 'You think they don't know, eh? You think they don't know?'

'They know?'

'Of course they know.'

'So what was all that bullshit last night, about the motherfucking computers?'

The Big Shilling laughed.

'The Brits must want this Russian son of a bitch executed, eh, before he can skedaddle back to Moscow, out of their reach. And if the Brits want him dead, you can be sure they're following orders given them by Washington. Britain is the fifty-first state, my boy, the fifty-first state, and don't you forget it, hey?'

American Troy considered this new information

as he impatiently ironed the Cypriot National Guard fatigues. The Big Shilling watched the cogs whirring. It was like observing a machine, a man-machine, completely automatic, with no one at home.

'And when you're done with that you can smarten up those boots, eh?' he said, lying down on the couch for a nap. 'I want us to look smart, real smart, because we are smart, eh, we are smart.'

'This is fucked up,' mumbled American Troy, 'this is totally fucked up.'

'The world is fucked up,' the Big Shilling corrected him, amiably, 'and I intend to fuck it up just a little bit more, eh? That which is falling deserves to be crushed, that which is crawling deserves to be pushed. Egypt.'

'Oh you're back on Egypt, are you?'

'Back on?'

'Your hobby horse.'

'You know nothing, boy, nothing at all. You are a nullity, a complete blank, you are empty inside. Egypt, now that was a civilisation. America? You think America is the greatest? It's a banana republic, my boy, a hollow empire. It's nothing more than a hollow empire and a banana republic.'

American Troy didn't know what to say to that. Empty inside? A nullity? A complete blank? He didn't know what to say to that, so he shook his head and sighed. The steam was making him hot.

'Fucking ironing,' he muttered.

Time dragged. Time dragged as the Big Shilling,

eyes shut, lectured American Troy on the Symbolist interpretation of the ancient Egyptian dung beetle.

'Therianthropy?' repeated Troy, angrily. 'What the fuck is that?'

When Frankie the Fish came to collect them just before five that afternoon, American Troy had to force himself not to burst out laughing, but he couldn't hide his characteristic smirk. The Royal Marine commando was dressed in a yellow cotton shirt, knee-length corduroy shorts, long mustard-coloured woollen socks that also reached to the knee, and a pair of brown suede chukka boots.

'The safari Land Rover,' Frankie announced, 'has been consigned to the knacker's yard. You'll be glad to hear, Troy, my dear, that I've replaced it with an old Range Rover that actually has working air con and a functioning set of front springs.'

American Troy looked askance at the Britisher: my dear? Did he just call me 'my dear'? What exactly had he got himself into with these two fruitcakes? Fucking dung beetles, and therianthropy!

'We look smart, eh?' the Big Shilling asked Frankie.

'My dear old thing,' said Frankie the Fish, 'you're the cat's pyjamas, you really are.'

'All set? Sure, we're all set. Let's go then, eh?' said the Big Shilling, apparently unconcerned by American Troy's disquiet.

Petulantly, Troy followed the odd couple outside, helped load the car, and climbed aboard. The Big Shilling's monologue began even before Frankie had started the engine. American Troy managed to tune it out, which made him feel a little better. He sat staring out of his window at the sunny, dusty Cypriot streetscape, trying not to think.

Frankie drove them to Kissonerga village, west of Paphos, where they collected the Greek kid Tryphon and the surly Albanian from the rented apartment. Both the newcomers were dressed in Cypriot military uniforms. The Albanian's girlfriend – big boobs, curved ass - clung to him, pawing him and kissing his unmoved face.

'You'll do, I guess,' said the Big Shilling, who'd got out of the car, 'you'll do. Hey, sweetheart, put him down, can't you see he doesn't like you being all over him like a rash?'

The Albanian looked at the Big Shilling insolently, and the Albanian's girl looked at the Albanian looking at the Big Shilling insolently.

American Troy happened to be watching her closely, and for a split second he saw a wicked look in her eyes. Oh yeah, thought American Troy, perking up, he'd seen bitches look that way before. They were all the fucking same, the world over: thots. She'd love you forever, that 'ho over there, right up until that moment when a better prospect hove into view. And as far as the Albanian girl was concerned, the Big Shilling was that better prospect. That wicked look meant she wanted them to fight, she wanted her man and the Big Shilling to fight it out, with her as the prize. That's what American Troy deduced. He snickered to himself.

Had the Big Shilling seen that wicked look? American Troy wasn't sure, since Shilling's eyes were locked with the Albanian's.

'Come along, chaps,' said Frankie the Fish, waspishly, 'no time like the present and all that.'

The moment passed, and everyone got in the Range Rover, apart from the Albanian's girl who drifted back to the door of the apartment. The Big Shilling suggested American Troy ride up front, and the kid knew from the way he said it that devilment was afoot. Even before the car began to move, the Big Shilling was telling them all about the Angolan Drill.

'Angolan Drill?' repeated the Albanian, sceptically. 'What is this?'

'The Angolan Drill?' said the Big Shilling. 'You've never heard of the Angolan Drill? You know, I'm glad you never have, eh? I'm glad, because that bastard, the bastard who claimed to have invented the Angolan Drill, he didn't invent it. I invented it, I invented the Angolan Drill, before that bastard even went to Angola. In fact, it's not called the Angolan Drill at all, eh, it's called the Big Shilling Drill, that's what it's called, hey? The Big Shilling Drill.'

'What is this?' asked the Albanian, frowning elaborately. 'What is this, the Big Shilling Drill?'

He was sitting in the back of the Range Rover, next to the Big Shilling, who was in the middle, with the Greek kid Tryphon on the other side. Troy was in the front next to the fruit Frankie.

'Two to the chest, one to the head,' explained the

Big Shilling, pleasantly. 'Two bullets to the chest, and one to the head. You know why, eh? Because two rounds from a pistol might not stop the bloke, so you put one in his head to make sure. That's the Big Shilling Drill.'

The Albanian's facial expression was by now even more unpleasant.

'Two in the chest, one in the head?' he said, sneering. 'You do not invent this drill. It is everywhere, this drill, everyone know it.'

There was a long, menacing pause before the Big Shilling said, 'What did you say? What did you just say, eh? Did you call me a fucking liar? Frankie, stop the car. Stop the car, Frankie.'

Frankie the Fish stopped the car.

It was a couple of minutes before he started driving again. When he did, the Albanian was holding a handkerchief, which Frankie had given him, to staunch the blood from the puncture wound the Big Shilling's vicious little stabbing knife had made below his eye.

'Next time, I'll fucking blind you,' the Big Shilling was saying, conversationally. 'You understand me? Next time you call me a liar, I'll fucking blind you. You understand what I'm saying to you, you dumb fucker, eh? Speak to me once more like that, and I'll blind you. Okay? Okay.

'Now where was I, eh? Oh yeah, I was telling you about how I came up with a drill in Angola in the 1980s to deal with attackers who were so hyped up on adrenaline or drugs that two shots to the chest were insufficient to drop them, hey? I call it the Big Shilling Drill. The Big Shilling Drill, got that? Not the Angolan Drill.'

There were no further problems. Not even when the Big Shilling mused aloud that he might not need the Albanian after all, that he might in fact, as an alternative, use the Albanian's girl instead of the Albanian. American Troy's chest was so tight he found it difficult to breathe. He stifled a snigger. Ever the diplomat, Frankie turned on the radio and tuned it to the British Forces Broadcasting Service.

'Want to hear the news, skipper?' he asked the Big Shilling.

'Sure, why not? Let's all listen to the fake news. Let's listen to what the WCs want nice people to think.'

'WC?' said Tryphon, laughing earthily.

'The world controllers, dumb ass,' explained the Big Shilling. 'World controllers, ha! Don't make me laugh. They want to control the world, when they can't even control themselves?'

It was a minute to the hour, and BFBS was nagging service personnel about not drinking enough water, and about how they shouldn't drink too much booze during celebratory catch-ups. When the news came on, there was no mention of Putin or the Russian exile, it was all Syria and Iran, and a speech in parliament by the Minister of Defence, and sport and more sport: football, cricket, and golf. Frankie turned off the radio. They were approaching a military checkpoint.

'Nice and easy, everyone,' said Frankie, cheerfully. 'It's all very friendly, smile and nod, smile and nod.'

Frankie the Fish was right. It was all very friendly, and his familiar and amiable face proved sufficient to get them through the security checkpoints at Akrotiri air base without any difficulty whatsoever. His name was on the clipboards the military police-men held in their hands, his upper class buffoonery earned from them some laughter, and once inside the wire they drove to the Killing House without further ado.

'Is this it?' asked Troy.

'Oh yes,' said Frankie.

The Killing House appeared to be a neglected former aircraft hangar situated on the very edge of the base. Frankie parked the Range Rover in the shadow cast by the rusting structure, and opened a padlock on the door with a key he kept on a length of hairy string attached to the belt loop of his shorts. The five of them, the Albanian hanging back, stepped through the door into an alternate reality. Frankie the Fish turned on the air con, then picked up a remote control and pressed a series of buttons.

'Gentlemen,' he said, after closing the door behind them, 'welcome to my world – I give you, the Killing House.'

And now, instead of a rusty, sun-heated metal hangar, the Big Shilling, American Troy and the two others found themselves in a computer-generated mock-up of the Paphos ice cream parlour. Even the sullen Albanian, whom everyone could tell was only biding his time until he could murder the Big Shilling, was impressed.

'This is where your tax dollars go, eh?' said the Big Shilling. 'This is what our lords and masters do with our tax dollars. It must have cost big shilling, eh. This must have cost big, big shilling.'

'It's only projections of the photos one took,' said Frankie the Fish, modestly, 'but it gives the general idea.'

'Where's the target?' asked Tryphon, the handsome Greek kid.

'At the back there,' said the Big Shilling, 'the round table near the fire exit, hey? He's there with his wife and two children. Frankie?'

Frankie the Fish played with the remote control, and up came images of the Russian exile's bodyguards taken from Brian Blee's illicit photography. Two of the bodyguards appeared to be seated with their master, the others were positioned in the corners, either side of the ice cream parlour's front door.

'These two guys at either side,' said the Big Shilling, 'they must be taken out first, or we're mincemeat.'

The Albanian shrugged unpleasantly. 'Is obvious,' he said. 'When you British teach us something we don't know? Every bank robber, jewel thief, know this.'

'Give the man a gun,' said the Big Shilling to Frankie. 'Give him a gun, and we'll see what he can do. And I mean a real gun, Frankie, loaded with real ammunition, not one of your toys.'

'Whatever you say, skipper.'

'You want me to teach you something, hey?' the Big Shilling asked the Albanian. 'You want me to teach you something, is that it? All right, I'll teach you something. I'll teach you how to take a gun off someone who's pointing it at your head.'

Frankie the Fish was returning from the gun cabinet with a pistol in one hand and a charged magazine in the other.

'Give them to me,' said the Big Shilling, and he showed the Albanian that the magazine was actually loaded with live ammunition. 'See?'

The Albanian saw. 'If,' he said. 'If, you take gun from me.'

'If I don't,' said the Big Shilling, 'you pull the trigger and shoot me dead, hey. That's what you want to do, am I right? I humiliated you, I cut you, you're my bitch and you want your revenge.'

'Give me gun,' ordered the Albanian, his fury mounting. 'We do this. We do this now.'

But the Big Shilling didn't give the Albanian the gun straight away, he gave him a lecture first instead.

He asked him if he'd heard of Jimmy Lichtenfeld, but before the Albanian could answer, the Big Shilling said, 'It was my father, God rest his soul, who taught Jimmy all he knew about hand-to-hand combat. Contact combat he called it, and Jimmy translated that into his own language as Krav Maga. I've simply improved on it, that's all, eh? Using my real life experience as a martial artist I have significantly improved upon Krav Maga.'

The Albanian was about to interrupt, but thought better of it, since the Big Shilling was still holding the loaded pistol. He muttered horribly instead.

'Superfast hands,' the Big Shilling said, raising his voice, 'and sloth hands, that's the key to this particular drill. You need superfast hands to beat your opponent, to take the pistol from him before he can fire. But you also need the sloth grip. What is the sloth grip? The sloth grip means you don't use your thumb, hey? The sloth has no thumb.'

'Now,' urged the Albanian. 'We do it now. Always you talk, yak yak, yak yak yak, like womans.'

'Nothing wrong with talking,' said the Big Shilling, infuriatingly reasonable, 'and there's nothing wrong with women, hey? Perhaps if you'd listened to that sweet girl of yours you might have learned a thing or two.'

In spite of being unarmed, the Albanian grew increasingly agitated. 'Fuck, give me gun, now, we do it, now, bastard.'

'You're going to shoot me in the head, eh?'

The Albanian spat explosively on the concrete floor.

'I blow out fucking brain, son-bitch.'

'Here, take the gun,' said the Big Shilling, grinning affably. 'Take the gun, and try and blow out my brains.'

The Albanian took the gun. 'Is shit for brains,' he said, aiming at the Big Shilling's face.

And then the Albanian was yelling with pain.

'You see,' the Big Shilling explained, once more holding the gun, 'there's something I didn't tell you. I didn't tell you because you were impatient, eh, and you didn't give me time to tell you. Don't put your finger inside the trigger guard. You know that now, eh, now you know that, because when I took the pistol off you with my superfast hands, I caught your finger in the trigger guard. Is it broken? It looks broken. Yes, it is broken.'

'Fuck!' yelled the Albanian, nursing his broken hand.

'Did you see?' the Big Shilling asked American Troy and the Greek kid Tryphon who were avidly watching the demonstration like they were back in school. 'Superfast hands combined with sloth hand. Did you see it?'

The Greek kid Tryphon stared gormlessly open-mouthed, so Troy said, 'The hand you put on his wrist, you didn't use your thumb, just the fingers.'

'Right, that's right, my boy. But why, eh, why?'

American Troy had to think about that, but he never got the chance to answer because the Big Shilling suddenly cracked the Albanian over the head with the butt of the pistol, and the Albanian's knees went and he collapsed where he stood, out cold on the concrete.

'No use to me anymore,' said the Big Shilling, 'no use to me without a trigger finger, hey? What use is a trigger man without a trigger finger? Tell me that.'

'Nice work,' said the Greek kid Tryphon, walking over and prodding the unconscious Albanian with the tip of an unpolished army boot. 'Very nice.'

'As I was saying,' said the Big Shilling, 'the men in the corners are the danger men, eh? We take them out first. You two, Troy, and you, Tryphon, are either side of me. You'll have Uzis. You put those two bastards down, and I'll take out the Russian myself, hey? I'll kill that motherfucker myself. Believing is seeing, boys, believing is seeing, and don't you forget it.'

'Eh?' said Tryphon.

'Forget about it, kid, don't fry your brains. Frankie? Over to you.'

'Thank you,' said Frankie, in a voice American Troy had never heard him use before. 'You two there! Stand to attention when I'm speaking to you! You idle pair of pillocks, I'll turn you into soldiers if it's the last thing I shagging do!'

CHAPTER THIRTEEN

Three hours later, as the sun was going down, Tryphon and American Troy, their ears singing from the noise of gunfire, lifted the Albanian into a hold-all and fastened the zip. The hold-all was the kind used by dive schools for scuba gear, and the oblivious Albanian was trussed up with rope and gaffer tape. The Big Shilling and Frankie the Fish carried the hold-all out to the Range Rover and swung it in the back. Next, Frankie the Fish loaded three other bags as well, containing incendiary devices and arms and ammunition. Then he locked up and they got in the car and drove off, not back to the air base's main gate, but along a bumpy track amongst the pine trees. When they came to a gate in the chain link fence, Frankie got out, unfastened a padlock and drove them out into the car park at Lady's Mile.

'A drink,' announced the Big Shilling. 'Who fancies a drink? I'll take you all for a drink, eh? Frankie, take us to the beach bar, my good man, the Big Shilling is in the chair, the Big Shilling is in the chair.'

They went for a drink at the beach bar, and the Big Shilling insisted everyone drink Leon beer. They didn't stay long. The Big Shilling chivvied them all into drinking up as quickly as possible. It was as though, thought American Troy, he wanted to keep them all on edge, and this after all the bonding they'd done at the Killing House.

Troy looked at the Greek kid Tryphon who was leering at passing females, some of whom leered back. Tree-phone was a klutz, a retard, and an animal, and it was obvious to American Troy what Tryphon's likely fate would be. He'd end up bagged and tagged like that other animal, the Albanian. Troy took a sip of beer, but it didn't taste any better than it had before. He massaged his belly. It ached.

'Tryphon did well,' the Big Shilling was saying, 'Tryphon can shoot, and Tryphon can swim, eh?'

'I was lifeguard,' said Tryphon, not for the first time. 'I was in Greek army.'

'So you said, my boy, so you said. Fashion model as well, a man of many parts.'

American Troy snorted.

'What's wrong, kid?' Shilling asked him.

'This beer tastes like piss. I'm getting a Keo.'

'Sit down and drink your Leon. Leon is the best beer. We're leaving, in a minute or two.'

American Troy sat down. He knew that if he

didn't, the Big Shilling would share a few home truths with the table, home truths he, American Troy, didn't particularly want to hear, such as the fact that Tryphon was a better shot than he was. American Troy did his best not to let his thoughts show. He chugged beer and stared out to sea instead. He was wondering how he could make himself indispensable. That seemed the only guarantee: to make himself indispensable. The question was, how? What he needed was an angle. Truth be told, what had happened to the Albanian had unsettled him. For all his bullshit, the Big Shilling was indeed the real deal. And so too was 007, Frankie the goddamn Fish. He might dress like a clown and act like a fag but there was no doubt he was a stone-cold killer. American Troy had caught Frankie looking at him, after Troy had fouled up yet again in the mocked-up ice cream parlour, and the look had been that of a hunter spying prey. Yeah, it turned out the guy was an animal too, another goddamned animal.

'Are we finished? Are we done?' said the Big Shilling, standing up. 'Then let's go.'

Even though they didn't stay long at the beach, it was well after nine o'clock by the time they reached Latchi. American Troy and the Greek Tryphon were dropped off at the house, tasked with packing up. Frankie drove the Big Shilling and the Albanian down to the harbour, and parked in front of the police station.

'Need a hand?' one of the cops called from the balcony when Frankie and the Big Shilling unloaded the Albanian from the back of the car.

'No, thanks, my wanker,' said Frankie.

The cop asked, 'What have you got in there anyway?'

'Why, the dead body, of an Albanian gangster, who couldn't keep his mouth shut,' Frankie said.

This caused the cop to lean forward and stare hard at the dive school hold-all, but only for a moment. His attention was drawn to Frankie who was acting the pantomime villain, melodramatically looking this way and that and throwing up his arms as though he had been caught in the act. The cop laughed, dismissed Frankie's histrionics with a wave of the hand, and lit a cigarette from the stub of the one he'd just finished.

'Chump,' muttered Frankie, and winked elaborately at the Big Shilling whose expression was that of someone tired of a companion's interminable repartee. 'Oh the irony,' the Royal Marine said to himself.

Together, Frankie the Fish and the Big Shilling struggled with the heavy bag. Sweating and sometimes cursing, they carried it past the crowded fish restaurant and between promenading holidaymakers and drowsing felines, down to the quayside where Frankie's dinghy was tied up. There they had a breather, then slid the Albanian in the hold-all into the dinghy. Frankie climbed in after him, reached up and shook the Big Shilling's hand.

'I'll see you when I see you, eh?' said the Big Shilling.

'Tally-ho,' said Frankie, 'and good hunting, skipper.'

The Big Shilling watched the dinghy leave the harbour before strolling casually back to the Range Rover. The cop on the balcony was speaking into a mobile phone and paid him no attention. At the house Shilling allowed American Troy and the Greek Tryphon to load up the car.

'You've checked everywhere, eh?' he asked American Troy.

'Checked everywhere twice,' confirmed American Troy.

'I'll go and have a check round myself,' said the Big Shilling.

That took fifteen minutes, and it was another hour on top of that before they reached the apartment at Kissonerga, the Big Shilling riding in the vanguard on Troy's motorbike, making it close to midnight before American Troy and the Greek Tryphon had finished unloading the car.

The Big Shilling had other things to attend to, namely the Albanian's girl whose name was Lena. He took her into the bedroom she shared with her boyfriend and spoke to her, quietly explaining the new dispensation behind the closed door.

At first, American Troy and the Greek Tryphon, coming in with bags and bits of kit, heard the girl protesting and weeping. Then they heard her loudly sniffing, and talking animatedly. Finally, they heard nothing at all. But by that time they were hot and sweaty and tired and dirty, and didn't care anymore.

'Looks like I have a roommate,' said Tryphon. 'He better not snore.'

'No,' said American Troy, who hated sharing a room (it reminded him of sharing a cell, something that he really didn't want to recall), 'you'd better not snore.'

'Since you are new here, I let you have first shower,' said Tryphon.

'That's big of you, friend,' said Troy, insincerely. Tryphon merely grinned at him, stupidly.

After Troy had showered, Tryphon went and showered. When he'd finished showering, he came out of the bathroom with a towel wrapped around his narrow waist. He was ripped and tanned, not to mention photogenic, and in comparison American Troy was the proverbial nine-stone weakling. It rankled. But I have one advantage, a major advantage, thought Troy, I've got brains and he hasn't. In the bedroom, Tryphon pulled on shorts and a t-shirt, and joined Troy in the living room.

The apartment was small - two bedrooms, a twin and a double, and two bathrooms, one of which was en suite - and the walls were thin. They could hear the Big Shilling taking a shower as well, and Lena quietly sobbing. When the Big Shilling finished showering, Lena stopped sobbing. She appeared at the bedroom door and, without meeting anyone's eye, went into the kitchen to prepare food. Shortly after, Shilling reappeared, a wolfish grin on his weathered face.

'Troy,' he said, 'set the table, Tryphon, you're barman.'

When the four of them were seated around the dining table in the living room, the Big Shilling said, 'Lena has something to tell you, haven't you, Lena, eh?'

'I am,' said Lena, hesitantly, 'I am your new member of the team.'

'No,' said the Big Shilling, gently, 'not quite, eh? I am the new member of your team.'

'I am the new member of your team,' said Lena.

'That's it,' said the Big Shilling. 'You are the new member of the team, eh? Well, say hello, boys. You heard what Lena said, eh? She's the new member of the team.'

American Troy and the handsome Tryphon raised their beer glasses to Lena, and so did the Big Shilling. Lena couldn't see them do this because she was looking at the table top.

'Lena,' said the Big Shilling, gently, 'Oh Lena?'

Lena lifted her water glass, and her eyes. 'Yammas,' she said.

'Yammas,' said Tryphon.

'Cheers,' said American Troy, thinly.

'Cheers!' cried the Big Shilling. 'That's more like it, eh? Now we can relax and have something to eat and a few drinks, and really get to know each other, hey?'

Lena burst into tears and fled into her bedroom, slamming the door behind her.

The Big Shilling was in no way fazed. 'What are you waiting for, eh? Tuck in, tuck in.'

It turned out later that neither the Greek kid Tryphon, nor American Troy snored. At least, neither of them did that night, because neither of them slept at all. The pounding and groaning and moaning from the next bedroom kept them both awake until the sun came up. Tryphon tossed and turned, and American Troy tossed and turned. At one point, Tryphon whispered, 'What are you saying?'

American Troy did not answer. Lying on his back, he'd been muttering, 'Animals, fucking dirty animals.' Angrily, he rubbed his eyes, which itched annoyingly, and launched himself onto his side so that he faced away from the Greek kid in the bed parallel to his, and only a few feet away.

Next thing he knew, Troy started. He must have drifted towards sleep. What had wakened him was an muffled orgasmic cry, but this time not from the other room, from the other bed.

Without turning to look, Troy said: 'Did you just do what I think you just did?'

Tryphon panted. 'You can do it too, Troy. I seen you, looking at Lena. Hey,' he laughed. 'Maybe we go in there and the boss'll let us join in, hey? How about that?'

'Sure, you go first. I'll stay here.'

'You think? Or maybe you want to join me over here and . . .'

'Shut your dirty fucking mouth or I'll shut it for

you,' spat American Troy with such fury that Tryphon was rendered momentarily speechless.

'Take it easy, take it easy,' he said, pretending he hadn't reacted at all. 'My joke, huh?'

'That was no fucking joke, Tree-phone.'

It was at least ten minutes before American Troy's pounding heart returned to its normal rhythm, all the time his mind beset with visions of bloody vengeance. Then he was struck by a revelation. He had remembered, but only dimly, the Big Shilling speaking about screenwriting and actors, and visualising what he wanted to happen. Yeah, the other night at the restaurant, that was it! His bullshit phrase: believing is seeing. That was his angle, the way forward, his way off the island, that was what BS had been trying to teach him, some woo-woo mystic horseshit about how you were the author of your own future. Troy suppressed a snigger. All in all, he felt a whole lot better.

'Hey,' whispered Tryphon, 'I'm sorry, American Troy.'

'Don't sweat it, bro,' said AT, and the words sounded almost genuine, even to him.

'We are buddies, yeah? Buddies, I'm glad we're buddies,' said Tryphon, contentedly.

Soon after dawn, they heard the Big Shilling visit the bathroom, the flush of the toilet heralding a new day. Soon after, he left by the front door, presumably to swim in the apartment complex's shared pool, or go down to the sea. Before he left they heard him lock Lena in the bedroom. She'd stopped crying now. At long last, American Troy and his buddy Tryphon fell asleep.

They surfaced just before noon to find the table laid for brunch. The Big Shilling was seated there, drinking coffee and munching hard-boiled eggs and the baklava that Lena had brought from the bakery.

'Lena went to the bakery?' asked American Troy.

'Sure she did, didn't you, sweetheart, hey?' said the Big Shilling, putting an arm around Lena's waist as she refilled his cup from the pot.

'Yes, daddy,' said Lena in a little voice.

The Big Shilling patted her shapely bottom. 'That's my girl, eh?'

Lena began to tremble. Not with fear but with bliss.

American Troy cleared his throat and exchanged a hooded glance with the Greek Tryphon who grinned gormlessly.

'Right,' said the Big Shilling, 'down to business. Troy, set up the comms, and I mean now, before you've eaten, not after you've eaten, right now. You should have done it last night. Tryphon, you help him, eh? No more lie-ins for you two. I want the weapons cleaned and loaded and ready to go. If my phone rings, then we have less than an hour, you understand me? My phone rings, and we have less than an hour to get down to the ice cream parlour in Paphos and do the business. Come on! Hustle, hustle!'

Troy said he didn't need any help to set up the

comms on the coffee table in the open-plan living room, so the Greek Tryphon carried the weapons into the bedroom he and Troy shared, and set about cleaning and charging them. There were two Uzis, three Glock 17s, a Heckler and Koch MP5 machine pistol, and an ancient British Army service revolver. Tryphon worked methodically, skilfully, and it was obvious to anyone who had seen his performance at the Killing House that this dumb, good-looking kid had an affinity for firearms and gun-fighting.

From the dining room table, the Big Shilling could see everything that was going on. He could see Lena in the kitchen, Troy hunched over the coffee table, and through the open bedroom door, he could see the Greek Tryphon expertly cleaning the weapons.

'The two Uzis are for you and American Troy,' he told him, 'right?'

'Right, boss.'

'Each of us has a Glock, apart from Lena. The MP5 is mine. The little Smith and Wesson revolver is yours, Lena darling.'

'Thank you, daddy,' called Lena from the kitchen.

The Greek Tryphon looked up from what he was doing. 'You want me to load it, boss?'

'Of course I want you to load it,' said the Big Shilling. 'What kind of question is that, eh? Do I want it loading?'

'Boss, I only ask.'

'Hey, Tryphon,' said the Big Shilling, cocking his head to one side. 'Are you saying Lena can't be trusted? Is that what you're saying? That our Lena cannot be trusted, hey, that one member of our team cannot be trusted?'

American Troy stopped what he was doing, the better to observe the unfolding spectacle.

The Greek Tryphon had developed a lump in his throat. Now he swallowed it. It tasted unpleasantly of bile.

'No, boss,' he said, remembering how the Big Shilling had strangled the Albanian with his bare hands at the Killing House at Akrotiri, 'I only ask if you need it loading, boss.'

'So you did, so you did, eh,' said the Big Shilling with a big grin. 'Well, you load it, and you load it good. And when we get to the ice cream parlour and you see Lena holding that little pistol, you make sure you don't shoot her, hey? Tryphon, make sure you do not shoot her.'

'Why I shoot her, boss?' asked Tryphon, but he didn't look up from his cleaning and loading.

'Why would you shoot Lena?' asked the Big Shilling. 'I don't know. Why would you? Why would you shoot American Troy? Why would you shoot me, eh?'

Now there was no one moving at all. The Greek Tryphon wasn't moving and neither was American Troy, and in the kitchen Lena had stopped drying the plate she was drying and stood there with it in one hand and the tea-towel in the other. The Big Shilling could see them all from his place at the dining table.

'Boss,' said Tryphon, slowly, 'what you want me to

say? I don't understand, please.'

'Half a million,' said the Big Shilling, 'that's a lot of money, eh? A lot of money to a punk-ass loser like you. Go ahead, boy, go ahead, pick up a gun, pick up a gun and collect that money.'

Tryphon didn't move, he didn't look up, and he didn't pick up a gun. He was pretty much certain that if he did move, if he did pick up a gun, that the Big Shilling would shoot him dead. He was pretty certain that the Big Shilling had a piece aimed at him right there and then from his place at the dining table.

'I work for you, boss,' said the Greek Tryphon, evenly, 'not this scumbag Russian.'

The Big Shilling waited half a minute before bursting out laughing. The raucous, slightly unhinged noise broke the tension, kind of. Shaking his head, the grinning Tryphon went back to loading a Glock magazine, American Troy once more tapped at a keyboard, and Lena finished drying the plate.

'I had you there, Tryphon, I had you there, eh?'

'You had me there, boss, you had me there!'

'The Commander's Intent,' said the Big Shilling, seamlessly, 'remember what I told you both about the Commander's Intent, hey?'

Tryphon looked like he didn't remember. 'Er,' he said.

'Auftragstaktik,' said American Troy, acidly.

He disliked the German term for 'mission tactics' that had been the subject of one of the Big Shilling's harangues at the Killing House. He also disliked the fact that the Big Shilling claimed to have been taught Auftragstaktik by an East German officer, an adviser to the Cuban army. American Troy disliked anything to do with Germany. He'd seen the movies, he'd watched the documentaries – they were insane, evil Nazis. He even disliked the fact that the Big Shilling intended to use a German machine pistol. At least he, American Troy, and the Greek kid Tryphon, would be armed with Israeli Uzis.

'You are a bigot,' the Big Shilling now told him, 'you are a bigot, hey? American Troy is a bigot. Stop reacting and start acting, eh? That's what he needs to do. That's the key to carrying out the Commander's Intent, eh, because no battle plan survives first contact with the enemy, no plan of battle survives contact with the enemy. I want you all to use your initiative tomorrow, eh, I want you to do what you think is necessary to carry out the Commander's Intent.'

'Yes, boss,' said Tryphon, loudly.

American Troy's eyes were locked on the screen of the laptop in front of him but he saw nothing. He was thinking about how much he would have enjoyed at that very moment to empty a seventeen-round clip into the Big Shilling's face and chest and belly.

He said, 'Believing is seeing.'

'What was that?' asked the Big Shilling.

Troy looked him in the eye. 'Believing is seeing.'

'So you have been paying attention, eh?' said the

Big Shilling.

American Troy tried to read his expression but Shilling's face was inscrutable.

'Tomorrow?' asked the Greek Tryphon. 'You said tomorrow, boss.'

'Yes,' said the Big Shilling, slyly. 'The hit will be tomorrow, hey? So, this afternoon we can relax, swim in the sea, swim in the pool, whatever takes our fancy, eh Lena?'

Lena had come into the room from the kitchen. She took hold of the Big Shilling's hands and tried to pull him to his feet.

'Take it easy, girl, hey?' he said, laughing, allowing her to drag him towards the bedroom. 'The Big Shilling's an old man, remember? She's insatiable, insatiable, I tell you, boys.'

'Not old man,' said Lena, pouting, 'powerful man, big man, huge man, man like god.'

I was right, said American Troy to himself, feeling vaguely disgusted. Thots, they're the same the world over.

'Hey Troy!' the Greek kid Tryphon said, excitedly. 'Want to go to the beach?'

'Nah, you go to the beach. I'm staying here,' he said, plugging the noise-cancelling headphones into the laptop and turning up the volume.

American Troy lay down on the couch, and closed his eyes as the track started: Misirlou, by Dick Dale and the Del Tones.

As soon as Tryphon had gone to the beach, Troy told himself, he'd google 'Believing is seeing.' It just might give him his angle, and if he had an angle, he told himself, he'd feel a lot better.

CHAPTER FOURTEEN

That afternoon, in Lena's bedroom, the Big Shilling burnished the image. Over and over, he acted in the screenplay he'd written and directed, rehearsing the death of the Russian exile until the scene had acquired a life of its own. Like all the best screenplays, it had been rewritten, tightened, and honed until it was perfect, and now it had crossed over from imagination into actuality. The Big Shilling sensed the moment it happened. So too did Lena.

When she had finished trembling and panting and moaning, she lay on the dishevelled bed sheets, utterly exhausted.

The Big Shilling said, 'You know what that was, baby girl, eh? That was an FBO.'

'FBO? What is FBO?'

'A full-body orgasm.'

'A full-body orgasm, no one ever gives me one of these before. I think I die. Oh God, is too intense. Oh, daddy, I love you. I love you so much, I die for you.'

'Sure thing, baby girl, whatever you say, but no one really dies.'

'No one really dies?'

'No, no one really dies. Everyone thinks that life is a straight line, hey, but it isn't.'

'It isn't?'

'No, life is a circle. At the moment of death, you don't die, eh, you return to the beginning, the moment of your birth, then you live your life over again.'

'Is very strange what you say. It make me feel strange.'

'Life is strange, eh, life is strange. Why existence, eh? Why not non-existence?'

'It make my head feel funny, this kind of idea.'

'Think: you will live this moment again, this exact same moment.'

'Is nice. This I like.'

'Until you wake up and remember.'

'What remember?'

'That you've been here before, baby girl. You must die to your old self and awaken, only then can you be reborn, eh, reborn in this life, not the next. It is only by awakening, eh, by attaining a higher level of consciousness that it is possible to escape eternal return.'

Lena placed a finger on the Big Shilling's lips. 'Hush

now,' she said, smiling hungrily. 'Lena want more.' And the finger travelled south.

A few minutes later in the living room of the Kissonerga apartment, American Troy ripped off the headphones, slammed down the lid of the laptop, and headed for the front door. Even with the volume on max, the renewed yodelling from Lena's bedroom had finally proven too much for him. That, coupled with what he'd been reading online, about the Barbadian and the black rabbi, had only served to stoke his foul temper.

Believing is seeing?

He hadn't believed a word of what he'd seen online. As far as he was concerned, believing was seeing was nothing more than a pile of bullshit, a lousy scam in the fine traditions of his own father, this Neville dude was nothing more than an accomplished and successful con artist.

BS equalled the Big Shilling and the Big Shilling equalled bullshit. But it was an angle, an angle at least, not that it made him feel any better. He let the heavy apartment door slam shut behind him, and headed for the beach and a beer. A Keo, that's what he needed, a bunch of Keos. That would put him right. Believing is seeing? Bullshit!

When a more mellow American Troy returned to the apartment around five o'clock, accompanied by the Greek kid Tryphon who'd been swimming and sunbathing and flirting with thots, he found the Big Shilling and Lena preparing food for the barbeque.

Chill-out music was playing and the atmosphere was kind of relaxed and benign.

'Hello, boys,' said the Big Shilling, amiably, and instead of the usual onslaught of questions, observations and orders, Shilling simply smiled at them and said nothing more.

It was about a half hour later, while Tryphon was taking a shower and Lena was occupied in the kitchen, that American Troy finally managed to speak privately with the Big Shilling. They were standing either side of the smoking barbeque in the small yard, the sliding patio door closed to keep insects and smoke out of the living room.

American Troy said, 'You're going to take out Treephone, aren't you? I want you to let me do it.'

The sun had gone down and it was dark in the yard in spite of the wall lights and the light from the living room. The Big Shilling's shadowed face was further obscured by grey and white smoke, pluming from the hot charcoal.

'Am I?' the Big Shilling asked him, apparently unconcerned. 'Is that what I'm going to do? You want to do it, hey? Why's that?'

'He's an animal, he's surplus to requirements. Last night, the things he said, about you and Lena.'

The Big Shilling continued in the same measured tone, 'Is that so? I'm disappointed, Tryphon's part of the team. Are you jealous of him? Is that it, because he did better than you at the KH? You know, maybe he'd make a better apprentice than you do, American Troy.'

The Big Shilling was speaking strangely – that is, like a normal person - with none of his usual verbal tics and repetitions, and Troy didn't know quite what to make of it, but there was nothing for it but to plough on.

'You think he could make the future?' Troy asked, speaking more urgently now, not wanting to be interrupted by Lena bringing out a bowl of salad or some such shit. 'He's dumb, terminally dumb. He's practically a retard, you know it. Do you think he could raise his level of consciousness, to feel that 'I am this' when all he can see is what is in front of him?'

The Big Shilling stepped aside from the billowing smoke and looked directly at Troy. 'You think you can do it?'

'Teach me how. Yeah, I think I can do it. I know I can.'

At that moment, Lena slid back the patio door and said, 'Daddy, can you open this for Lena?'

She was holding a big jar of mayonnaise.

'Allow me,' said Troy.

'Oh thank you, it is tight.'

When American Troy had unscrewed the heavy jar and handed it back to Lena, the Big Shilling said, 'That's nice. I like to see you kids get along together, gives me a warm feeling inside.'

Lena beamed. 'Thanks, Troy.'

'You're welcome.'

'Troy's all right,' said the Big Shilling. 'Isn't he, Lena?'

'We like him,' Lena affirmed, before going inside and closing the door.

'Here's the plan,' said the Big Shilling. 'You listening, my boy?'

'I am,' said American Troy.

So the Big Shilling told American Troy what was going to happen at the big ice cream parlour at Paphos the following day.

American Troy and the Greek kid Tryphon were early risers Friday morning. They'd slept like the dead, and now they were wired and ready for the fray.

The Big Shilling had expected this, knowing that his troops would be nervy and tense what with action so close at hand, and so he had deliberately left some tasks unfinished. He emerged from his bedroom just after eight to find American Troy and the Greek kid drinking coffee, seated amongst their kit and equipment by the comms centre.

'Ready to leave?' he asked them. 'There's hours yet, hours, hey, but if you're ready to go already. American Troy, I want you to take the Range Rover to the place I showed you on the map, east of Paphos centre. Tryphon, go with him, take Troy's bike, and the two of you come back on it. When you get back, Troy, you will remove the silencers from both bikes, understand? That's what the garage is for, you see? That is why Frankie the Fish chose this apartment complex for us, eh? While Troy is removing the silencers, Tryphon, I want you to man the comms centre, understand?'

'Okay.'

'And make sure you take Troy's bike, not yours. Got it?'

'Okay.'

'Me, I'm going for a swim.'

'Can I come?' asked Tryphon, stupidly.

'Shut up, you klutz,' American Troy told him. 'You heard what the boss said: we're going to Paphos, and you're riding my bike, not yours.'

'Oh okay,' said the Greek kid Tryphon.

Shilling just smiled.

There was a hotel near the apartment complex with a natural salt-water swimming pool enclosed by rocks. The Big Shilling jogged down the road in the early morning sun, a towel around his shoulders, wearing swimming trunks and flip-flops. His heart rate was slow and his breathing deep and even. He felt relaxed and glad. It was always the way with him. Whenever there was the chance for daredevilry he was the happiest man alive. He went down the metal steps and into the pool, enjoying the freshness of the water first thing in the morning, and ignoring the flabby British tourists and unwashed East Europeans who splashed and paddled around him. A few minutes later, he clambered over the rocks and launched himself into the sea proper, battling against the waves, putting distance between himself and the land and pointless humanity. He stayed out for half an hour, floating on his back, the life in him exultant, imagining the future.

'I am! I am, I am God! Ha ha ha ha ha!'

The future fixed and golden, with powerful strokes he swam back to shore

As he walked back to the apartment he thought about Lena. He did not doubt she would do what he wanted. It was natural after all, and you could always rely on Nature. He was the alpha male and Lena, this beautiful embodiment of the eternal feminine, was a lowly pack bitch. Since he had disposed of her mate the Albanian, himself a lowly pack dog, it was only natural that she would acquiesce to the alpha dog's commands. It was natural and therefore good. Problems arose only when you attempted to go against Nature, and since the Big Shilling never went against what was natural, he never had any problems. That's what he was telling himself as he walked along the dusty pavement by the side of the banana plantation as he returned to the apartment complex.

The Big Shilling approached the heavy apartment door. It was cool here in the covered car park, and the Range Rover was gone. He thought he knew what would happen when he entered the apartment. He was right. When he entered the apartment he saw Lena peering round the bedroom door. As soon as she saw he was alone, she opened the door wide, went down on her hands and knees and crawled towards him. She was naked, and her eager fingers were dusty from the floor as she unfastened his swimming shorts.

'You are like god,' whispered Lena.

The Big Shilling did not deny it. That morning in London, the morning of his sixtieth birthday, he had imagined that the powers were deserting him, but he had been wrong. It was he who had put himself out of their reach. But he had repositioned himself, and the powers had immediately returned to him. Lena could sense it. She was a woman, and attuned to such things. She had sensed the reality of it in the dingy basement flat in west London. Soon others would know his power as well. The Big Shilling craned his neck, stared up at the revolving ceiling fan, his hard face lupine, seeing the future. As soon as he was finished with the female he'd go out to the garage and attend to Tryphon's motorbike.

It was mid-morning before American Troy and the Greek Tryphon returned from dropping off the Range Rover. The Big Shilling was drinking coffee, seated at the dining table with Lena, who was by now reluctantly wearing clothes, nestling in his lap. The clothes she was wearing were unusual, but if American Troy and the Greek kid noticed them, they said nothing. Instead, they went into the kitchen in search of ice-cold water. When Troy had gone out to the garage, closing the heavy front door quietly behind him, and Tryphon was seated slack-jawed at the laptop monitoring the news, the Big Shilling made Lena unload the British service revolver again, and practice drawing it from the pocket of the apron she was wearing.

'Be natural, eh?' he said. 'Take it nice and easy, like you do this every day of your life. It's natural, eh, taking this thing out of there and levelling it and squeezing the trigger, hey? Natural, that's right. Now load it again, eh, and take your time but hurry up. That's good, baby girl, that's very good.'

'I did it!'

Lena threw her arms around his neck and hugged him like her life depended on it. 'Thank you, daddy,' said Lena, 'oh thank you, thank you, thank you.'

'You're welcome, baby girl, papa loves you.'

At lunch, no one but the Big Shilling ate very much. He did not belabour them, much. They were nervous, and it was the heat.

'In winter,' pronounced the Big Shilling, 'the Cypriots get fat. In summer it is too hot to eat, they have no appetite, so they get slim. Every year it is the same, eh? It's the same every year because it is natural, it is Nature's way, hey? Do what Nature tells you and you can't go wrong, you cannot go wrong if you do as Mother Nature says, hey? Cycles, you see? Mother Nature works in cycles.'

Lena beamed at him, nodding vehemently.

'Tryphon,' said the Big Shilling, 'go through the plan for me, eh?'

'Again?'

'Yes, again. If you don't mind, eh, if it isn't too much trouble, hey?'

'Sure, boss, I go through the plan.'

And so Tryphon went through the plan for the Big Shilling. He went through the plan diligently and without mistakes, if a little slowly.

The plan was this: Tryphon and American Troy were boy racers, they'd ride their silencer-less bikes into Paphos old town and wait by the bus station, making as much noise and drawing as much attention as possible. The Big Shilling and Lena would already be in situ, watching for the arrival of the Russian exile, his wife and children, and their bodyguards. At a signal from the Big Shilling, American Troy and Tryphon himself would enter the ice cream parlour and commence firing. American Troy and Tryphon would take out the bodyguards, paying particular attention to the two men expected to have stationed themselves either side of the entrance, and the Big Shilling would waste the Russian exile. That was the plan.

As soon as it was completed, they would leave the scene of the assassination by bike, and ride to the Range Rover which was parked less than a mile from Paphos harbour.

'You've forgotten one thing,' said the Big Shilling.

'No,' said the Greek kid Tryphon, 'no, I do not forget it. Don't shoot Lena.'

'That's right,' said the Big Shilling. 'If you see her, wearing this pink shop-coat and an apron, don't shoot Lena.'

'Don't shoot Lena,' said Lena in a baby voice. 'Please, no shoot Lena.'

'I won't shoot Lena,' said the Greek Tryphon.

'American Troy?' asked the Big Shilling.

'I won't shoot Lena,' said American Troy, gallantly.

'That's right, no one shoots Lena, eh?' said the Big Shilling.

'Papa, Lena scared,' said Lena.

'Scared? There's no need to be scared, baby, hey?' said the Big Shilling, hugging her. 'Come on, come with daddy, daddy has just the thing to stop little Lena from being scared, eh? We'll cuddle up together and have a little nap. What do you say to that?'

'You are so good to me, daddy, cuddle up together again.'

And the Big Shilling took Lena into the bedroom and closed the door.

'Well, there's a first,' muttered American Troy.

'Extreme stunt rider,' said Tryphon, enthusiastically, 'yeah?'

'Yeah, okay.'

American Troy and the Greek Tryphon moved over to the couch by the comms centre, and American Troy found the video he'd been telling Tryphon about while they'd been driving to Paphos.

'This is it,' he said. 'Man, you've never seen anything like this guy. Kirk Schmidt, extreme stunt rider.'

'Extreme stunt rider,' repeated Tryphon, relishing the words. 'Never seen anything like this.'

Troy turned down the volume, glancing at the bedroom door as he did so: there was complete silence.

And so the early afternoon progressed.

If any of the four outlaws had given a thought to opening fire with automatic weapons in an ice cream parlour likely to be packed with families and children, none of them mentioned it. The Big Shilling was too busy imagining the Russian exile dead, and in his arms Lena was sleeping, a joyous smile on her face. As he watched the motorcycle stunts on the laptop screen, three-quarters of American Troy's attention was given over to what he would spend his cut on, and as for the Greek Tryphon, whose conscience was as stunted as his IQ, he was sometimes watching the video, and sometimes thinking of what he'd like to be doing to Lena, if the Big Shilling hadn't already been doing it to her. In fact, thought Tryphon, he really would not have minded making up a threesome.

American Troy sighed, and checked the time, yet again. Slowly, the afternoon progressed.

Sometime later, the Big Shilling's phone pinged. As Lena began to stir, the Big Shilling propped himself up on a rumpled pillow and read the text. It was from Brian Blee: the Russian exile's wife had just left by Mercedes, presumed to be heading for her daughter's school. The Big Shilling sent an acknowledgement. He knew that Betty Blee was at the school. In due course, he would receive word that the Russian exile had left the house in the Akamas as well. But that didn't mean there wasn't time for a shower. The Big Shilling took Lena's hand, and, as she was now used to doing, Lena followed her man into the bathroom, rolled up her sleeves and washed him lovingly under the lukewarm spray. She was used to the scars by now, and made no mention of them.

Slowly, the afternoon progressed.

When the Big Shilling was dressed once more in clean clothes, he went into the living room. American Troy and the Greek kid Tryphon looked at him expectantly.

'On your feet,' ordered the Big Shilling. 'Weapons check.'

The Big Shilling checked their weapons. He checked that the Glocks were loaded with seventeen rounds, and that there were two extra magazines for each gun. He checked that the Uzi submachine guns were locked and loaded, with selectors on safe. He checked his own MP5. Finally, he checked that Lena's pistol, which she'd left on the dining table, was loaded as well.

'Let me look at you,' he said to American Troy and the Greek Tryphon, looking them up and down. 'Yes, you look the part, eh? You look like a pair of boy racers, hey? You put clothes in the Range Rover, yes?'

'Clothes,' said American Troy, 'and shit for the beach.'

'Shit for the beach, eh?' said the Big Shilling. 'You mean the things I told you to pack for the beach, hey?'

'Yeah.'

'Then why don't you say so, eh? Be accurate, from now on be accurate. Say what you mean and mean what you say, hey?'

'Right,' said American Troy.

'Right,' echoed the Greek kid Tryphon.

'You're nervous?' the Big Shilling asked them. 'Now don't lie to me. There's nothing wrong with being nervous. It's natural, and nothing to be ashamed of. Some people suffer from nerves. You're nervous?'

Both American Troy and the Greek Tryphon admitted to being a little nervous.

'You are fortunate,' said the Big Shilling, 'because today Doctor Shilling is in the house. Here, take one of these each, hey? Diazepam, make you nice and relaxed. Lena, do you want another happy pill?'

'Yes, please, papa,' called Lena, hurrying from the bedroom, once more smartly turned out as a shop girl.

'There,' said the Big Shilling, paternally, when his three charges had washed down the tablets. 'It's time Lena and I were leaving. As soon as I get the word, boys, I'll tip you the wink. There's plenty of time, and you won't have any problems with the traffic on your bikes. Just remember to set the time bomb before you leave, eh?'

'I won't forget,' said American Troy.

'I know you won't,' the Big Shilling told him. He looked around at them, nodding. 'I am proud of you all. No captain had a better crew than you three, hey? No captain alive.'

'Let's do this thing!' cried Tryphon, suddenly.

'Shut up, you mutt,' said American Troy.

CHAPTER FIFTEEN

This time it would be different. That's what the Albanian girl Lena was thinking as she looked over her shoulder at the man she loved so desperately. The Big Shilling winked imperceptibly at her, and her heart almost burst.

Suppressing an enormous smile, she crossed the road by Paphos bus station and entered the larger of the two ice cream parlours. It was very busy everywhere today. The streets around Paphos harbour were very busy and so was the ice cream parlour. Lena felt a little faint. It was very hot today, and also she was nervous. She held her stomach like she had a tummy ache, but really she was supporting the weight of the revolver in the pocket of the apron. She went straight to the chiller cabinet and selected a bottle of water. She didn't look around her, she looked at the floor as though she was feeling a little faint from the heat, but she could hear the hubbub of parents and children and of the women selling take-away ice cream at the counter.

She could also hear the noise of the motorbikes without silencers that these two guys kept riding up and down the street next to the bus station. Motorbikes were really very, very noisy without silencers, and she wanted the irritating noise to stop as soon as possible.

Lena had the correct money. Daddy had told her how much a bottle of water from the chiller cabinet cost in the ice cream parlour. Lena smiled weakly at the woman behind the counter and handed her the correct change, but she didn't meet the woman's eye. Next, Lena went and sat on one of the couches near the toilets at the rear of the ice cream parlour, unscrewed the bottle and took a sip of water. This time it would be different. Daddy had promised her that this was his last job. It is time to retire, hey? That's what he had said, a smile on his beautiful face. They would live by the sea somewhere warm, and they would go fishing, and cook the fish over a barbecue on the beach, and they would sleep naked under the stars, and they would be alone, no Tryphon, no American Troy, just her and her papa. This time it would be different, Lena said to herself. Daddy was not like the other outlaws she had dated. Daddy was older and wiser and therefore knew that if he didn't retire he would surely be killed or would go to jail for the rest of his life like all the other outlaws she had dated.

Later, she could not be sure whether she heard the sound of the explosion before she saw the bike explode, or vice versa. She remembered wondering if it was the Greek Tryphon's bike or American Troy's. She hoped it was Tryphon. She didn't like Tryphon. American Troy was not as handsome, but he had a nice name and was polite to her and was clever. Tryphon was a pain. She'd felt his eyes on her ass and her titties all the time they were in the apartment together.

Lena got to her feet, feeling definitely sick now. There was a commotion. One of the big plate-glass windows had shattered. A child with blood on its face was screaming. Some people were crouching down, other people were rushing for the fire exits. A woman knocked Lena out of the way. Lena thought at first that the woman was one of the Russian exile's bodyguards but she quickly realised that the woman was simply terrified. The Russian exile and his family were crouching down, surrounded by big men who were looking round. One of them looked at her hard, and Lena pretended to be terrified, and the man looked quickly away.

Lena waited for the stampede to abate. People were shouting and crying, and everything was confused. There was ice cream and broken glass all over the floor near the entrance. American Troy appeared amongst the people who were escaping through the front doors. Lena saw the machine gun in American Troy's hands, and she was glad it was him and not the Greek Tryphon. She thought that

Tryphon might have shot little Lena, despite what he had said at the apartment in Kissonerga. American Troy didn't shoot at Lena. He shot at the ceiling above the table where the Russian exile and his family were sheltering.

After that, Lena became increasingly confused. There was more gunfire, pistol shots she thought, and then American Troy wasn't firing at the ceiling but at a target on his left. There were potted plants and a pillar in the way so Lena could not see who or what Troy was firing at, but she could hear screams. Next, one of the Russian exile's bodyguards threw his arms wide and fell backwards across a neighbouring table, smashing glasses and sending ice cream and dishes flying across the room.

Daddy, thought Lena, daddy is here, just like he said!

The Russian exile and his family were by now in some disarray. Their bodyguards were distracted, returning fire with pistols towards the emergency exits. Lena could see the Russian exile's face and neck and shoulders. His head was in profile. He was a handsome man, cultured, refined and brave. He was protecting his wife and their children as a good husband and father should, shielding them with his body. He was unafraid. He looked at Lena in surprise. He looked at her and at the revolver she had produced from the pocket of the apron. That was when he brought up his own pistol. Lena fired the gun. It jumped in her small hands, and the bang was loud and she could smell the smoke it made. She fired once more and saw that the second bullet hit the Russian exile in the head.

'Uh,' said the Russian exile's mouth, and the pistol he'd been holding dropped onto the tiled floor.

Lena inhaled, clenched her jaw and fired three more times. She aimed the shots at the Russian exile's shoulders. She didn't want to shoot him in the head again. There was blood now, and the blood mingled with the spilled ice cream on the tiled floor. She was sure the Russian exile was dead. Then someone grabbed her by the arm and dragged her to her feet.

'Daddy!' she cried. She hadn't even realised she'd been squatting down.

The Big Shilling dragged the girl to her feet and pulled her towards the fire exit. The Big Shilling had killed all the Russian exile's bodyguards, he was certain of it, but still he scanned the room, the Heckler and Koch machine pistol moving in concert with his head. Look all around, forwards, backwards, side to side, up and down: that was the way you kept alive, by seeing the target before the target saw you. The Big Shilling pulled Lena through the doors of the fire exit, and told her to walk not run.

'Oh daddy,' said Lena, 'I did what you told me! I always do what you tell me!'

'You did good, baby,' said the Big Shilling. 'Now go!'

The Big Shilling returned to the Russian exile's table, dragged the screaming wife out of the way and fired a burst point blank into the Russian exile's skull to make sure. The Russian exile's head exploded like a watermelon. The Big Shilling crouched down and moved a few metres sideways and to the left. He could see American Troy exiting the ice cream parlour by the front doors. American Troy smoothly reloaded the Uzi and fired bursts into the sky. The Big Shilling heard muffled screams, and people running in the street outside. Inside the ice cream parlour it was much quieter, or seemed to be, since the Big Shilling realised he was partially deafened by the noise of gunfire, but most of the people who could, had by now made their escape.

It appeared that American Troy had killed an extended family seated at a table to the left of the entrance. There were two children, two grandparents, and the mother and father. The Big Shilling guessed the father was a cop. He had a cop's gun in his dead hand, a cop's holster on his belt and a cop's paunch overhanging the belt.

'Bakgat,' said the Big Shilling, lips pursed and eyebrows raised. It was one of South African Troy's favourite expressions, back in the day. Its English equivalent was the word 'cool,' in the sense of appreciation of great skill.

The Big Shilling decided it was time to leave. He could have killed American Troy right there and then, firing through the open space where the plate glass window had been, an easy shot, thirty metres at most, American Troy walking on stiff legs down the street across from the bus station, presumably on his way back to his bike. But the Big Shilling decided not to kill his accomplice. He'd already given the police the Greek kid Tryphon, and the police would leave no stone unturned in hunting down the man who had killed one of their own.

Just as, in the same way, the Big Shilling had decided not to kill the Albanian girl Lena after she had shot the Russian exile. Part of him would have preferred to have exfiltrated alone, with both the girl Lena and American Troy dead, but it made better sense to keep two irons in the fire, so to speak. Getting off the island was always going to be the tricky part of the operation, and he might need to take diversionary measures in order to ensure his own escape. He'd just rewrite the script.

And so, as the Big Shilling left the ice cream parlour by the fire exit, he was feeling very pleased with himself, all told. The Russian exile was dead, the job had been done, and all was right with the world. No, the Big Shilling told himself, life did not get much better than this. And what better end to an enjoyable afternoon was there on a holiday island than a cold beer at the beach and a swim in the sea?

There was no pursuit. They saw no police cars, although they did hear emergency vehicle sirens, but that may have been the fire brigade and not the police, for that Friday afternoon there was an unprecedented spike in calls to the emergency services reporting explosions and fires in the Paphos area. A minute before the Big Shilling had detonated the charge secreted under the petrol tank of the motorbike the Greek kid Tryphon had been riding, he'd also made the call that set off the fire bomb American Troy had planted in the kitchen of the Kissonerga apartment. And Brian and Betty Blee had made a number of diversionary calls to the emergency services that afternoon as well.

No, the only cop they saw all day had been the off-duty detective who had so fatefully decided to take his extended family out for ice cream.

The Big Shilling kept an eye on American Troy. He kept an eye on him as he strapped the rucksack containing one of the Uzis, the MP5 and Lena's pistol to the seat of the motorcycle, and primed the fire bomb that exploded a few seconds after the three of them, the Big Shilling, Lena and American Troy, had driven off in the Range Rover. He kept an eye on him during the drive to the car park at Lady's Mile, where they changed out of their stained clothes, and he kept an eye on him on the beach as well, where American Troy proved to be uncommunicative and sullen.

The Albanian girl Lena, on the other hand, was no problem at all. She behaved like nothing had happened, that she hadn't just murdered a man for the first time in her life, and in cold blood. No, she behaved like it was a summer Friday and she'd just got off work and was at the beach with the man she loved. The Big Shilling sent her to the bar for three beers.

'Leon, hey? Not Keo,' he told her.

'Not Keo, Leon,' she said, blowing him a kiss.

'Something wrong?' the Big Shilling asked American Troy when she was gone.

'No.'

'Then start smiling.'

'Maybe I'll just lie down on a sunbed and close my eyes.'

'And brood some more? No way, my boy. You're going to party with me and the girl. We're going to get a little merry and we're going to have a little swim and you're going to flirt with those pretty Cypriot girls over there. Or else. You understand me? Or else.'

The Big Shilling watched American Troy gather his spirits together and get a grip on himself.

'Better?'

'Better,' said American Troy.

'Good man, because this isn't over yet, eh? We're only half way home.'

CHAPTER
SIXTEEN

merican Troy couldn't think straight. There was a movie playing in his head that demanded, and held, his attention. It was a horror movie. American Troy wanted it to be an uber-cool auteur-directed crime thriller, but it wasn't. It was a horror movie, and he was the monster slaughtering the innocents.

Whenever he looked away from the screen he could still hear the sound track, the gunshots, the screaming, the off-key, ear-lancing music. Only gradually did the alcohol deaden the pain. But even through its foggy numbness, the ghosts reached out to him, asking him why, imploring him to explain, because they didn't understand, they would never understand why he had done what he had done.

Why hadn't he stopped firing? Jesus! He'd killed the cop first, he'd killed the cop first, goddamn it. He'd seen the cop go for his gun, thank Christ, seen him bring up the piece, and nailed him with a double tap that hit him in the chest. But the Big Shilling Drill was at the forefront of his mind: you had to make sure, two to the chest, one to head, make sure, make sure. And so he'd walked forward a couple of steps, to make sure, and drilled the leo through the skull. And then the woman was on her feet and so was the old guy, he could still see their dreadful, contorted faces, and he flipped the switch to full auto and hosed them all to hell, woman, pops and grandma, and the kids as well. Jesus, the kids as well!

Now he shuddered, and was for a moment aware of the relentless noise: the Big Shilling in the middle of another one of his ninety-minute-long monologues, the thumping music over the speakers from the beach bar, the squawking of dozens of kids splashing in the sea.

Jesus wept, what had made him do it? It was the Big Shilling Drill, was what it was, the An-fucking-golan Drill, two to the chest and one to the head, two to the chest and one to the head. That's what had made him do it.

'Hey. Hey. Hey!'

It was the Big Shilling. It was always the Big Shilling, goading him, needling him.

'All right,' said American Troy. 'Jesus, I'm all right.'

The Big Shilling, lording it on the sunbed with the Albanian girl Lena, pointed a finger in warning at American Troy.

'We're having a sun-downer, eh,' said the Big Shilling. 'You're having a sun-downer?'

American Troy jerked the plastic beaker of lukewarm beer that he gripped in his right hand. 'I'm having a sun-downer.'

'That's all right then, hey?' said the Big Shilling. 'We're having a sun-downer along with our good friend, American Troy, and all is well with the world. Now where was I, before I was so rudely interrupted?'

'You were saying, daddy, about how is the best way to barbeque sable.'

'That I was, that I was. You were listening, hey, you were listening to daddy, baby girl?'

American Troy inhaled mightily, and turned his back on his companions. As he slowly exhaled he looked at the sun. As was the case at this latitude, at dusk the sun did not tarry on its journey to the horizon. You could see it moving through the ribbon of haze that blurred the region where sea met sky. In less than a minute it would be gone, extinguished by the curvature of the turning earth.

Just like the Albanian and the Greek kid Tryphon were gone, extinguished by the Big Shilling.

Jesus, thought American Troy, looking at the beer in the plastic beaker and seeing reflected there the life-giving sun, now I can think, and I don't want to.

This is what he was thinking: it's me next. That's what American Troy was thinking, that he would be next, coshed and strangled like the Albanian, or blown to bits by a bomb like the retard Tryphon.

American Troy closed his eyes, but there was no escape. Even with his eyes closed he could see a negative of the sun, a black sun, and hear the Big Shilling's voice.

'Where are you off to?' the Big Shilling asked him.

American Troy was on his feet. 'To get another brew. Want one?'

The Big Shilling took his time considering, and finally decided after a certain amount of deliberation that he and Lena were okay for drinks at the moment, thank you. Irritated, American Troy stomped off. He was irritated by the idiotic Euro-pop pumping out of the beach bar loud-speakers, irritated by the sand on the bottom of his feet and by the flip-flops he had to wear, irritated by the stupid holiday-makers and their lousy kids, and irritated most of all by the funk he was in.

He had to queue at the bar. He looked around at the pounded sand on the worn concrete steps, the litter everywhere, the cigarette butts and the drinking straws, and the rolls of fat on the Russian girl showering, and was filled with disgust for humanity. Christ, he wished he had that Uzi with him right now, he'd waste the whole goddamned lot of them, that Russian peasant and her ugly off-spring in their spangled white-blue-and-red tops, those Cypriot boys and their hook-nosed girlfriends, the par-boiled Brits in their stupid sun hats playing pad-ball. When he realised what he was thinking, American Troy almost sniggered.

He was still smirking when the barkeep approached him. There wasn't any tequila, but there was whisky.

'A bottle of Keo and a whisky, then,' said American Troy. 'And turn down the goddamned music for me as well, buddy. Jesus.'

When the beer came it was in a plastic beaker not a bottle, but it was definitely Keo and not Leon, and when he tasted it, it tasted to American Troy like triumph. The whisky didn't hurt either, and neither did the fact that the barman did indeed go and turn down the music a notch. American Troy propped up the bar for the short while it took him to finish the scotch.

Yes, all in all he was feeling a lot better. He'd come to a decision. All he had to do, obviously, was kill the Big Shilling first, before the Big Shilling killed him. Nothing to it, was there? He still had the Glock 17 in the rucksack under the sunbed. The guy slept. The guy turned his back on you. The guy suspected nothing. If you have a problem, thought American Troy, yeah, you can solve it.

He sang along to the tune that was playing, about ice, babies and vanilla.

Be like ice. Be cool, like ice, he told himself. Be ice cold, and waste that bullshit motherfucker before he wastes you.

'So where is he?' he asked, when he got back to the sunbeds with his half-drunk beer. The Big Shilling was watching Lena as she dreamily danced about in the surf.

'Good boy,' said the Big Shilling, 'he's a good boy,

eh? Got him to turn down the music, did you?'

'So where is he?' American Troy repeated, persistent.

'Where's who?'

'You know who: Frankie the Freak.'

'Frankie? Oh, Frankie will be along. As soon as it's real dark and everyone has gone home.'

'Where's he taking us?'

'You'll find out soon enough, my boy,' said the Big Shilling, scowling at him. 'Me? I'm going to catch a little shut-eye. My advice to you would be to do the same, hey? Conserve your energy, conserve your energy, eh? And lay off the booze. Had a sneaky one at the bar, hey? Think I wouldn't notice?'

'I thought this was a beach party,' American Troy said, but the Big Shilling affected deafness and closed his eyes.

Troy shrugged and sat down, a little unsteadily.

After he had finished his beer, sniffing because his nose was a little fizzy, he did indeed fall asleep on the sunbed, and when he awoke it was very dark, and Lena and the Big Shilling were collecting their things together. Troy checked the time. It was 10.35. His mouth tasted foul. He rinsed it with lukewarm water from the bottle and spat into the sand. The alcohol had done its familiar work, his formerly high spirits replaced by a fug of despondency, or maybe that was down to the fact that he'd wasted an entire family that afternoon. Yeah, maybe that was why he was feeling a little low, the fact he was a child killer.

Fuck, thought American Troy as he levered himself upright, I could use another whisky. He looked along the beach and confirmed what he already knew to be the case, that the beach bar was closed and all the people had gone home. At least it was quieter, and cooler.

'Present from Lena,' said the Big Shilling in an undertone, tossing a small object Troy's way.

It was insect repellent. 'Thanks, Lena,' said American Troy.

He tore open the wipe and swabbed his bare legs and arms, his face and his neck.

'Come on,' said the Big Shilling in the same quiet tone. 'We're moving down the beach.'

American Troy was wrong. Not all the people had gone home. There were still a few couples and foursomes and lone dog-walkers here and there along Lady's Mile. And there was RAF Akrotiri as well, in the distance to the west, and the sound of a helicopter hovering or on the ground. Planes had been landing and occasionally taking off all evening, delta-wing jet fighters, cargo aircraft, a giant AWACs airplane with a radome on its back. Now, American Troy saw the Big Shilling checking out those giant listening aerials again, and felt a watery unease in his guts.

After five minutes' walking, the Big Shilling called a halt, and they settled down in the sand to wait. They waited almost four hours. The Big Shilling barely said a word the whole time. Around midnight the animal took the Albanian girl Lena into the dunes and they returned half an hour later, American Troy forced to listen to their rutting yet again, and to Lena's giggling and gagging, but it did at least give him time to check out the Glock. He removed it from the waterproof zip-lock wallet, and considered killing his two companions when they returned from whatever it was they were doing. Next, he wondered whether it would be better to stash the pistol in the side pocket of the rucksack, rather than have it inaccessible in the main body of the bag. There was no way he could conceal it about his person, wearing as he was swim shorts and a t-shirt.

He still hadn't made a decision when he heard the Big Shilling and his squeeze returning from the dunes. He slipped the Glock into the waterproof bag and put the bag in the side pocket of the rucksack. He wasn't going to waste the guy now, not when Frankie the Fish might solve all their problems and whisk them off who knew where.

But Frankie the Fish never arrived. Instead of a leaky old wreck named the Melissa, American Troy was astonished to witness the beaching of Omar the Sailor's vaunted stealth boat.

He was alerted by the Big Shilling, who had more than once claimed to have the hearing ability of a dog.

'Dog's ears, I've got dog's ears, hey? Not human ears, dog's ears, dog's ears.'

That night it certainly seemed true, for American Troy heard nothing for many minutes after the Big

Shilling had gotten to his feet, turned his head sideways, and cupped a hand to the side of his head.

'A new biz,' Shilling seemed to say.

'What?' asked Troy.

'He's coming,' said the Big Shilling. Then, half a minute later, 'He's here. Do you hear him? He's here. Get your things together, children, we're going for a boat ride, hey?'

But it was another two minutes before American Troy, straining, heard the noise of the stealth boat's muffled engines above the sighing of the sea. He looked at the Big Shilling with new respect.

'How did you do that?'

'I grew up in the desert, my boy, far from civilisation, that's how I did that, eh? Ever been to the Lebanon?'

American Troy was staring out to sea, his mouth open. 'It's not Frankie.'

'Does it look like a yacht?' The Big Shilling pointed. 'There. Do you see him? That's Omar, Omar the Sailor.'

'Omar the Sailor,' said Lena, clapping her hands together silently, and jumping up and down on the spot. The Big Shilling reached out a hand to still her.

Finally, American Troy saw the stealth boat. The craft was so low in the water that it looked like a semi-submersible, and its smooth radar-repellent lines were coated with some kind of matt material that seemed to absorb what little light there was, from the stars above and from the port of Limassol away to their left. This was more like it. James fucking Bond!

'He's brought a cargo,' said the Big Shilling with a chuckle. 'Hey, I knew he'd bring a cargo. He's brought a cargo, hey? Put your flip-flops in your bags, put them in your bags or you'll lose them in the sea.'

The cargo was disembarking in a barely controlled frenzy. There were eight of them - irregular immigrants, economic migrants, asylum seekers - six men and two women, ecstatic now to have touched the sand of mother Europe. They struggled through the shallows, the sea sucking at their legs as though it didn't want to let them go, the women round-faced in their head-dresses, the young men of fighting age, fit and eager, bearded and bright-eyed.

They must have been warned there would be people on the beach, for they barely glanced at the Big Shilling, American Troy, and the girl Lena in their hurry to get to the dunes. American Troy could smell vomit. He pulled a face. One of the migrants must have had puke on their clothes. The smell got stronger as they neared the stealth boat. A young man was swilling it out with buckets of sea water.

'Quickly,' said Omar the Sailor in English. 'Take your time but hurry up, please.'

It was one of the Big Shilling's favourite phrases, and American Troy guessed that Omar the Sailor was an old friend of the Big Shilling.

'What took you so long, hey?' the Big Shilling demanded, and American Troy saw a flash of white teeth as Shilling and Omar clasped hands.

As soon as the three of them were aboard, the young man, who was Antoine's older brother, the student of accountancy and lover of smuggling, dipped into the water and shoved the boat off so that Omar could start the engines. Omar helped his son back aboard, and told them to get strapped into the seats. This took them half a minute, what with the boat turning and the sea slopping over the sides that had them sliding about, and by the time they were under way Lena had already thrown up over American Troy's bare feet.

'Jesus,' said Troy in disgust, tightening his harness as Omar opened the throttle. He glanced back at the beach, and saw a spotlight from a vehicle that was travelling at speed from the west. The Big Shilling had seen it as well. He turned his back on it definitively, not caring what was happening to the off-loaded cargo, already scanning to port and starboard, the sea and the sky, searching out danger like he had done all his life.

And danger there was, suddenly, in the form of two patrol boats, one Cypriot, the other British. Omar the Sailor, urging the stealth craft onwards with imprecations to heaven, headed for the gap between them.

They won't fire, thought American Troy when he realised what was happening, they never fire. Instead, they rescue you. But this time he was wrong. The Cypriot maritime patrol opened fire. The British boat illuminated the target, and the Cypriot boat fired. It fired wide, American Troy saw the red tracer rounds striking the sea, but then there was a huge bang from aft and the engines cut out and they immediately began to lose way.

For the space of a few seconds, American Troy was flummoxed. He had the strangest feeling that this self-same situation had happened to him before. Stranger still, he was thinking that Shilling was the cause of all this! That he had somehow caused the engines to blow up, but how was that even possible? The Big Shilling's opinion, so often repeated, now sounded inside Troy's brain: getting off the island would be almost impossible. Troy could not move.

But the Big Shilling did not hesitate. 'Over the side!' he cried, unfastening his harness.

Acrid black smoke began to roil and billow from the engines.

'Want to burn, kid?' Shilling asked him.

There was nothing for it. Troy went over the side. The Big Shilling was looking out for Lena. American Troy was on his own. He tried not to panic. He was trying to swim and trying not to panic. There was nothing underneath him but the sea and he tried not to panic. He was swimming, or trying to, but not making any headway. Panic rising, he rolled onto his back. As he did so he got a mouth full of seawater. Coughing and gagging, he tried not to give in to the panic. He could see the boat on fire and in the boat were two figures and they were on fire. He flailed with his arms and kicked desperately with his legs, but he wasn't making any headway.

He cried out. Suddenly, there was an explosion that blinded him, and a welling up and a rush of water. The wave took American Troy bodily and dragged him under like he was nothing, and his head was filled with gushing and his lungs were screaming at him for air.

Twice American Troy got his head above the surface and twice he was submerged again. He could feel his vital energy ebbing away. He flailed again, but it got him nowhere. He was going to die! He was drowning! Where was Shilling? Where was he? Help me, you animal!

What happened next was something that he'd heard about, but never for one moment thought he'd actually experience. He was drowning and there was nothing he could do. A calmness came over him, and the most perfect tranquillity took the place of the terrible panic that had gripped him. His senses were deadened but not so his mind. Quite the opposite, in fact, his mind appeared to be working with such clarity and rapidity that he was astonished. He was thinking how his death would affect his mother and his other family members, and his thoughts spread out at astonishing speed, first back over the events of that day, then the weeks before, then his whole life right back to when he was a kid. It was amazing. He was seeing his whole past life in the minutest detail. It was all there, everything he had thought and done, travelling backwards, the whole of his existence viewed as if from a panorama.

Rough hands gripped him, an arm got him about the waist. He could breathe, his head was above the water. He was on his back, a hand under his chin, being towed to the shallows.

Fifteen minutes after leaving Cypriot soil, the three of them, the Big Shilling, American Troy and Lena, were back on the beach. Troy lay there on the strand, coughing and spluttering, overjoyed to be alive. Lena tended to him while Shilling went off on a recce.

'That's a hell of a way,' said Troy, panting, 'to learn to swim.'

'Oh Troy, Troy!' said Lena, stroking his face and his hair. 'We think you are dead.'

'No,' mumbled Troy, 'I didn't die. It was weird.'

He heard padding feet approaching.

'Save your breath, boy,' the Big Shilling told him. 'Can you walk? Back to the car, as quick as we can, eh?'

Lena was sobbing quietly. The Big Shilling gathered her into his arms and carried her along the beach.

'Come on, kid, move it! Or we're done for!'

Troy got to his knees, then to his feet, the urgency of Shilling's words giving him the energy to stand up. He stumbled after them, every step leaden. Shilling waited for him to catch up, and when they reached the rows of sunbeds, he called a halt so that Troy could catch his breath as well. Beyond the dunes they heard the sound of a heavy truck's diesel engine passing by at speed.

The truck was a desert patrol vehicle belonging to the RAF Regiment, and it reappeared when the three of them emerged from the path at the side of the beach bar into the car park. A powerful lamp suddenly illuminated the shipwreck survivors.

'All right?' called a British voice, playfully. 'Stop right where you are, guys, and everything'll be just fine.'

The voice belonged to an RAF flight sergeant, a scouser or Liverpudlian. He was wearing a blue beret and holding a rifle, which he now brought up to his shoulder and took aim.

'Not your night, is it?' he said, laughing.

He recognised the two men, the younger one defo. Yeah, that was the little blurt who'd been eyeing up Nicole, on the beach at Latchi the other day.

CHAPTER SEVENTEEN

The sun was coming up when they reached the dump in the Troodos mountains. The air was clean and cool and there was a smell of pine from the trees all around. A raptor circled below in the clear sky.

'I told you,' said the Big Shilling, 'I told you it would still be here, hey?'

American Troy had done a lot of moaning on the drive from Lady's Mile to the dump in the mountains. American Troy had done so much moaning that the Big Shilling had felt compelled to set him straight about one or two things. A back-hander delivered to the kid's face had sorted him out, but now he was sulky and resentful. Some thanks for being saved from drowning!

'You're an ingrate,' the Big Shilling now told him, 'an ingrate, that's what you are. Here, help yourself to water, and to food. There's a tent, clean clothes, everything we need, eh, everything we need. And it's here, just like I said it would be. You know why? High trust, that's why. Cyprus is a high trust society. Everyone knows everyone else, so there is no crime, practically. That's how I knew the kit I dumped here would still be here when we needed it, hey?'

He ripped open the plastic wrapper on the six-pack of water and lobbed a two-litre bottle to American Troy.

'Say thank you to the widow woman.'

'Thanks,' mumbled Troy, after uncapping the bottle and taking a few long swigs. He didn't know what that meant and did not care.

The Big Shilling supposed that was as close to an apology American Troy was going to make. He said as much. The girl Lena was in the back of the Range Rover, sleeping and exhausted. The Big Shilling expected problems from her as well, but nothing he couldn't handle. Problems, problems, all they gave him were problems. He said as much, and more than once.

'Today,' said the Big Shilling, 'today is a day of rest. We rest and we regroup. Tonight, or maybe tomorrow night, we make use of our fall-back plan.'

'That guy Joshua,' said American Troy.

American Troy's voice sounded a little funny, what with the thick lip the Big Shilling had given him. Or maybe there was another reason. The Big Shilling searched the kid's face: had the light finally dawned? He'd been whining about the stealth boat's engines, about how he couldn't understand how they'd failed.

'So now you're an expert in marine propulsion?' he'd asked him, more than once, and the kid had shut up.

'That's right. Remember him, my little Shona friend from the glorious nation of Zimbabwe, hey? So you see, there is nothing to worry about, nothing at all. In fact, everything is working out wonderfully.'

American Troy said, interrupting, 'The authorities have had a victory. They can say they foiled our escape attempt, sank a stealth boat, and caught a bunch of migrants.'

The Big Shilling pointed a finger at him and nodded his agreement. 'Watch and learn, my friend, watch and learn, eh?'

When the Big Shilling started unpacking the two-man tent, American Troy came over to help him. Not that he was much help. The Big Shilling recognised the signs, the kid had had enough, he'd had as much as he could handle for the time being. Be careful what you wish for, eh? You wanted to be a bad man, a killer, an outlaw? Well, now you were, my boy, and this was how it felt.

'Let me,' said the Big Shilling, almost gently. 'Let me do it. Sit down, and let me do it.'

American Troy sat down on the ground, and watched the Big Shilling work.

Once the tent was up, the Big Shilling unfurled the bedrolls and told the kid to get some sleep. American Troy simply nodded, crawled inside the tent and immediately fell asleep. The Big Shilling was made of sterner stuff, and brim-full of energy in spite of being a sexagenarian, set about organising the rest of the camp. He moved the Range Rover closer to the undergrowth, so that it was hidden from the trail through the trees, he sorted through the clean clothes, and made a mental inventory of all the kit they had with them. He checked the weapons were clean and dry, he removed the SIM cards from the remaining mobile phones, scorched them with the Zippo's powerful flame, and buried them between the roots of a tree.

He felt good as he worked. He was a force of Nature, that's what he was, nothing could stand in his way, and nothing could stand in his way because he came from nothing, he came out of nothing, he was nothing. He remembered the look on the RAF sergeant's face when word came over the radio that the prisoners were to be released. Crestfallen, that was the word for it, the guy had been crestfallen. And the words had stuck in his craw when he'd told them they could go.

'Maybe we don't want to go,' the Big Shilling had told him, grinning wickedly. 'Maybe we want to stay here all night and party on the beach.'

'Please your fucking self, fella,' the RAF sergeant had said, stalking back to his truck. 'I'm out of here.'

'Aren't you going to search us?' the Big Shilling had goaded him. 'For all you know we could have weapons and explosives in the car over there.'

'Leave it,' American Troy had hissed. 'Jesus Christ, man, leave it! He's letting us go.'

The Big Shilling had laughed. He laughed long and hard, laughed so much he teared up, and American Troy was staring at him, bug-eyed, like he was crazy. No, the kid still didn't get it. He still thought they'd be paid, and he'd be able to buy a fleet of motorbikes, and they'd swan around Europe like they were in some cockamamie movie. Now, as the Big Shilling lay down on one of the sleeping bags under the cool of the pine trees and prepared to rest, he laughed again, but quietly this time, so as not to wake the children. A force of Nature, a force of Nature is what I am.

'Ha ha ha ha ha!'

As the drifted towards sleep, relaxed and happy, the Big Shilling imagined future success.

All was peaceful at the campsite, save for the bird-life, the squirrels and the insects. At some point, the Albanian girl Lena left the back seat of the car and came and snuggled up beside her papa, and just after that, American Troy cried out in his sleep. It was early afternoon before the three of them awoke. American Troy checked the time. It was five before two.

'No,' said the Big Shilling to pre-empt him.

'Why not? We need to know.'

'I need to know. You need to know what I decide you need to know.'

'Fuck it, man.'

'Listen to me, boy, and listen good. I've given you one slap today and I can give you another, if you like. No more of your whining. From now on, you call me boss and like it.'

American Troy's mouth was sullen but he managed to straighten it enough to say, 'Yes, boss.'

'Yes, boss,' repeated the Big Shilling. 'Yes, boss. Right, you two, clean yourselves up. There's water and soap and toothpaste, and you'll find a towel in the back of the car. I'm taking a constitutional.'

'Can't I come with you, daddy?' asked Lena in a little voice that boded ill.

'Clean yourself up,' he ordered, striding off down the hillside.

It had been a mistake to tune into the British Forces radio news on the drive from Lady's Mile to the Troodos mountains. He'd done it without thinking. Well, so what? Even I, the Big Shilling, am allowed to make a mistake once in a while. The story was the second lead, and there was already a soundbite from some senior law enforcement officer that had set American Troy flapping his mouth. No doubt the public relations people would have a further spin on it by now. Every police officer on the island mobilised in the search for these cold-blooded killers, Turkish authorities informed, Interpol have issued a red notice, no word yet from the Kremlin on the brutal slaying of President Putin's former ally, blah, blah, blah. The Big Shilling shook his head. What was needed was a clean start, drain the swamp and start again.

The Blees' campsite was about half a mile from the dump. He spotted the Irish widow's campervan from afar, the big England flag it was flying catching his eye immediately. Brian Blee was tending the barbeque, his wife Betty sunning herself in a deckchair beneath the improvised washing line.

'Here he is!' said Brian. 'The man himself. What did I tell you, Bet?'

'Hello, love,' squawked Bri's breadknife, 'fancy a cup of rosy?'

The Blees had the radio on. Brian Blee was turning sausages over on the griddle and singing along to a lyric about clowns and jokers.

The Big Shilling stopped and stared at him.

'Bet,' said Brian, quickly, 'turn that shite off.'

'You think I'm a clown?' the Big Shilling demanded. 'You think I'm a joker?'

The Blees laughed it off, of course they didn't think he was a clown, or a joker! They laughed it off, and he let them. He let them feed him tea and sausage sandwiches as well, and at two twenty-nine Brian obediently turned on the radio again. The story of the murder of the Russian exile was now the lead item.

'A body believed to be that of an Albanian national sought by police in their investigation into the brutal killings at a Paphos ice cream parlour yesterday has been washed ashore near Aya Napa.'

Good old Frankie, thought the Big Shilling, as good as his word as always.

'More tea, love?' asked Betty, gesturing with the

pot.

'No. No more tea.'

Brian glared at his wife to keep quiet.

'Eleven people died in the massacre near Paphos harbour yesterday, including two children,' read the announcer, 'and four people remain in hospital, two of whom are said to be in a critical condition. Police are not treating the incident as terrorist-related and say that the general public should not be alarmed by the incident. Ministry of Justice spokeswoman...'

'Turn it off,' ordered the Big Shilling.

As though he'd been anticipating such a peremptory command, Brian Blee immediately snapped off the sound. There was a tension in the ensuing silence. The three of them sat there in their deckchairs, the Big Shilling, Brian and Betty Blee, the smell of barbecued sausages, pine resin and burnt charcoal eddying around the campervan in the gentle breeze.

'Get what I asked for?' the Big Shilling asked, eventually.

'Right here, chief,' said Brian, passing over a plastic carrier bag.

'Thanks.'

'No problemo.'

The Big Shilling turned, and focused on Brian Blee's sweaty beetroot face. 'Let's have a look at the map.'

'Bet, love?'

Betty Blee went and fetched the map from inside the van. She was sweating as well, the Big Shilling noted.

'Warm today,' he said.

'Just nice, up here in the hills,' chirped Betty.

'Boiling, down there on the coast,' croaked Brian.

'You'll both feel the heat if you let me down,' said the Big Shilling, darkly. Noting the downcast faces, the downcast eyes, he grinned and said, 'Now, let's have a look at the map.'

He went through it twice with them, so that there could be no misunderstanding he went through it twice.

'Meet me there, it's only fifteen kilometres from the crossing point, that's if I call you, eh? If I don't call, you stay this side and we'll rendezvous at this point here, understand?'

'Understood,' said Brian Blee.

'One more thing, Bri, eh? Take off your shorts.'

'You what?'

'Take them off.'

Brian Blee barely hesitated. He sniffed, stood up, and dropped his shorts. The Big Shilling held out a hand for them.

'Here,' said Betty to her husband, reaching up to the washing line as though embarrassed. 'Cover it up.'

'Camouflage,' the Big Shilling explained.

The Blees had a good laugh about it, once Bri had covered his meat and two veg with the beach towel Bet had lobbed him.

'Camouflage,' said Brian to Betty, encouraging her.

'Camouflage,' she said, joining in.

So good a laugh in fact that Brian felt emboldened to broach the subject of cash.

'Kitty's getting a bit depleted, like,' he said. 'Few hundred would be much appreciated, say six hundred, or maybe a bag of sand, only if you've got it, like?'

The Big Shilling didn't react for some time. Then he said, 'You people, hey? You people, all you people ever want from me is money. You want some money, hey? You want money? Here's your money, here's your money, another lousy grand.'

He put Brian Blee's shorts, which were unpleasantly warm and damp, into the carrier bag which contained amongst other things two unused mobile phones, and walked back the way he'd come. As he left, he could hear the Blees bickering horribly as they tried to rescue the wad of banknotes that he'd slipped under the barbeque griddle into the smouldering charcoals beneath.

The first thing he said when he arrived back at the camp was, 'Did you listen to the radio?'

'No, I didn't,' said American Troy without emphasis.

The Big Shilling turned to Lena, and said, 'But you did.'

Lena was sitting on the ground beside the Range Rover, hugging her knees and rocking back and forth.

'You killed him,' she said, and her voice sounded cracked. 'You killed him! You said you let him go, but you lied to me, you lied to little Lena.'

'Lena,' said the Big Shilling, considering his options, 'oh Lena. Shut up, Lena. Shut up, or daddy will have to chastise you.'

'No no no!' screamed Lena. 'Keep away! Keep away from me!'

She was on her feet, running away, weeping and crying out and running away.

'Mustn't be hungry,' said the Big Shilling, as though puzzled.

CHAPTER EIGHTEEN

American Troy was feasting on the fresh bread and canned tuna that the Big Shilling had brought back, courtesy of Betty Blee. The Big Shilling was eating as well, eggs, raw not hard-boiled, tapping them on a rock to split the shells, then emptying the contents into his upturned open mouth.

'Protein,' he said, 'tuck in, tuck in. We need protein to replace all the energy we've expended. That canned tuna's good, hey?'

'It is good,' said American Troy, trying to ignore the unappetising sounds the Big Shilling was making as he crunched egg shell and washed it down with glugs of water from the bottle they were sharing. But Troy was ravenous, and he wolfed down food until he could hardly eat any more. He couldn't think, he was just his appetite and was glad.

The Big Shilling himself ate six raw eggs, shells and all, before starting in on the bread and tuna.

'Bring her over here,' he ordered, eventually.

The Albanian girl Lena had stormed off, but she'd not gone very far away. She was rolling on the ground about a hundred yards away, kicking her legs and beating the pine needle-covered earth with her little fists. She'd been doing that on and off for ten minutes now, and sometimes they could hear her sobbing and crying, and occasionally screaming in frustration. It sounded like a kid having a tantrum, which, American Troy guessed, was what it was. How old was Lena anyway? Nineteen? Eighteen? He wiped his hands on the legs of his shorts and took the bag of miniature pains-au-chocolat with him as a bribe.

The Big Shilling stopped chewing, observing them closely, American Troy and the Albanian girl Lena. When he'd decided they were not in collusion, and that they posed no immediate threat to him, he began to chew again.

'Aw, man,' he said to himself, 'this bread is good. And the tuna, mmm.'

When American Troy came back, the Big Shilling watched him finish his meal, rounding it off with a few green grapes and bites at a small banana. Lena refused to eat, and not even the pains-au-chocolat, her favourites, could tempt her. She sat on top of the sleeping bag a short distance from them and sulked, her tantrum for the moment played out.

'Maybe Lena wants to eat something else,' said the Big Shilling to American Troy, opening the bag of pains-au-chocolat.

'I hate you!' said Lena.

'I think baby Lena wants a taste of papa's spicy sausage.'

'No!'

'No?' said the Big Shilling, looking at American Troy with eyebrows innocently raised. 'Have one of these.'

'Thanks,' said American Troy, taking a miniature pain-au-chocolat.

'Looks like Lena doesn't want to smoke dada's cigar.'

American Troy, alerted by the change in the Big Shilling's tone of voice, said nothing. He took a bite of the pastry but his mouth had gone dry and he found it difficult to masticate. He'd been ravenous but he was ravenous no more.

'No!' said Lena.

'No? No?' repeated the Big Shilling. 'Well, one of you is going to smoke my cigar. I'm like a rhino, hey? I'm a like a rhino with the terrible horn. So one of you kids is going to help me out, or the rhino's going to charge, hey? The rhino is going to charge.'

It had gone quiet. It was that silence which the Big Shilling was happily familiar with, the silence of fear and high tension that he was able to produce in others, that silence which showed him to be top dog, the alpha male, king of everything.

'Troy,' he said, 'take off your shorts.'

The Big Shilling heard the kid swallow. 'I don't want to take off my shorts.'

The Big Shilling silently counted to ten before saying, 'Either you kill me, right now, or you take off your shorts.'

'No!' cried Lena. 'No more killing! Do it to Lena, you beast!'

Lena had jumped to her feet and was ripping off her t-shirt and shorts. When she was wearing nothing but a thong, she ran over to the tent, ducked inside and lay down on the bed roll, whimpering.

The Big Shilling slowly turned his head and looked directly at American Troy. Eventually, Troy sat up and slipped off his shorts. Unlike Bri, Troy wasn't naked underneath, he was wearing boxers. The Big Shilling smiled at him, warmly.

'What passport are you carrying?'

'It's British. You know it's British.'

'Camouflage,' said the Big Shilling, taking Brian Blee's Union Jack shorts out of the plastic bag and flinging them in Troy's face.

Then he laughed, the Big Shilling, long and hard, and American Troy put on the damp shorts that were three sizes too big for him.

'You're afraid to die,' said the Big Shilling when he had finished laughing.

He watched American Troy consider how to respond.

'Aren't you?'

'I don't mean just now, hey, I mean in the sea. You were scared. You were crying like a little bitch.'

American Troy, ashamed, didn't deny it.

'At the ice cream joint, I wasn't scared then.'

'What happened to you in the water? Something happened to you. What was it, hey? I could see it in your face when I got you back to land. What happened, Troy? What happened?'

Troy didn't know what to say. What had happened in the water? It was so strange it no longer seemed real. This was real, being needled by the psycho, BS.

'You didn't need to be, at the ice cream parlour,' Shilling went on. 'You knew the Russian's bodyguards were more than likely unarmed. This is Cyprus, not Chicago. Guns at the house, okay, but not on the streets: against the law.'

'When I saw the cop go for his gun, I wasn't scared then either.'

'Of course not, you didn't have time to be scared, hey? Your training kicked in, you were on autopilot, the training I gave you at the Killing House kicked in. But you've changed the subject, eh. I see you've changed the subject. I said that you are scared to die, and you are.'

'I don't want to die, if that's what you mean.'

'You mean because you're still young, and you think a man my age wouldn't mind dying, eh?'

American Troy shrugged. 'Something like that.'

'You're scared now.'

'All right,' said Troy, mumbling, 'I'm scared now.'

'You have to overcome this fear,' the Big Shilling advised him. 'You're no use to me if you are scared half the time. Why didn't you kill me on the beach when I came back from my little lay down with Lena?'

American Troy was about to lie. He was about to lie but he checked himself, knowing that it would be obvious that he was lying.

'I thought I was next,' he admitted.

'You have to overcome this fear, my boy,' the Big Shilling persisted. 'If you can overcome this fear you have of your life ending, it will make you powerful, and men will fear you. You know why men fear me, hey? Shall I tell you why men fear me?'

'I know why.'

'Because they know I will fight anyone, even if it means I am killed. Even if it means I am going to be killed, I will still fight. People know this of me, eh, and that is why they fear me. They think I am a monster, a maniac, a mad man. Well, maybe I am, maybe I am.'

'Or maybe you're just smarter than everyone else.'

'Oh, I'm definitely smarter than everyone else. And you know why this is? Because I observe people, I'm always alert, eh? I never tire, and I'm always on the look-out – for danger, for information, for whatever gives me an edge, an angle.'

The Big Shilling could see that American Troy was now hanging on his every word. The boy knew that he wasn't about to be killed, or raped, that he was instead being offered an education, the kind of education you'd never get in school or from the TV or from the government.

And so the Big Shilling talked, he talked and talked

the afternoon through. He needed an audience. That was the problem with being a successful out-law. You could never tell your story without in-criminating yourself. You could never be famous unless you were caught. The Big Shilling had a theory about that as well, about how many ageing criminals had allowed themselves to be taken, just so they could tell the world what they had done. And even when he saw that American Troy was no longer listening, was overloaded with new insights, the Big Shilling still kept on talking.

'Shut up,' said Lena, eventually. 'Shut up, shut up, shut up! I can't stand it, he never shut up!'

'Oh, you're awake, are you?' the Big Shilling asked, a big smile on his face. 'You've been listening to what I have been saying, eh? Well, I have a question to ask you, girl. Are you listening?'

'Yes!'

'Tell me, then, what did you see in the Russian's face when you shot him?'

'I tell you,' moaned Lena. 'I already tell you.'

'You told me he was noble and brave and hand-some,' said the Big Shilling, mocking her. Then, his voice harder, he said, 'Do you know what I saw when I killed him? Do you know what I saw when I shot him in the head, hey? I saw fear, I saw fear and weak-ness. That is what I saw. You always get to the truth of a man when he is about to die. How does he die? Does he die bravely, does he die with contempt for his killer? Or does he die like a cur, like a whipped dog, defeated and broken and abject? It is your decision. You alone decide how you are going to die.'

'Stop,' said Lena, sobbing and shaking once more, 'please stop. Stop talking about killing, stop, killing.'

'You see what I mean?' the Big Shilling asked American Troy, pointing a finger at the tent. 'She is a slave. Lena, you are a slave. And you are too, boy, you are too. You are weak, like this Russian was weak. You are frightened of dying, both of you, but to me there is something more frightening than death, and that is living as a slave, living as a slave, eh? Think about that the both of you, think about that.'

The Big Shilling got to his feet and stretched his arms. Without further ado, he went over to the tent, crawled inside and closed the flaps behind him.

American Troy got to his feet as well, not wanting yet again to have to listen to the animals rutting. He got to his feet and pulled up his shorts, his clown shorts, his slave shorts. He wondered if he should take them off. He walked a few paces, undecided. He felt shattered. It wasn't just listening to the Big Shilling's interminable monologue, it was the content of the monologue as well. It had caused in him deeply unpleasant emotions. His brain was fried and he couldn't think straight. He kept the shorts on, even though he had to hike them up every few paces. Finding himself near the Range Rover, he opened the passenger door and perched on the seat. Sitting down was unpleasant, the shorts being damp from another man's sweat, but Troy didn't get up.

Now he knew what movie he was in. The famous misquote sounded inside his head. It was from Nietzsche originally, he knew that, he'd seen it online: that which does not kill you makes you stronger.

American Troy began to say the line out loud, 'Whatever doesn't kill you . . .' but his voice trailed away.

Well, the Big Shilling was certainly strong, and strange, you had to give him that, he was probably the strongest, strangest man Troy had ever met.

A Trickster, a teacher, far more than just garbage who killed for money.

American Troy didn't think anymore after that, he just lolled in the car seat, enjoying the breeze that stirred the warm aromatic air beneath the pine trees, his mind blissfully in neutral. Even the urgent beastly noises coming from the tent could not disturb him. He must have fallen asleep, because the next thing he knew he started and the Big Shilling was standing in front of the Range Rover, talking into a phone. He was talking a strange mixture of English and some other tongue.

'Give me the money back?' the Big Shilling was saying in surprise. 'You want to give me the money back? No, my friend, that money is yours. You took the money, and now you are going to earn your pay. Meet me tonight, meet me tonight, Joshua, and keep the money I gave you. Why are you crying, eh? Don't call me bwana. There's no reason to cry, hey?

We are friends, you and I, we are friends.'

And the Big Shilling looked over his shoulder, a wicked grin on his face, and winked at American Troy who was watching him.

CHAPTER NINETEEN

T hey were being followed. It was after midnight, and the three of them, the Big Shilling,
American Troy and the Albanian girl Lena,
were riding in the Range Rover, negotiating a long
curve in the road down out of the Troodos mountains. The Big Shilling was behind the wheel. He
adjusted the rear-view mirror and eased his foot off
the gas. The first of the following vehicles grew in
size in the mirror, headlights dazzling him.

'Cops?' asked American Troy from the back seat.

'No,' the Big Shilling told him. 'They're Brits. RCS
from Mount Olympus, I shouldn't wonder.'

'What's RCS?'

The Big Shilling did not answer. Instead, he opened
his window and waved a hand, telling the driver
behind them to pass. 'Nothing to worry about,' he
said.

The two Royal Corps of Signals Land Rovers overtook them, the drivers pipping their horns in thanks.

The Big Shilling watched the British army vehicles pull away, thinking about the signals intelligence base on top of the mountain. The phone he'd used to call Joshua had been purchased in Paphos by Brian Blee and so was clean, but he did not doubt that the British had been listening in on his call. That was why he'd made the most important part of it in Shona, Joshua's native language, and not in English. He wondered if the British Government Communications HQ in Cheltenham, England had Shona speakers, or whether there was software that could identify every language in the world and translate it instantly into English. It did not matter. The British had his back. In spite of what had happened to the stealth boat, the British obviously had his back. The Big Shilling smiled, reached out, and squeezed Lena's bare thigh.

'You okay, baby girl?'

'Yes, papa,' said Lena, dreamily.

'Papa's medicine works wonders, eh?'

Lena flopped her head about, and giggled.

'How about you in the back there?'

'I'm good,' said American Troy, who'd ingested only one 10mg tab of diazepam, not the cocktail that the Big Shilling had fed the Albanian girl.

'Looking forward to a kebab, eh? I'm looking forward to a kebab. Those Turks who invented work, they sure know how to cook a kebab.'

There was nothing the Big Shilling liked better than a captive audience, nothing in the world. He began to talk. As they rode down the mountain, he told them about the history of copper mining in Cyprus, and about the Turkish invasion of the island in 1974, and about Kemal Ataturk and the Freemasons, and about Lawrence of Arabia's motorbike, and about the Great Bitter Lake and the recent completion of the by-pass on the Suez Canal.

'You're a walking encyclopaedia,' American Troy managed to interject at one point.

'Piracy,' the Big Shilling was saying, 'Somali pirates. Piracy's made a big dent in the Suez Canal Company profits. Profits are ten per cent down, ten per cent. That's big shilling as far as the Egyptians are concerned, big shilling they're losing out on, hey? But this is what happens, this is what happens when you try to steal everything, when you try to control the whole world. The guys you're thieving from pick up guns and steal right back, eh? Because they have no other choice, no other choice. Greed, greed - that is what drives the world controllers.'

On and on he went, the Big Shilling, talking constantly, endlessly, one subject following on from another, seamlessly, in a tsunami of words.

'I could end it tomorrow,' he now insisted, 'piracy, I could end it tomorrow, but the world controllers show weakness. I could end it tomorrow, just sink the pirates' boats, bomb their villages, slaughter their families. That would be that - ended, finished. The same with the migrant crisis, so-called.

Extreme violence. Sink the smugglers' boats, that's all you have to do, sink the smugglers' boats. When the migrants, so-called, come ashore impale them on stakes, impale them on stakes just like Vlad the Impaler used to do. Impale them on stakes for the television cameras.'

For a moment, repulsion troubled the face of the Albanian girl Lena. The Big Shilling patted her knee and she briefly smiled before subsiding into pharmaceutical sleep.

'Yes, Vlad the Impaler, eh? He knew how to deal with invaders. He captured the invading Turkish soldiers and had them impaled on sharpened stakes inserted into their rectums or through their bellies. Dreadful way to die, hey? Dreadful, dreadful, but it worked. If it had not been for Vlad, Europe would be Moslem already, Europe would be Moslem.

'Violence, you see, beautiful violence. Ah, violence is the key.'

This natural pause in the monologue allowed Troy to interject: 'Jesus, finally.'

'You're saying I talk too much?' asked the Big Shilling, suddenly belligerent, glaring at American Troy in the rear-view mirror.

'That's exactly what I'm saying,' said American Troy, made careless by the powerful benzodiazepine he'd taken.

The Big Shilling, who knew that it was the drug that was talking, laughed raucously and said, 'My one failing, my one failing, eh? I love to hear the sound of my own voice, I love it, love it, hey?' He nudged Lena in the passenger seat. 'You awake?'

'Hmm?' said Lena, half opening one eye. 'Lena awake, mmm.'

'That's right, that's right, my love, get some rest, get some rest.'

The Big Shilling paused for a moment to gather his thoughts, then it began again, the relentless monologue, this time, following on from the last time, regarding the state's monopoly on violence.

'Refuse to pay your taxes and what happens? You get a knock on the door and it's the police, the police to take you to court. You resist, you resist the police and what happens? The police knock down your door, they knock down your door, eh, and they subdue you, cuff you and haul you away to a cell. In other words, they use violence. They haul you away to a cell and take you to court in a black maria. You defy the court, and what happens? The judge sentences you to jail, and you resist again. What do the cops do? They put you in chains and haul you off the jail. How can they do that? Because they are stronger than you, they are stronger than you are, eh? They're willing to do more violence to you than you are willing to do to them.

'They dress it up in legalese, sure they do, but it all comes down to violence. The powers that be have a monopoly on violence, or they think they do, and the ovine majority acquiesce, they acquiesce. But not me, not me, eh? I fight back. I'm not your slave or your sheep, I'm not a normie. You do violence to me, I do greater violence to you. I don't care who you are, I don't care how big you are, or how many you are, I will do violence to you, hey? I will do more violence to you than you will do to me. That is my philosophy, that is the way I have lived my life, hey? And here I am, still alive, still strong, still vital, an old man in a game where most men die young.'

'Yeah, beware of an old guy in a business where guys tend to die young,' said American Troy, dopily.

'That's it! That's it exactly!' the Big Shilling cried. 'Now come on, come on, wake up, wake up, my children. We're nearly there, we're nearly home. Is that my good friend Joshua? I think that is my good friend Joshua from Zimbabwe, in his little white clown car.'

It was Joshua, the Zimbabwean mine clearance operative, waiting up a farm track in the darkness on the edge of no man's land on the Green Line that divided Cyprus between Turk and Greek. When he saw the approaching Range Rover he got out of his car, a worried look straining his face, and when he saw the Big Shilling waving at him, he waved back, his expression turning sickly.

'Think you can set the time-bomb?' the Big Shilling asked American Troy.

'Yes, I can do it.'

'Wide awake now, eh?'

'I'm good.'

'You're good? I thought you were bad, I thought you wanted to be bad. Set it for six tomorrow morning, my boy.'

'Right.'

'Then help Lena. Oh, Lena? Wake up, Lena.'

'Lena wake up,' said Lena, stirring, rubbing her face.

The Big Shilling turned off the headlights and the engine, and climbed out into the sultry night.

'Joshua, my friend,' he said, but the African did not return his greeting.

Instead, the Zimbabwean Joshua pleaded with him. He pleaded with the Big Shilling to be allowed to return the money he'd already received. He pleaded with him to be allowed to leave. He pleaded with him to be allowed to leave and not to have to lead the three of them, the Big Shilling, American Troy and the Albanian girl Lena, through the minefield along the cleared path.

'It is clear,' repeated Joshua, 'it is clear path. I clear the path, there is no danger. Go through, go through and I go home.'

'No,' said the Big Shilling. 'Go home? To Zimbabwe? You're not going anywhere. No, you will lead us through the minefield. You will go first and we will follow you along the cleared path.'

'Please,' begged Joshua, 'I have money. Here, please take money. This is the money you give me, sah, and this is my savings. I withdraw it from bank. Please, you take all the money and Joshua go home, keep quiet, never happen, never happen. Please, I beg you, bwana, please.'

The Big Shilling, it appeared, had had enough. He withdrew the Glock from his waistband and lazily waved the gun at Joshua.

'Your choice, make it now. Take us over to the other side, or die, right now.'

The Zimbabwean placed his shaking hands together in prayer.

'No, bwana, please.'

The Big Shilling aimed the pistol.

'You should have looked, Joshua, before you leapt, Joshua, eh? Who did you think I was? The Free Money Man, shovelling big shilling your way? There's no such animal, no such animal. You made the bargain, you did, eh, no one forced you to do it, you greedy little man. Now, stop your snivelling and lay on, Macduff.'

And so, tearful and defeated, Joshua led them to the wire fence that marked the beginning of the minefield. The only sound was that of their footfalls, that and the chirruping cicadas. Mournfully, Joshua showed them the different coloured tapes he had used to mark the clear path through the minefield. He was a big man with powerful shoulders and arms, and even though he was bow-legged, the result no doubt of some childhood illness, he was still more than six feet tall. And so, when the US M2A4 bounding mine exploded as they were nearing the Turkish side, it was the six-foot African who took the brunt of the fragmenting shrapnel.

The bounding mine did what it was designed to do. As soon as the inadvertent Joshua triggered it, by standing on one of its exposed prongs, it leapt into the air and exploded at waist height. The Big Shilling, ever vigilant, walking ten paces behind Joshua, his arm around Lena's waist, heard the mine's firing pin engage and immediately threw himself and Lena to the ground. Behind them, American Troy did the same a split second later. But for Joshua there was to be no salvation. The exploding mine all but cut him in half, and when the noise abated and the smoke had cleared, his ragged carcass lay in a bloody tangle in the Cypriot dirt. It was several seconds before the survivors stirred.

As soon as the Big Shilling checked Lena he knew she was dead. He couldn't find the wound and his searching hands did not encounter any blood, but there was no denying that she was gone to another place.

'We're nearly there!' cried American Troy in a desperate whisper.

That was when they saw movement on the Turkish side. It was a man in uniform, armed with a flashlight, who appeared to be beckoning to them.

'No,' said the Big Shilling, crouching low. 'We go back.'

American Troy whimpered in frustration. 'What about Lena?'

'Dead,' said the Big Shilling, laconic.

'Dumb ass nigga,' spat American Troy. 'That dumb fucking bastard.'

'Another word and I'll shoot you myself,' hissed the Big Shilling, grabbing American Troy by the jaw and twisting his head towards the lights on the Greek side. 'Move!'

As the two men ran back the way they'd come

there were no shots from the Turks, and when they reached the Range Rover the Big Shilling climbed up the ladder that led to the roof rack, took aim at the approaching police car, and emptied the magazine of the Glock 17 at its blue flashing lights. The car kept coming and American Troy started shooting at it as well, pumping off well-aimed single shots with the Glock. Up above him, the Big Shilling reloaded. The cop car was closer now, its siren screaming. The Big Shilling fired again, saw the windscreen shatter, and the car turned sharply away, crashing into the roadside ditch.

The Big Shilling jogged over, smashed a side window with the butt of his gun, and stuck his head inside. A couple of seconds later, American Troy heard two single shots.

CHAPTER
TWENTY

The Big Shilling strolled back to the Range Rover like nothing had happened. He was checking the Glock. A smile of satisfaction on his face, he changed magazines and smoothed his hair.

'What are you doing?'

'What am I doing?' asked American Troy. 'What does it look like I'm fucking doing? I'm disarming the motherfucking bomb is what I'm doing.'

'Don't,' said the Big Shilling, grinning. 'Set it for ten minutes, hey?'

So American Troy set it for ten minutes. While he was setting it, or trying to, the Big Shilling drove Joshua's car, the white Peugeot hatchback, over to the Range Rover and started transferring gear from one vehicle to the other. He worked methodically, the way he always did, which was in stark contrast to American Troy's fumbling with the time-bomb.

'Why won't my hands do what I want?' he mumbled, desperately.

His hands had worked fine when he was popping off at the leos, but now his fingers would not obey him.

'Take a breath, and calm down,' said the Big Shilling, which only served to annoy American Troy even further.

'What?' he demanded. 'Take my time but hurry up?'

'That was then, this is now. That was just for a limited period, so that you revealed yourself.'

'What the fuck is he talking about?' yelled Troy.

'Do you want me to do it? Do you think you can load the car before the cops get here? Do you know which gear to take and what to leave behind? Do you want me to do it?'

American Troy cried out in frustration. 'Just shut up for one goddamned minute, can't you!'

The Big Shilling laughed at him, and went on loading gear into the white Peugeot.

'There!' cried American Troy a few seconds later. 'The bomb is armed and timed to explode in ten minutes.'

'But that was three minutes ago,' said the Big Shilling. 'Better set it for seven minutes, no, six, make it six. And stop shouting, eh? There's no need to get upset. It's just a waste of energy.'

American Troy punched the back of a head-rest over and over again, but when that didn't help reset the bomb he gathered himself together and reset it himself.

'Five minutes,' he said. 'I've set it for five minutes, all right?'

'Five? Man, that's cutting it fine. Are you sure we'll be clear in five?'

'Yes!' American Troy yelled, slamming shut the door of the Range Rover.

'Drive it over to the cop car,' the Big Shilling ordered. 'I want them both to go up. And get the cops' radio, eh?'

American Troy quickly got behind the wheel, turned the ignition key, stalled, and tried again. This time the engine started, and he did as he'd been told, parking the Range Rover right beside the cop car that was upended in the ditch. Getting the radio was more difficult. He had to slide down into the ditch and reach through the smashed driver's window and haul the dead cop off of the steering wheel, and the cop's head was leaking blood and there was congealed blood on the radio and on American Troy's hand, and he had to crouch down in the road after he'd taken the radio and wipe his hand in the dirt to get rid of the blood, or try to. He hurried back.

'How long do we have now, do you think?' the Big Shilling asked him brightly.

The Big Shilling was standing beside the little white Peugeot with his hands on his hips, as though he didn't have a care in the world. He glanced across the minefield to the Turkish side where American Troy could now see the beams of flashlights moving towards no man's land.

He ran over to the Peugeot and jumped in the passenger seat.

'No,' said the Big Shilling. 'You drive, you drive.'

'For fuck's sake!' said American Troy, throwing open the door.

The radio came alive in his hand, almost making him jump. It was in Greek of course, but you couldn't mistake the sound of a worried despatcher telling a fellow law enforcement officer that help was on its way.

'Come on,' urged American Troy, 'get in.'

But the Big Shilling was in no hurry. He was fiddling with the Glock. That was when American Troy discovered there was no ignition key. The Big Shilling had hot-wired it.

'Things would be so much easier if you'd just calm down,' the Big Shilling observed, getting settled in the passenger seat. 'Hear that?'

American Troy couldn't hear anything, apart from the Big Shilling's infuriating voice.

'Cops,' said the Big Shilling, 'coming from the south, and from the north. If you don't get a move on they'll cut us off.'

'There!' yelled American Troy in triumph when the Peugeot's engine roared into life. He turned on the headlights.

'Take that road,' ordered the Big Shilling when they reached the highway.

It was a side road, little more than a track. American Troy didn't need telling twice: there were sirens and flashing lights converging on their position from both sides.

'Turn off the lights.'

Troy turned off the headlights. As he did so there was a tremendous explosion behind and to the right.

'Nice work,' said the Big Shilling, laconically.

They drove along the track, at low speed in order to avoid the ditch on the left hand side. American Troy glanced back at the flames from the Range Rover and the cop car. There was no one following them. It appeared the pursuing cops had diverted towards the conflagration.

'I have to hand it to you,' American Troy began, shaking his head in admiration.

'You see?' said the Big Shilling, vociferously. 'You see? All you have to do is do as I say and I'll get you home safe and sound, eh?'

'Yeah.'

'What was that? You don't sound convinced.'

'Yes, boss,' said American Troy with more enthusiasm, not wanting to point out that once more their escape had failed.

American Troy looked at the little man in the little car's passenger seat, the little man whose eyes were closed and who was smiling, relaxed, as though he were lying on a beach in the sun. He had the cop radio in his little hand with the volume turned low, and American Troy could hear the voices of the Greek cops gabbling away. He supposed that was why the Big Shilling was smiling –

another victory. American Troy stopped the car suddenly, but the Big Shilling didn't open his eyes.

'Turn right,' he said, 'turn right, and when we get to the main road make another right, all right? We're going to the big city, my boy, Nicosia, the capital of this delightful little island. I'll buy you breakfast, eh? I'll buy you breakfast. Man, I'm hungry. Are you hungry?'

American Troy said nothing. Food was the last thing he wanted. He felt sick to his stomach, and there was an unpleasant taste of bile at the back of his throat. He was filthy as well, and he now realised that the smell he could smell was coming from him. His hands were caked in dirt, and there was congealed blood under his fingernails and his clothes felt so soiled he wanted to tear them off and throw them into a fire. The image of the smoking, mangled corpse of the African returned, and American Troy instantly pushed it away.

'We can't go to a restaurant, not looking like this,' he muttered.

'We'll shower first,' said the Big Shilling. 'Turn on your headlights. We're clear now, I reckon, hey?'

American Troy turned on the headlights. 'Shower? A real shower, with hot water and soap?'

The Big Shilling only smiled.

'Pity about Lena,' he said.

'What happened to her? I mean, it looked like she was okay, compared to the other guy.'

'Strange thing shrapnel. One tiny sliver can sever your spinal cord, or enter the brain and kill you instantaneously. In a way I'm glad. She was a pretty girl. Better that than being ripped into offal, eh?'

American Troy gulped. 'I guess,' he said thickly, and swallowed a pellet of foul-tasting puke. He wiped his itchy eyes with twitching fingers, and told himself to get a grip.

They were approaching the main road. There was a sign, Nicosia right. American Troy even signalled, the law-abiding road-user, but there was no need, for the road was deserted. Troy looked left and right but all he could see were a few blameless houses and the occasional street light. There was a sharp click as the Big Shilling turned off the police radio.

'Relax, my boy,' he said, quietly. 'Let the tension go.'

American Troy shook his head. 'Can't. Can't do it.'

The Big Shilling said nothing.

Fifteen minutes later, and the white Peugeot was approaching the outskirts of the city. The Big Shilling sat up straight in his seat, the better to see, and glanced about him.

'Just up ahead,' he said, 'slow down and take a good look.'

American Troy did as he was told. Not that there was much to see, just the usual jumble of stores and apartment buildings that made up the average streetscape in Cyprus.

'There,' said the Big Shilling. 'That lay-by there, with the kiosk. See?'

American Troy saw.

'I want you to make sure you can find your way back here, all right? So pay attention.'

'Right,' said American Troy, paying attention. He knew better than to waste his breath asking why he needed to be able to make his way back here.

They drove another couple of miles into the city. They passed only a few vehicles, taxis, an empty bus, a cop car heading out of town with its blue lights flashing but absent the siren. The quality of the buildings and of the road surface improved as they neared the centre of the capital. American Troy noticed that as well.

'Here,' said the Big Shilling, who American Troy knew had been monitoring him since the lay-by with the kiosk. 'Take the second left.'

Second left was the entrance to an underground car park. American Troy guided the little Peugeot down the ramp, and the Big Shilling pointed to a parking space beside double doors which led to the elevator. Beside the doors was a collection of scooters, pushbikes and motorcycles.

The Big Shilling motioned that Troy should stay in the car, got out, and disappeared for a minute or two before returning with a door key.

'Shower?'

'Sounds good,' said American Troy, weakly. He was just about all in.

The apartment was on the top floor and the Big Shilling insisted they walk up rather than take the elevator and wake the neighbours. It was five am and the stairwell was silent and baking hot. The apartment was hot as well, no air con, only fans. The Big Shilling turned on the dim lighting, kicked off his walking boots, and motioned Troy to do the same. American Troy knelt down and laboriously unlaced his Nikes. He could hear the Big Shilling padding about in bare feet, opening windows and shutters as silently as possible. When he returned, he was carrying two plastic bottles of iced water. American Troy took one gratefully, and drank. The water was like nectar and he almost groaned with pleasure.

They'd brought with them from the car only the rucksacks containing their personal belongings. The Big Shilling carried both rucksacks into the bedroom and dumped them on the two single beds.

'Six star luxury,' said American Troy, meaning it. 'Sure beats camping.'

The Big Shilling was looking at him strangely, the sharp tip of his tongue perched on his lower lip.

'You take first shower,' he said.

American Troy found his washbag and went into the little bathroom, closing the door behind him. He didn't lock it. Tentatively, he regarded himself in the mirror over the wash basin. What was that movie about the French penal colony, Dustin Hoffman in those Coke bottle-bottom specs? Devil's Island, where no one ever escaped? He couldn't recall. Steve McQueen was in that one too, but the title still evaded him. American Troy stripped off, letting his filthy clothes fall on the floor. When he peed, his pee, what little there was of it, was an unhealthy dark brown. Man, he was seriously dehydrated.

He turned on the shower and found a worn bar of soap in the tray. It felt wonderful to step under the trickle of lukewarm water and to begin getting clean. He washed himself all over, paying particular attention to his face and fingernails, then rinsed himself off. Something was nagging him, but he couldn't think what. Then he suddenly remembered the name of the prison movie, but that wasn't what had been nagging him. He shut off the water and hauled back the curtain.

'Enjoy your shower?' said the Big Shilling.

American Troy hadn't heard him come in. The assassin was standing there naked, the bathroom door closed behind him.

'Yeah,' said American Troy, like nothing was amiss.

They'd shared the service apartment in London, but there they'd had separate bedrooms and separate bathrooms, just like the house at Latchi, and the apartment at Kissonerga, and never before had American Troy seen the Big Shilling butt naked.

'Lena,' said the Big Shilling with a sigh, 'daddy misses his baby girl.'

That would account for the soft-on the Big Shilling was sporting, thought American Troy, trying not to look at the growing member. But of course he did look at it. He looked because the Big Shilling turned to the side to show him something. Scars, terrible scars, half-hidden by greying ginger pubes.

'Jesus Christ,' said Troy, gasping, 'who did that to you?'

But the Big Shilling just stared at him with that basilisk stare. Then he took a step closer to bath tub, and said earnestly: 'You know, Troy, you may not believe this, but there was a time in my life when some people considered me completely insane.'

CHAPTER
TWENTY-ONE

In the bedroom, American Troy slowly got dressed. From the bathroom came the sound of the shower running, and all there was was the here and now. For American Troy, nothing else existed. He felt dizzy, as though he'd been stunned.

On his bed was laid out a miniature armoury: two Glocks, loaded, four magazines, charged, the little stabbing knife, and a stiletto that American Troy hadn't seen before. There was also the inner packaging of a Kinder egg, not that Troy really registered its presence, for lying ominously next to it was a tube of lubricating jelly.

The message was clear, wasn't it? Either kill me, or lube yourself up.

American Troy slumped down on the bed. 'Jesus, man,' he said, holding his head in his hands. The words of his uncle Nathan now came back to haunt him. Have you smoked his cigar? Have you smoked the Big Shilling's cigar? Jesus, is that what he wanted? Or worse?

It was only then that he remembered that night at the Hotel Mercurius, and the two hookers, Marina and Marianne, though he could not for the moment remember which was which. Doggy-style, he remembered that, one of them behind him, he couldn't believe it. First, the hot, soft tongue, then a cold finger, then fingers plural, hotter, followed by, what? He'd wanted to look but couldn't, because of the unprecedented explosion massively building.

'Jesus.'

Troy grabbed one of the Glocks, checked that it was indeed loaded, and slipped it into the waistband of his shorts, his own shorts, his regular khakis, not the clown shorts which he'd left in the Range Rover. He went quickly into the kitchen, a gloomy nook off the tiny living room. In the fridge he found a bottle of milk, a glass bottle, not a carton. He opened it and drank. When he heard the shower stop running, swallowing became too complicated. He put the milk back in the fridge and rinsed his mouth with water from the sink.

Was he going to kill the bastard? Is that what he was going to do? Because there was no way he was going to let him do whatever it was he wanted to do.

American Troy drew the Glock, and held it like he meant it. But what if he did kill him? A gun shot in this place, with its tiled floors, right up here at the top of the building? He crossed to the sink again and slid open the window. He opened the shutters as well, and reflected sunlight blinded him for a couple of seconds. When he could see properly again he realised he was looking across to the Turkish side at the two gigantic flags – one Turkish, familiar, the other representing northern Cyprus less so – that the Turks had fashioned into the hillside facing the Greek south.

The Big Shilling was his ticket home. Without him, he was fucked.

With him, maybe he was fucked as well.

Or maybe it was another one of his sick jokes, another screwed-up mind game. What was that movie? With Ray Liotta. Christ, why wouldn't his brain work anymore? There was a blank inside his head like a missing piece in a jigsaw puzzle. They're having drinks, these wise guys, with their stupid shirt collars, and one guy, was it the little fellow, what's his name? Were they breaking his balls? Or was he breaking somebody else's balls? Was that was it was? Another one of the Big Shilling's wind-ups?

But who'd broken the Big Shilling's balls? Who had done that terrible thing? Who had tried to cut off the Big Shilling's back wheels?

The bathroom flew door open. American Troy could see down the narrow hallway through the living room door which was also open. He saw the Big Shilling emerge from the bathroom, look right, and eyeball him standing there, guiltily, in the kitchen.

Thank Christ, American Troy said to himself, the

son-bitch is wearing a towel.

'Forgot my razor,' explained the Big Shilling.

He disappeared into the bedroom and returned carrying a pack of Gillettes, but rather than go back into the bathroom the Big Shilling came into the living room instead.

'See this?' he asked, turning round. 'See these scars on my back? You've seen them before, hey? I know you have. You've been looking at me, haven't you? I've seen you, hey? Don't think I haven't seen you, checking out my body, eh?'

The Big Shilling looked over his shoulder and pouted at American Troy. Then he turned round again and stood legs apart, fists on hips.

'My old man did that to me. I was fourteen. He took an Angolan sjambok to me. Do you know what a sjambok is?'

'Yeah,' croaked American Troy. He coughed, to clear the milky phlegm that suddenly clogged his throat.

'Yeah?'

'It's a whip. The South African cops use them.'

'It's a whip, it's a whip. It's more than a whip, the sjambok, it's the whip of whips, eh? Man, you don't know what a whip is until you've seen a sjambok. It's made out of rhino hide, rhino hide or hippo hide, one of the two. You kill snakes with them. One blow from a sjambok and bam, that snake is dead meat, man, dead meat.'

The Big Shilling turned round again, pulling the skin of his shoulder tight with one hand.

'You see what it does to human flesh, hey? You see it? Yes, my old man, that bastard, he was never the same after he came back from the war, the Western Desert, fighting Rommel, then Italy and up into Austria, then after the war, Palestine. Oh yes, did I never mention it? My old man, after the war fighting the Nazis, they sent him to Palestine to fight Frankie's friends, the Jews. Did I never mention that?'

'No, you never mentioned that.'

In fact, the Big Shilling had said something quite different. He'd said his dad was a communist who'd refused to fight for the British Empire and had spent the war years on the run or in jail.

'Jewish terrorists,' the Big Shilling was saying, his eyes strange, 'the Irgun, the Stern Gang, the Hagannah, a dirty war, a dirty war all right. Man, he hated the Jew boys, hated them. The King David Hotel, he was there when the Jewish terrorists blew it up. He was there when they killed Lord Moyne, he was there when they killed Count Bernadotte, oh yes and the irony was not lost on him. Here he was, you see, fighting Jewish terrorists, after spending five years fighting the Nazis who'd been hell bent on eradicating Jews from the face of the earth. No wonder he came home all screwed up, eh? Ingrates, ingrates the lot of them, that's what he used to say.'

Why the lies? Why the stories? Helplessly, American Troy tried to figure it out. Was Shilling saying the past didn't matter? Did he mean that you could rewrite the past just as you could write the future?

Troy didn't know what he was expected to say, so

he said, 'Why did he whip you?'

'Why? Because he caught me shagging a goat.'

American Troy stared at the Big Shilling who was staring at him.

Do I laugh? wondered American Troy. Do I burst out laughing? Is he joking? Or is he serious? Oh Christ, he is serious, isn't he?

'You see, I have always had a powerful sex drive,' the Big Shilling was saying, 'right from the age of nine or ten. Girls, boys, women, men, didn't matter which. It was all about getting it wet, hey? Getting it wet. When I needed to get it wet, then I had to get it wet. Goats, sheep, donkeys, I've done it with all of them, when there was no human handy. It was a compulsion, an overwhelming compulsion, and I had to put a stop to it.'

American Troy wished there was a farm animal to hand right now. Then the Big Shilling brandished the packet of razors and Troy understood: the scars, the terrible scars. Shilling had done it to himself. He'd tried to cut off his cock and balls. Troy felt dizzy.

'I'm going to shave now,' the Big Shilling said, casually. 'Shave my face and shave my legs. I want my skin to be as smooth as marble. Go and have a look in the wardrobe, would you? There's a little suitcase you'll find in there, hey?'

When the Big Shilling went into the bathroom and closed the door behind him, American Troy let out the breath he'd been holding, and his heart, which was already thumping, accelerated a little more.

'Jesus Christ,' he mumbled. 'This guy.'

There was a time in my life when some people considered me completely insane? No shit, man!

In the bedroom, he removed the small red suitcase from the wardrobe in trepidation, and laid it on the bed to open it. When he did so, the contents of the suitcase made him laugh out loud.

Jesus! A wig! A ginger wig! And a dress! And pantyhose!

The Big Shilling was a tranny, the guy was a cross-dresser, a chick with a dick!

American Troy wept with laughter, and with relief. He collapsed on the bed and laughed until he could hardly breathe, then he laughed some more. When he heard the Big Shilling burst out of the bathroom, he sat upright and tried to stop laughing but it was too late. The little man was on him, flailing at him with his hard little fists, punching expertly, everywhere except in the face. American Troy curled up, too scared to hit back, trying to parry the blows or avoid the worst of them. He felt his attacker take the Glock from the back of his shorts and the next thing he knew his head was being pulled back by the hair and the barrel of the pistol pressed between his lips.

'Open your mouth or I'll smash your fucking teeth in,' hissed the Big Shilling.

American Troy tried to object but it was useless: he opened his mouth, and felt the gun barrel being inserted into his throat. He gagged and his face burned. He could feel with his lips the Big Shilling's finger on the trigger of the Glock.

'I was born to ride,' he heard the Big Shilling whisper hoarsely, 'I was born to ride, hey? And you, you were born to be ridden. You remember that, boy. Any time I want, I can do what I want with you. You're my bitch, until you prove otherwise. Do you understand me? Hey?'

American Troy nodded enthusiastically.

'What are you? Mind, or muscle? Me, I'm both. I am mind and muscle. The Big Shilling is mind and muscle. But you, you, you're a fucking disappointment, an embarrassment. You make me sick, eh, you make me sick.'

When the gun barrel was removed from his throat, American Troy rolled over on the bed, retching and coughing and fighting for air. Ropes of snot and phlegm and sputum hung from his mouth and nostrils. He wiped them away with his hand as best he could and lurched across to the bedroom door, utterly disgusted and humiliated.

This time he locked the slammed bathroom door behind him, crouched over the toilet bowl and retched into it, reaching up blindly to tear toilet paper from the roll with which to wipe his slimy hands and boiling face.

Suddenly, the Big Shilling hammered on the bathroom door. Troy stopped what he was doing. He could hear Shilling's voice mimicking a tough Irish-American mobster.

'Troy? You in there, Troy? I should've wasted you in the mountains, you no good, small time shyster.

Can you hear me, Troy my boy? Listen to this then! Men who are not afraid of death, they are infinitely superior to the most powerful temporal power. Remember that, you yellow streak of piss, just remember that.'

Then Shilling went away, laughing, laughing that crazy laugh of his.

American Troy stayed in the bathroom a long time, lying on the clammy floor tiles amongst the dirty clothes and damp towels, clutching his knees to his chest and sometimes silently weeping.

Why me? he asked himself.

I can't take much more of this.

I'll kill the motherfucking bastard!

No.

He knew he wouldn't do that. He couldn't. Without Shilling, there was no way off the island.

What then?

What does he want me to fucking do?

But he knew the answer to that as well: he had to prove himself. Prove he wasn't a slave, prove he was a man. Prove he was mind and muscle, like the Big Shilling.

But he didn't know if he had inside him what made a man like the Big Shilling. That was why he'd given up motorcycle racing, because he knew that he'd never be a true champion. Oh he could beat a bunch of light-weights all right, but when it came to the top flight he knew was strictly second division. And he knew why as well: he was scared to die. That's what champion bike riders had and he didn't: they

wanted to win so much they were willing to die trying.

He lay there brooding on that. He lay there a long
time, brooding and feeling sorry for himself, and
hating himself for brooding and for feeling sorry for
himself. It reminded him of his old man, and Uncle
Nathan, his inheritance. Shysters, snivelling shysters. Then that line popped into his head and repeated itself:

'I should've wasted you in the mountains, you no
good, small time shyster.'

It was a moment of epiphany for American Troy.
Insight upon insight crowded his mind so suddenly
that he had to slow down, go back and examine
them one by one. His brain was working again, the
fog had cleared, he could think clearly.

He could see the scene: the loyal lieutenant taking
him into the forest to waste him, but the shrieking,
hysterical grifter begs for his life, and the stand-up
guy, disgusted by this undignified, grovelling creature, spares him.

The next insight was a line half-remembered from
a book whose title he could not recall: a man who
had been cowardly his whole life could not be
called a coward because it was within his power not
to behave cowardly the next time.

Yes.

Yes, that was it.

Soon after, American Troy got to his feet. He
would try. That's all he could do. He would try,
but he knew he wasn't a snivelling shyster. He knew

that at least. Maybe he would fail, but at least he would have tried, and that was something.

By the time American Troy had cleaned himself up for a second time and emerged from the bathroom, the Big Shilling had made a pot of coffee and set the table for breakfast.

'I decided we'd eat in, eh?' he said when American Troy came into the living room.

American Troy sat at the table, shuffling out a chair and squeezing himself into the gap between the table and the dusty TV on its crochet-covered stand. He didn't look at the Big Shilling straight away, preferring to catch glimpses of him as he busied himself between the fridge and the stove and the sink.

'Inside every man,' pronounced the Big Shilling, 'there is a woman. Real men know this, Adam and Eve entwined, Adam and Eve entwined, eh? These tough guys who beat up faggots, who never read books or listen to a symphony or paint a beautiful picture? They're missing out, I tell you, they'll never be whole, they'll never be whole, hey?'

Something landed on the table cloth in front of American Troy, almost making him jump. It was a passport, issued by the Irish government. American Troy picked it up and looked at the photo inside, which depicted an elderly woman with ginger hair. Her name, according to the document, was Kathleen Assumpta O'Gurley.

'This you?' he asked.

'Yes, that is I,' said the Big Shilling. 'Look at me and

tell me what you think.'

American Troy looked. The Big Shilling was wearing a summer frock patterned with sunflowers, a ginger wig that looked exactly the same as the one Kathleen O'Gurley was wearing in the photograph, and make-up. American Troy had to admit that the disguise was surprisingly convincing.

He nodded a couple of times. 'Yeah, not bad. Not bad at all.'

'You like the dress? I like the dress, hey. It's by J K Snazz, J K Snazz of Kissonerga, Cyprus. Mrs O'Gurley bought it for me herself. She's a widow woman, her old man died twenty years ago now, a former Dublin gangster, and she's lived in Cyprus on his ill-gotten gains ever since.'

'Don't you have a dress for me?'

The Big Shilling cracked a smile. 'Feeling better? I like it, I like it: don't you have a dress for me. No, no dress for you. A coffin, that's what I've got for you. Hey! Don't look so worried, not a real coffin, just a tight space. And now for the piece de resistance.'

That said, the Big Shilling uncapped a bottle of cheap, foul-smelling perfume and sprayed it liberally all over himself.

Before they left, the Big Shilling made a call. He called Ahmet Bey to find out if he'd made the transfer, now that the authorities had confirmed the death of the Russian exile. American Troy could hear only one side of the conversation, but he got the drift all right.

The Big Shilling was saying, with mounting anger, 'Bad for business, is it? I have caused you many problems, have I? A great deal of trouble, you say? You didn't want a massacre, you wanted a clean kill. I see. Oh, legitimate businessman, are you?

'Now listen to me, Achmed, or whoever the fuck you are. Either you pay me the fucking money, eh, or I come gunning for you, you dirty fucking Turk cunt! I come gunning for you, and do to you what I did to the Russian, eh!'

The Big Shilling ended the call. He didn't smash the phone to pieces or hurl it at the wall, he placed it on the table top, and smiled amiably at Troy.

CHAPTER
TWENTY-TWO

American Troy said it was tight, real tight, but that he thought that he could do it. The Big Shilling, dressed in the old lady's frock, ushered him out of the camper van and into the blazing sunshine of a Nicosia noon. Traffic streaked past only feet away.

'We'll sit down first and have a drink,' said the Big Shilling in the high-pitched Irish-accented voice he'd adopted since arriving at their rendezvous.

The Brits were still seated at the little metal table, under the arbour beside the lay-by kiosk, a couple of miles outside the Cypriot capital. The old fat guy, who sounded like Sir Michael Caine, American Troy now recognised. He was the dipstick who'd been conducting the singing at the birthday party in the restaurant, near the Russian exile's house in the Akamas. His wife, terminally wrinkled and the colour of oiled mahogany, bared her false teeth in a grimace.

'No luck?' she asked, ironically.

'It's no problem at all, it's not,' said the Big Shilling, encouraging American Troy to sit. 'Brian, be a love and get the lad a drink, will you?'

The Brit lumbered to his feet. 'Whatcher 'avin?' he seemed to say.

'He'll have a beer is what he'll have,' said the Big Shilling. 'A Keo.'

American Troy sat down under the arbour of grape vines. Here, in the middle of the island, away from the cooling sea breezes of the coast, it was infernally hot, and American Troy felt enervated, not just sapped physically, but mentally and spiritually as well. All he had left was his will power.

'I can do it,' he told the Big Shilling.

A cop car cruised by, but the pair of leos didn't even glance their way.

The Big Shilling was searching through the contents of his handbag. American Troy heard the rattle of pill bottles and the crinkle of foil-wrapped plastic trays being extracted from stiff cardboard packs. Doctor Shilling had brought his dispensary with him.

'Here are, son,' said the cockney, passing American Troy a bottle of not quite cold enough beer, 'get yer larfin' gear round that then.'

'Thanks,' said American Troy wearily. He tasted the beer. It was gassy and tasteless, and reminded him of home. Hicksville, Illinois, how he wished he were there right now.

'Drink it,' ordered the Big Shilling, glaring at him playfully from under false eyelashes.

American Troy drank, and when the Big Shilling dropped four or five white pills into his cupped hand, American Troy didn't bother to look at them, he just tossed them into his mouth and washed them down with pulls on the bottle.

'God love him,' said the Big Shilling, 'wasn't he always my best boy?'

The cockney's wife tittered at this, and sucked orange juice through the straw from a plastic beaker. The cockney winked encouragement and toasted American Troy silently with a bottle of water. Only the Big Shilling was without a drink. Instead, he was fussing with the corner of a tissue and a compact mirror.

'I'm running,' he said. 'It's terrible warm.'

'Take yer knickers off,' advised the cockney's wife before emitting a cackle of laughter.

'There'd better not be vodka in that OJ, Bet,' said the Big Shilling, smiling dangerously.

That shut the old lady up. She cleared her throat nervously and puckered her mouth.

American Troy was suddenly feeling very, very relaxed. He sipped his beer with newfound pleasure. He had to admit it, now it tasted pretty darn good. The sunshine dappling the tables was beautiful, and he was no longer troubled by the intense heat, or by the noise of the traffic that kicked up dust and irritated his eyes. In fact, the dust itself appeared to be . . . friendly. American Troy experienced a loving surge of emotion. The Big Shilling and the two Britons were infinitely appealing, why hadn't he noticed that before? People, man, they were beautiful, and connected, to everyone else and to everything else.

'Well?' asked the Big Shilling. 'All right now are you?'

'More than all right,' said American Troy, the words catching in his throat.

'You'll be feeling a bit emotional,' the Big Shilling went on, 'but it'll pass in a few minutes, then you'll be feeling relaxed, very, very relaxed indeed.'

'Relaxed,' said American Troy, and the word seemed to be imbued with special meanings which he had never before apprehended.

'I'll have what he's having,' said the trouble and strife, 'bless him.'

'Time to make a move?' asked her husband.

'There's no hurry,' said the Big Shilling. 'Finish your drinks.'

'Take your time,' American Troy heard himself say, 'and don't hurry up.'

They had to help him up the steps into the campervan.

'It'll be like being reborn,' said the Big Shilling, holding his hand as American Troy stepped into the coffin, the smuggler's compartment hidden beneath the bench seat. 'It'll be like being unified, having a soul.'

'Awesome,' said American Troy, and meant it.

It was awesome. The prospect of being reborn was awesome indeed. How had he ever doubted? How could it have been any other way? The Big Shilling was Odysseus, navigating the way home across the wine-dark sea.

'Beautiful,' said American Troy, 'you're beautiful.'

Again, the words caught in his throat and he thought he was going to cry.

The false bottom was laid on top of him, and he listened to the turn of the Allen keys as the screws were fixed into place. Next came the clothes and innocent odds and ends to fill the storage compart-ment, then the seats fitted on top of that, the sounds growing more muffled now. American Troy, lying on his side in the foetal position, closed his eyes, a big, beatific smile on his face, and drifted off to sleep.

When he awoke, he remembered the sound of the engine and the noise of the moving vehicle, of being pushed against one side of the coffin then the other as the campervan negotiated bends and corners and traffic. He discovered he couldn't move. It wasn't confinement, he really couldn't move: he was para-lysed. He heard creaking above him as someone sat on the bench seat. Then he heard the Big Shill-ing speaking in that high-pitched Irish accent, or at least he thought he did. He wasn't sure if he was truly conscious, or dreaming. The fact that he was paralysed did not bother him in the slightest and that made him think he was dreaming, listening to the Big Shilling speak.

'Even the outlaw, even the murderer,' the voice was saying, softly, distantly, hypnotically, 'even the basest creature ever to have walked the earth, if he was initiated into the Mysteries then he was assured of everlasting life in the hereafter. That is what the normal person cannot understand. It has nothing to do with morality, achieving immortality, with being a good person, with doing good deeds, nothing whatsoever. It has everything to do with secret knowledge, with actual experience of that secret knowledge. Finding it hard to breathe? Yes, you are finding it hard to breathe. It's getting hotter. Of course it is getting hotter. You are nearing the infernal regions. You are nearing the other side, and you cannot breathe.'

American Troy could not breathe. There was no air in the coffin. He tried to drag air into his lungs but his lungs did not inflate. With every exhalation his lungs grew smaller, tighter, harder. There was a pain in his heart. He could not move. Sweat leaked out from every pore. He felt like he was broiling in his own broth. Panic rose in him. Surely he was dreaming. A red mist filmed his sightless eyes, and strange creatures, baleful, inhuman, rose from the darkness, disturbed by his presence. He'd seen them before, in Amsterdam: therianthropes, half-animal, half-men. One of them came closer, a dog-headed monster that seemed to examine his very heart, and then was gone.

Again he heard the Big Shilling speaking with an

Irish accent, but he could no longer understand what he was saying. He could not breathe.

Make a soul?

He was burning up.

You are many?

He wanted to scream, to thrash about, but his vocal chords were as paralysed as his limbs. Was this death? Was he dying? Was this the end? This time his life was not relayed to him backwards.

Then he heard the Big Shilling's Irish brogue, saying, 'A gift of unity.'

A great black wave welled up and engulfed him, and he fainted. And when he came to, American Troy underwent the strangest experience of his life. He was on the other side, in the absolute elsewhere. It was as though he were dead but still conscious. It was indescribable. Ultimate freedom, infinite joy – but the words meant nothing compared to the actuality. It began to fade, as though he were being dragged backwards by a silver cord. No! He wanted to stay, but the pull of life was too strong. Back he went, back into the coffin, back to the island, Cyprus, the island from which it seemed impossible to escape!

He could hear again, and breathe, and was no long panicky.

It sounded like the police were searching the van. This everyday reality appeared massive, solid, utterly mundane. The van was stopped, and it rocked slightly as heavy feet plodded through the cabin.

Outside, men with official voices were speaking Greek. Michael Caine was having a laugh and a joke. Cupboards were opened and closed, drawers searched, walls tapped. American Troy realised he could move, and that his breathing had returned to normal. It wasn't even that warm anymore. He had the idea that the van was parked beneath a sunshade. Then he heard the bench seat cushion being removed and the contents of the storage tray being moved about. A sliver of brightness as a flashlight was shone.

Then it was over. The bench seat cushion was roughly replaced, and the customs officers or cops or whoever they were, disembarked. Shortly thereafter, he heard three people get aboard, the engine started up, and the van rolled forward slowly in bottom gear.

American Troy felt sick. He wasn't sure how much more of this he could take. Had the drugs worn off? They couldn't have, not yet. But at least he could breathe. He concentrated on that thought, and on the inhalation and exhalation his body automatically made. Calm, he told himself, stay calm, but an insistent inner voice started whining – why me, why me? Then he slipped into sleep once more, and not even the distant sound of men speaking Turkish could disturb him.

The next time he awoke it was because he was about to be released. The bench seat cushion was removed, then the clothes and assorted items, finally the tray was unfastened, and blinding daylight poured in along with humid fresh air.

'Will you look at the state of him?' said the Big Shilling in his Irish voice. Then, in his more familiar white-colonial accent, he said, 'Like a real sweat box, hey? Here, my boy, drink this.'

American Troy chugged gratefully on a bottle of cool water, glugging it down his parched, sore throat until the bottle was empty. He gasped for air, his chest heaving.

'Are we through?'

'We're through,' said the Big Shilling, amused by the ambiguity of the question.

To American Troy, reborn from the smuggler's coffin, the Big Shilling's colonial accent sounded as fake as his Irish one. The Big Shilling was whatever he wanted to be, he was the man with a thousand faces. It seemed to American Troy that he knew nothing at all about the Big Shilling, that everything he thought he knew about him was a lie, was a fabrication, an act, and that it did not matter. The only thing he knew for sure about the little man was that he possessed the kind of knowledge that normies never even dreamed of.

This surreal experience continued for the next few minutes until it dissipated and American Troy was left feeling weary and disquieted. He had the impression that he knew things he had no right knowing, that he had glimpsed not only the future but some kind of strange afterlife as well. And then the rational part of him was telling him that was just a bunch of bullshit, a drug-fiend's dream. But ...

'He's not going to pay,' he now said, seated on the bench seat opposite the Big Shilling, who was still dressed incongruously, and patently falsely, as an old Irish woman. 'We won't get our money, whatever we do.'

Another insight accompanied this certainty but it stayed tantalisingly out of reach, as though it could only be accessed from inside the coffin and from within a drugged consciousness. American Troy clenched his fists in frustration. He had an inkling that Ahmet Bey was acting too, but in what way he couldn't quite grasp.

'It was never about the money,' said the Big Shilling, the twinkle in his eye contrasting sharply with his grim visage.

American Troy averted his gaze. The make-up on the Big Shilling's face was smeared and runny, the lipstick licked off by that sharp tongue, the mascara smudged, false eyelashes coming unstuck. It was a clown's face or a joker's, the kind of clown or joker who'd entice children into the woods, or criminals into a try-out, the kind of face of a man who'd soak a billion dollars in gasoline and negligently toss a lit match.

'What we need are better kinds of criminals,' said American Troy.

'You saw it then?'

'I don't know what I saw.'

'But you saw it.'

'Yeah, I saw it.'

'Are we through?'

'Not yet,' said American Troy.

'No,' said the Big Shilling, getting up and moving towards the cab. 'Not by a long chalk, not by a long chalk, eh?'

It was never about the money. No, it had never been about the money. It had always been about domination. The Big Shilling had a will to power, a will to dominate everyone around him, a will to dominate life itself. And that was the prize he was offering American Troy. Overcome yourself, rise above your weakness, and you too can dominate. And now he had gone further still. Not only could you dominate life but you could, in some still undefined way, overcome death as well. That was today's lesson. Why be afraid of death when death wasn't the end?

What was that he said, back in the apartment? Something about men who are not afraid of death being infinitely superior to the most powerful temporal power?

But American Troy still wasn't sure. He wasn't at the end, but he had been helped along the way, that much was certain.

'Here we are,' said the Big Shilling from the cab of the camper van.

He was seated between the Blees, Brian was driving and Betty Blee was reading directions from the sat nav. American Troy began to take notice of his surroundings once more. The van was turning into a dusty suburban street, and from nearby came the roar of a passenger plane taking off.

Half an hour later and the Blees had left in the van. American Troy and the Big Shilling were drinking beer in the living room of Mrs O'Gurley's rented villa.

'Man, I'm tired,' said American Troy. 'I need to sleep.'

'Good,' said Shilling. 'You can go and have a nap in a minute, when I've finished instructing you, so pay attention, eh. Are you paying attention?'

'Yes.'

'It's all about visualising, of visualising the outcome, remember? I want you to visualise the successful outcome of our escape from this island, I want you to visualise it as you fall asleep. The question you must ask yourself is: what would I see? What would I see, eh, when I succeed? What would I see? What would I say? How would I feel? And once you've answered those questions, you write the scene, eh, the scene of fulfilment. But you must convince yourself absolutely, convince yourself to the point of self-persuasion. You must convince yourself that we've already escaped.'

'Can't you do it?'

'We're both going to do it,' said the Big Shilling, getting annoyed.

American Troy pulled himself together. 'Yes, all right, I'm going to do it.'

'What is the scene of fulfilment?'

'The two of us, a bottle of tequila and the finest Havana cigars, drinking a toast: we did it.'

'We did it,' chimed the Big Shilling. 'We did it. I like it. But how about, we made it? Wouldn't that be better?'

'Yes,' said American Troy eagerly. 'We made it!'

The Big Shilling was beaming with pleasure. 'That's my boy,' he said. 'Now, you get off and have a nap. I'll wake you in a couple of hours, because I want you to make a phone call for me, a phone call to Ahmet Bey.'

'What about?'

'About how you're going to betray me,' said the Big Shilling, amiably, 'about how you're going to betray me, eh, in return for an obscene amount of cold hard cash.'

CHAPTER TWENTY-THREE

The woman known as Sam to her colleagues in the British Secret Intelligence Service left the headquarters building at Vauxhall Cross on the river Thames and caught a number 2 bus to Brixton, south London. It was late afternoon and the sunny skies of that morning had been replaced by lowering dark clouds. A cold front was moving in from the west, bringing strong winds, heavy showers and the possibility of thunder.

It was a short journey of less than two miles but the London traffic was, as usual, atrocious. If it hadn't been pouring with rain, Sam told herself, she would have got off the bus and walked, but the English summer had been disappointingly cool and wet. She consoled herself with a large bag of chili peanuts and a can of pineapple-flavoured fizzy drink. Today was supposed to be a diet day, but she was nervous, and when she was nervous Sam had a compulsion to eat.

She was nervous because she'd received a letter that morning informing her that Internal Security wished to speak to her. The date was set for the following Monday, at 11.45. Sam had immediately taken the letter into her boss's office and asked Petra what she knew about it. The cow had been her usual stupid self, fortunately, and had got straight on to the head of security and started going on at him about victimisation and stereotyping and some such shit. She'd even complained about the timing of the interview, on a Monday, so that poor Sam would have to stew over the weekend.

It was probably something and nothing, she told herself, finishing the large bag of nuts. If it was serious they'd have come straight to the office and hauled her off to an interview room. With food in her stomach, the woman known as Sam felt more optimistic.

The Progressive Muslim Women's Centre stood in a dreary row of shops near Brixton Market. Sam used the computers there regularly. She said hello to some familiar faces gathered in the reception area, and chatted briefly with a friend about an upcoming protest march, before seating herself at a work station at the back of the computer room. Less than an hour after leaving MI6 headquarters, the traitress was in secure contact with Mr Fraidoon-Pour, her handler at the Iranian Embassy in London.

Using their family-based code she informed him

that her grandfather had arrived safely in Lefkosia, which is the Turkish name for the Cypriot capital, Nicosia.

Mr Fraidoon-Pour asked if her grandfather had his pet with him.

Sam thought for a moment before keyboarding a reply: 'Not that I know of but his friends from London took him in their camper van.'

Her heart was beating a little faster now, because she had left the best till last. She actually knew where her 'grandfather' was staying. She typed: 'Grandfather is staying at Mrs O'Gurleys in a villa near the airport.'

How nice for him! wrote Mr Fraidoon-Pour.

Sam typed the address.

The single word reply made her beam with pleasure: Excellent!

At work, Sam's boss, the cow Petra, or to give her her full name Petronella Plumleigh-Gorse, was having a less enjoyable time handling some news.

'No, really,' she was saying into her phone, 'that's wonderful, darling. You'll absolutely shine in the role. I am happy for you, sweetie, it's just that there's a bit of a flap on. Yes, when isn't there? We'll talk later, I put champers in the fridge. Oh. Well, I shall probably be in bed by then. I'll be leaving before six tomorrow. I've not got a clue what to wear. Do you know what the weather's going to do?'

Petra was relieved but also saddened when Caro rang off.

'Well that's that then,' she said to an empty office.

It was probably for the best. Now that Caro had got her heart's desire – editorship of BBC Radio's flagship afternoon news programme – it was inevitable that they'd see even less of each other than they did now. And if the gutter press had got wind of their relationship, well, it wouldn't have done either of their careers a jot of good, would it?

To fend off tears, Petra Gorse briskly blew her nose on a Kleenex, and got on with the task at hand.

'KBO,' she said to herself, 'KBO.' It was one of her mother's: keep buggering on.

She decided she needed a drink. The sun was over the yard-arm, after all – somewhere in the world. She crossed to the sideboard and poured a small measure of 12 year-old malt into a cut-glass tumbler. It was one of the perquisites which came with being senior management, having a drinks cabinet. She took the whisky over to the chaise-longue, sat down, adjusted the soft leather cushion, and stretched out. She did some of her best thinking here, but only when there was no chance of being disturbed. She didn't want word to get round that she was sleeping on the job. She began to review the situation.

Cheltenham had a tap on the Cypriot police computer, naturally, and as soon as BASKERVILLE – the SIS codename for Rickardo Hanratty, the man also known as the Big Shilling – had crossed into the north on the O'Gurley passport, Operations had immediately let her know. And thanks to the widow

O'Gurley, who'd stupidly paid for the villa rental by credit card, they even knew where BASKERVILLE was staying. Petra had ordered their northern Cyprus stringer to get eyes on, and conformation had come at teatime that their man had been positively identified at the address.

Then, twenty minutes ago, the head of Ops, Teddy Fitzgerard, had waltzed into her office and told her the individual also known as South African Troy had filed a flight plan, Sofia, Bulgaria to Lefkosia, northern Cyprus. It seemed the dirty dog BASKER-VILLE was going to fly away, who knew where, leaving poor old Frankie bobbing up and down on the briny like a spare whatsit at a wedding.

Slippery Fitz was still in damage control mode, but his flabby face was a good deal less ashen than it had been when news had broken about the ice cream parlour massacre. Naturally, Teddy's first objective had been to pass the buck, and when Petronella declined to accept it, they had all been mightily relieved, and somewhat surprised, when the team's foreign signing, Mortimer Parron, seconded to MI6 from the CIA's Directorate of Operations, had taken the blame - after a fashion.

As Mort had explained, he accepted the significant and demanding responsibilities that came with juggling multiple classified time-sensitive projects, but, that being said, it was only right that he owned results that some might think of as being subpar.

That was all right then.

Subpar: Petra had looked it up. It meant 'of a lower

standard than traditionally accepted norms, but not entirely unacceptable.' One supposed that this was an example of Mr Parron's supposedly legendary chutzpah. He certainly appeared to be completely unmoved by the massacre, whereas she had suffered a sleepless night of sickly recrimination.

Petra closed her eyes. There was a way out of this bloody tangled mess, and if she could find it there might be glory to be had. Her mind wandered, and she day-dreamed about being the first female Director-General of Her Majesty's Secret Intelligence Service.

Long overdue. Smash the glass ceiling. Dame Petronella. But who would accompany her to the Palace investiture? Her mother?

The day-dream faded away. Again, Petra Gorse felt the prick of conscience. What a filthy business she found herself in. No place for a woman, not really, her mama had once insisted. They'd argued, Petra citing another of her mother's axioms: if you can't stand the heat, then go back to the kitchen.

'Not bloody likely,' said Petra, crossing to her desk and picking up the phone.

'Operations,' said a familiar voice.

'Hello, Rangana, can you get hold of Major Frankish for me?'

'Yes, ma'am,' said the young Sri Lankan, 'putting you through.'

Poor old Frankie, one did feel for him. She wondered if he actually believed her assurances about his daughter. Of course, one would do what one could, but the poor lamb was so desperate he simply wasn't thinking straight. You were after all dealing with the Israelis here.

'Hullo?'

'That you, Sailor Sam?'

'How lovely to hear your voice, dear heart, how are things?'

'Can't complain,' said Petra. 'KBO, and all that.'

'What news with you then? Nothing untoward?'

'Had my heart broken once again, that's all.'

'My dear old girl.'

'I know, you'd think I'd learn, wouldn't you? Settle for alcoholism and rescue cats somewhere down in Sussex.'

She heard Frankie laughing like he didn't believe her one bit, his voice slightly distorted by the satellite phone or the scrambler, she wasn't sure which. Whatever it was, it made him sound slightly deranged. She was a little cross. She knew there was unfriendly, and unfounded, gossip about her and single-minded ambition. She didn't expect it from Frankie.

'Anyhow,' she said, hiding her annoyance. 'It looks like chummy's making his own way home with his South African friend, due to land Lefkosia tomorrow at 1600. I think you should be there, a little welcoming committee.'

'Watching brief?' said Frankie.

'Sceptical?'

'You know what I think, ma'am. I speak my mind, always have.'

'That's why we love you, Major.'

'He's quite something, isn't he?'

'Yes, he is, though I'm not quite sure what.'

'His patron, I'm pretty sure, thinks along the same lines.'

'You mentioned...'

'And you thought it was a lot of old nonsense, but there it is.'

'What was the word?'

'Karaconcolos.'

'I looked it up.'

'Yes, but reading about it in your smart office on a computer screen is one thing,' said Frankie, 'actuality quite another.'

'I don't disbelieve you, but it is rather irregular.'

'There are more things in heaven and earth than are dreamt of in your philosophy, Horatia.'

Smiling, because Frankie was such a dear really, even if he did sound like he'd been reading too much Conrad, Petra came to a decision.

'Watching brief for now,' she ordered, her voice crisp and calm, 'but if I send word... Could you do it?'

Frankie the Fish didn't respond straight away, and the crackly silence was weighted with meaning.

'For Melissa I'd take on the very devil himself,' he said.

'Oh Frankie, you're such a dear.'

At that same moment, in northern Cyprus, not thirty miles from Frankie the Fish on the yacht Melissa, Ahmet Bey, the man who believed in the existence of the malevolent goblins, was also taking a phone call from London.

'You have surpassed yourself,' said Ahmet Bey.

'I am only glad to have been of service, my friend,' said the deputy military attaché of the Turkish Embassy, whom Petra's personal assistant, the traitress Sam, knew as the Iranian spy Fraidoon-Pour.

'I thank you again,' said Ahmet Bey, ending the call.

Ahmet Bey thought for a moment, and was about to order his men to the cars when he heard the phone ring in his briefcase. When he answered it, he spoke again in English.

'Hi, do you recognise the voice?'

'Yes,' said Ahmet Bey, 'I do.'

'I want to do a deal,' said American Troy.

'What kind of deal?'

'You're Ahmet Bey. I mean, that's who I'm talking to, right? Not his tea boy.'

'You are an intelligent man, Mr Troy.'

'We do a deal. The deal is, I get my money, and I give you him. His plan is to wack you.'

'It is what?'

'To wack you.'

'I see.'

'Is it a deal?'

'That depends on where you are.'

'On your side of the line.'

'You escaped. I congratulate you.'

'Listen, listen. Do we have a deal? He plans to kill you. Pay me my end and I'll deliver him to you on a plate. I mean, you can come and get him.'

'Northern Cyprus is a very small place, Mr Troy.'

'Do we have a fucking deal, or don't we?'

'Yes, we have a deal.'

'All right. Transfer the money to this account. If I don't get the money within five minutes, we're out of here.'

'It will take longer . . .'

'Five minutes.'

'Very well. You will have your money, Mr Troy. It is a small price to pay.'

'That's what I thought.'

'You are an intelligent and resourceful young man.'

American Troy read out the account number and the address of the rented house.

'Yes, we should do business in the future.'

'Let's get this one deal under our belts first,' said American Troy, and ended the call.

CHAPTER
TWENTY-FOUR

American Troy heard the Big Shilling come out of the bathroom in the vacant rented villa near Lefkosia airport. It was early evening in Cyprus and very hot. Troy adjusted the air con. He was feeling a little nervous, and something else as well: he had the idea that he'd been promoted. It was like one of those war movies where some guy's been made up to sergeant. It kinda takes time to get used to it.

'Wanna eat?' he called up the stairs.

'You hungry?' said the Big Shilling. 'Sure, I'm hungry. There's food in the fridge.'

'You're right,' said American Troy, opening the fridge which was half filled with groceries and assorted beverages. 'You're always right.'

When the Big Shilling came downstairs a short while later, he was looking at his phone and saying,

'Bakgat, bakgat.'

Troy pricked up his ears. 'Bakgat?'

'It means excellent, cool,' said the Big Shilling.

'I know what it means,' said Troy. 'It's Afrikaans, you told me, remember? It means South African Troy is on his way.'

'Oh? Is that what it means?' said the Big Shilling, but his sly smile meant that American Troy's intuition was correct.

'Outstanding.'

'How did you find it,' asked Shilling, 'visualising your fulfilment?'

'I did just fine,' said Troy, who suspected that in some uncanny way he could not even begin to fathom the Big Shilling had assisted him.

'So you did,' said the Big Shilling.

He sat down gingerly, checking (to divert the kid's attention) that American Troy was wearing his Nikes, and proceeded to pull on the walking boots. He saw that American Troy had put a selection of dishes on the dining table – hummus, taramasalata, olives.

'Nervous?' he asked.

'Not much,' said Troy.

'Uneasy?'

Troy thought about this for a while. He said, 'In what way?'

Shilling didn't answer. He finished fastening the boot laces and stood up. 'Ahmet Bey is mind, not muscle. He is weak, a fool, a superstitious fool. Surprised, were you, hey? To find out who he really is.'

'A little,' said American Tory, honestly.

'You sneered at him. You thought he was a fag-got, eh, always fawning. But he was clever, eh? As though he'd divided himself into two, showing the world this false personality named Ahmet Bey, but hiding his essence.'

The Big Shilling stopped in his tracks. He'd been buttoning up his shirt and walking over to the fridge, but now he stood there, alert, head cocked. He'd heard something.

'What?' said American Troy.

He too listened, and heard nothing, but he intuited that the nothing he was hearing was unlike the background noise he had grown used to since taking up residence in this their latest temporary home.

That was when the front door was smashed open, and men in black uniforms stormed across the sud-denly illuminated patio at the back of the villa. Within seconds, both the Big Shilling and Ameri-can Troy were tackled to the floor, within a minute, both of them were handcuffed, within five, they were sitting facing each other, knees touching, in a cage in the back of a paddy wagon.

'Did you make another call while I was taking a shower?' asked the Big Shilling. 'Sure you didn't call 911? Is that who you called? Did you call the po-lice? Why would you call the police?'

'Maybe they're not cops,' said American Troy, iron-ically.

'Maybe they're not,' the Big Shilling admit-ted. 'Maybe they're something else altogether, eh?

Maybe they're Ahmet Bey's boys. Is that who you are? Did Ahmet Bey send you, boys?'

But there was no answer from the cops in the cab of the speeding paddy wagon.

The Big Shilling lowered his voice. 'Everything's going to be all right, kid,' he said, leaning forward. 'All we have to do is get to the airport by midnight tonight. That's when your namesake, South African Troy, is scheduled to take off.'

'That's all?'

'That's all.'

'I don't think we're getting nearer to the airport,' said American Troy. 'I think we're getting further away from the airport, and from the city.'

The Big Shilling nodded. 'You're right. They're not taking us to police headquarters, eh?'

'They must be taking us to Ahmet Bey.'

The Big Shilling merely smiled one of his sly smiles.

Ahmet Bey lived in a gaudy palace overlooking the sea near the port of Famagusta. It was an enormous building and heavily guarded, not only by armed men but with the very latest in security technology as well. It was virtually impregnable, and not even a daredevil like the Big Shilling could have gained entry, unless, that is, he had invited himself in.

The small convoy consisting of three police cars, the paddy wagon, and a motorcycle outrider, entered the perimeter defences of the palace via a checkpoint. A short drive took them to a gate in a chain-link fence, which an armed guard opened. Finally, the convoy drove through an archway and into the palace courtyard.

'Thanks,' said the Big Shilling when the cage was unlocked and the door opened.

He reached out a hand to one of the cops, and stepped down from the paddy wagon like he was royalty. For half a second no one reacted, then the Big Shilling was howling with laughter as he was slammed up against the side of the wagon, the cops angrily shouting at each other. Somehow, the Big Shilling had escaped from his cuffs.

'Easy, boys, easy,' he said, 'just a bit of fun to get the evening off on the right footing. Now, take me to your leader, eh? Take me to your leader, and let's get this party started.'

He tossed the key he'd used to unlock the cuffs to one of the cops, who caught it and glanced at it stupidly before pushing the Big Shilling in the middle of the back towards the palace steps. American Troy, still cuffed, followed on behind. He was apprehensive, but kind of elated as well. The audacity of the little man!

Then something very strange happened.

The Big Shilling turned into a king.

There was no other way that American Troy could describe it to himself: the little man turned into a king! His gait changed, he grew taller, the line from the crown of his head down to the leg was suddenly elegant, integrated, powerful. It was remarkable. And as the Big Shilling's feet touched the steps in

those heavy boots, it was as though he was weight-
less, gliding. It wasn't just Troy, it was the cops
as well. They saw the transformation too. It was
as though the Big Shilling had emerged not from a
paddy wagon but from a gilded coach. The cops
exchanged glances, dumbstruck. They followed respectfully in the Big Shilling's wake.

The marble steps led not to a doorway but to
another arch which took them through to a vast
courtyard where a fountain was lit with garish
green lights, and the sound of trickling water made
American Troy nervously want to pee. There were
flowers and bushes and trees, and the warm evening air was scented with roses and bougainvillea. It
would have been idyllic if it hadn't been for the men
with guns, and the caged dogs, and the garish green
lights.

'Remember this guy?' the Big Shilling asked American Troy. 'Bulgaria, the bear fight, eh. That's the
Kangal that killed the bear.'

American Troy eyed the giant dogs warily. They
all looked the same to him: dangerous, aggressive
and unpleasant.

'Welcome,' said Ahmet Bey's double, appearing
from a pathway between the rose bushes.

He looked as weary and as unimpressive as he had
in Bulgaria. His rounded shoulders, pot belly and
big nose gave him a ridiculous, lugubrious air that
was out of place in a palace, even one illuminated
by garish lights. He spoke rapidly in Turkish, and
the most senior of the police officers answered him

scornfully.

Annoyed, Ahmet Bey's double turned to the Big Shilling and raised an eyebrow.

'You makes fool of my mens,' said Ahmet Bey in execrable English.

'It was just a little key,' said the Big Shilling with a grin.

'Time for jokings is over. Now is time you die.'

'I wanted it this way,' said the Big Shilling, 'I wanted to be captured. How else would I get in here?'

'You want moneys?'

'I don't want my money, I've come here to kill. I've come here to kill you, Ahmet Bey.'

Ahmet Bey's double opened his hands, indicating the police with their guns, and the guards, also with guns, who were stationed around the courtyard.

American Troy piped up, 'I brought him here like I said I would, Ahmet Bey! Ahmet Bey, get me out of these cuffs and let me go, like we agreed!'

The Big Shilling glanced at American Troy as though angered and surprised. Then both men looked up, in the direction of the sound of hands clapping, not in applause but as a way to attract everyone's attention. On the balcony, in the shadows, was a slight figure.

In its cage, the Kangal shepherd dog named Gazi barked once.

The senior cop gave an order, and American Troy's hands were freed. The senior cop was a sweating, corpulent man with a black moustache and glittering eyes. Now, he unbuttoned his holster and stationed himself in front of the Big Shilling.

'You're not going to feed me to the dogs, are you?' the Big Shilling asked him. 'I thought you were going to set the dogs on me. I thought that was what was going to happen.'

'No,' said the fat cop, drawing his pistol. 'This is what is what will happen.'

'This is what is going to happen? Are you sure? Maybe something else is going to happen.'

If he hadn't been so fat, the cop's gun hand would not have had to travel so far. As it was, his gun hand had to negotiate the tubular apron of blubber that flopped over his belt, and by the time the gun was levelled at the Big Shilling, the Big Shilling with his super-fast hands had grabbed the gun that was aimed at him, reversed it and shot the cop in the chest.

Right after that it was all noise and fury and turmoil and confusion.

American Troy shoulder-charged the cop nearest to him, and sprinted for the shadows, and there was gunfire on all sides, and chips of marble hit him in the face and sent him ducking and scurrying along the wall into cover. He found himself in a doorway. There were light switches mounted on a metal panel. He swept his hand upward and the courtyard was immediately plunged into darkness. Then someone was firing at him again and he was through the door and running scared along a slippery marble passageway that led past Turkish baths to a swimming pool.

In the courtyard, the Big Shilling picked up a Sarsil-maz machine pistol from the dead body of one of the bodyguards he had felled with a double-tap to the chest and a single bullet to the head, just before the lights had gone out.

All the cops had scattered as soon as he'd begun shooting. He could hear them moving about amongst the roses and potted plants. He stuck the pistol in his pocket and flicked the Sarsilmaz's selector to auto. He fired bursts first one way then another, changed position, fired at a running shape, heard a womanish scream, and emptied the magazine at the balcony.

For a moment there was silence. Then American Troy came out of the swimming pool changing room and spied the motorbike cop who was holding a helmet in one hand and a pistol in the other. Unseen, Troy went back the way he'd come. The firing had stopped, but now he could hear Turkish voices, shouting, calling, giving orders. Suddenly, the lights came on, and the motorbike cop clocked him and started to shoot, but Troy was already running back the way he'd come. He was almost at the light switches when he saw a small, unmistakable figure in the shadowed doorway. He threw himself full length on the floor, calling, 'Look out!'

Over his head was a fusillade of shooting. He rolled over, cowering against the wall, and saw the motorbike cop was dying, and not well. Hand over hand,

American Troy used the wall to help himself to his feet.

'Jesus,' wailed American Troy, 'put him out of his misery, can't you?'

He and the Big Shilling were marching towards the dying, screaming man. The screams were horrible, like those of a tortured animal. The Big Shilling shot him dead with a pistol, and the two of them continued through the changing rooms to the loggia that overlooked the drive.

'Move it,' warned the Big Shilling.

American Troy began to run, the Big Shilling firing single shots to cover him, but even so he was being targeted by automatic fire that made the hair stand up on his scalp and caused him to cry out and wince and pull in his neck. The automatic fire stopped abruptly, as though a magazine was emptied. Troy looked about desperately.

There was no one guarding the police vehicles. Eagerly, American Troy ran and leapt into the saddle of the BMW motorbike, turned the key and started the engine. Moments later, the Big Shilling mounted up behind him and they were off down the drive and through the gate in the chain-link fence. But there was no way out. A big black Mercedes van was parked athwart the road in front of the checkpoint and American Troy could see armed men in cover behind concrete blockwork. There was a footpath left. He gunned the bike and took it, all too aware of the bullets that were striking the trees on all sides and shredding greenery and bits of wood, rounds zinging and whizzing past them.

Down the paths they went, deeper into the landscaped gardens, then steeply uphill onto a terrace that led to an infinity swimming pool overlooking the sea. Again there was no way through, and Troy slowed and turned the big bike around.

'Whadda we do?' he cried.

'There,' said the Big Shilling, pointing. 'Think you can make it?'

'Yes,' said American Troy immediately.

There was no other option. There were gunmen on the balconies and flat roofs of the palace, eager to get a clear shot at them through the trees, now that someone had turned on the floodlights. American Troy readied himself, bringing the bike round the pool to get as much run-up as possible. He felt the Big Shilling's small body behind him urging him on, and suddenly American Troy was certain that they would make it. He twisted the throttle and the bike hurtled forward, launching itself off the end of the terrace, across the slope of the moated lawn and over the outer wall of the palace, smashing off coping tiles and lumps of concrete as it went.

American Troy landed as best he could, standing tall and lifting up the front wheel, but the BMW was heavy and the landing was a terrible jarring crash that threw both of them out of the saddle. The Big Shilling grabbed onto Troy and American Troy hung onto the handlebars and both of them slammed back onto the seat with a sickening, neck-compressing thump as the bike smashed through undergrowth, across compacted sand and onto a dirt track.

'Did you get him?' American Troy asked, shouting.

'Did I get who?'

'Ahmet Bey! Did you get him!'

The Big Shilling shouted back, but American Troy couldn't hear him, and then he was too busy building up speed and negotiating the rough ground on the damaged bike to waste time talking. He felt exultant, thinking of Steve McQueen and The Great Escape!

Had he done enough? Had he turned the corner? Had he proved himself?

He didn't know for sure, but he thought he had.

CHAPTER TWENTY-FIVE

T he police bike gave up the ghost and died before they got to the winery. They left it in the ditch, the engine block ticking, broken pipes spluttering and steaming, stinking of leaking petrol and hot coolant. All the way from Famagusta no one had looked at them twice. In Cyprus, crazy joyriders on beat-up bikes were ten a penny.

The Big Shilling wasted no time. He got his bearings, and pointed.

'Down there, see? Those buildings, that's where we're going.'

'Do we have time?' asked American Troy.

'He'll wait. There are always delays at airports, hey.'

The Big Shilling was already haring ahead, and American Troy had to jog to catch up with him. The track was dusty and dark, and rutted with deep potholes, but the Big Shilling was as sure-footed as a mountain goat. On either side were olives trees, and from amongst them came the comforting sound of cicadas and the scents of sun-warmed countryside.

'Quite a jump,' said the Big Shilling in admiration. 'Yes, that was quite a jump. Evel Knievel couldn't have done it better himself, eh?'

American Troy didn't know what to say. He wanted to ask again if Ahmet Bey was dead but he doubted he'd get a straight answer. He had the idea that things were far from over yet.

'Cat got your tongue?'

'My back hurts.'

'If you're a good boy I'll give you a massage, eh? Come on, pick up the pace. What you need is a big glass of chilled white wine.'

A few minutes later, American Troy saw the lights of the winery. Soon after that he saw that there was a big illuminated sign by the main road with wording in Turkish and English: winery, finest wines, tastings each afternoon at appointment, proud supplier for airline industry.

So that was it! They were going to be smuggled in.

Eagerly, American Troy followed the Big Shilling through a vegetable patch where strawberries and watermelon were growing, and onto the side-road that led to the gates where a white van waited. American Troy could smell what he supposed was Turkish tobacco smoke.

'Hullo! Hullo!'

A small hairy man in a dirty white shirt got out

from behind the wheel of the van. He was smoking a cigarette and eating nuts at the same time.

'You are friends of Bulgaria?' he said in English.

'That's right,' said the Big Shilling. 'We are friends of Uncle Bulgaria.'

The two men stood there, eyeing each other up in the dim yellow light cast by the cab lights.

'Come,' said the Turkish Cypriot. 'We go now. Ten minutes only, we are there.'

He had them climb into the back of the van through the cab, handing them plastic bottles of chilled water as they went.

'Down, down,' he coaxed, as the van began to move. 'Is okay, relax, peoples see me all time. I come, I go, I bring wines for airplanes.'

The back of the van was hot and stuffy, and half-filled with cardboard boxes. American Troy found a seat and eased himself down onto a stack of boxes. His lower back hurt like hell now and his neck felt like it was out of skew. But the cold water was welcome. The Big Shilling loomed over him, not that much taller even though Troy was seated, methodically emptying his own bottle of water with glug after glug.

'Well,' he said, after belching a couple of times, 'you got your money, hey? Whatever happens, they can't take that away from you.'

American Troy slowly lowered the bottle of water from his lips. His intuition had been correct. 'I made that jump,' he said.

'So you did, so you did,' the Big Shilling allowed.

Then his demeanour changed yet again: 'Without you, I s'pose I'd never have got out of the place.'

'Fuck you,' said Troy, his anger mounting.

'Exactly, exactly,' said the Big Shilling in a hoarse whisper. 'That's what you wanted to do to me, wasn't it? When you were speaking to the Turk on the phone, that's what you wanted, wasn't it, eh? You wanted to do the deal, and you wanted to do the dirty on me at the same time. That's what you wanted, you rat fink ingrate bastard.'

'No,' said American Troy without thinking.

'And I say, yes!' said the Big Shilling, those strange eyes glinting.

At that moment the van driver braked sharply, causing the two of them, American Troy and the Big Shilling, to fall about and grab hand-holds. There was a police truck blocking the road, headlights blazing. The van driver mashed his cigarette out in the overflowing ashtray, and unhurriedly crunched up the nuts in his mouth.

American Troy did not see what happened next, but he guessed that one of the Turkish cops had got out of the truck and was approaching the driver's side.

The driver got out of the cab and spoke a Turkish greeting, but he was answered by a familiar English voice.

'All right, my wanker, what have you got in the back there?'

'Frankie the fucking Fish,' said Troy, pushing the Big Shilling out of the way. 'Hey, Frankie!'

And American Troy slipped between the boxes of wine bottles and slid behind the driver's seat and out the door onto the road. Shilling did nothing to try and stop him.

'Well, if it isn't old whatshisname,' said Frankie the Fish.

'Hey, it's great to see you, shipmate.'

Frankie the Fish looked at the Turkish driver, and American Troy looked at Frankie the Fish. After a few seconds of this, the three of them looked at the van.

The Big Shilling hadn't appeared. They could hear him inside the van, ripping open corrugated cardboard boxes. When he did appear, the Big Shilling was clutching small bottles of airline wine in both hands, and holding an empty bottle between his teeth which were made wet by the wine, and so were his lips, and his chin where the wine had run down it.

When he was standing on the roadway, he spat the empty bottle at Frankie the Fish's feet. It bounced once, and rolled between the treads of the polished black boots Frankie was wearing. They were the sort of black boots a cop might wear, so too the black rip-stop pants, and the navy blue, short-sleeved shirt with breast pockets and epaulettes, and the gun belt as well. Once the Big Shilling had taken in what Frankie was wearing, he looked him in the eye.

'He'd do anything for his daughter, Melissa, anything at all,' he observed, loudly, 'including betray dear old Blighty.'

'Flight's cancelled, skipper,' said Frankie the Fish.

'Have a drink, Frank,' said the Big Shilling, gesturing with the miniature bottles in his fists. 'Been in touch with London, eh? Operations ordered this, did they? Or was it Tel Aviv, hey? Was it your wife's pals ordering Frankie the fucking fool what to do, yet again?'

When Frankie the Fish drew the Taser that was tucked into the back of his belt, the Big Shilling flung the little bottles of wine at him, but they did not deter Frankie the Fish. He squeezed the trigger that fired the barbs connected to the gun's powerful batteries and hit the Big Shilling square in the chest. As the electric shock coursed through his body, the Big Shilling bared his wine-darkened teeth, and bellowed. He stood it for as long as he could – much longer than any of the three watching him thought possible - before his legs gave way and he dropped, twitching on the blacktop.

'There's a dive-bag on the back seat,' said Frankie the Fish to American Troy. 'Get it.'

For a moment, American Troy hesitated, then went and fetched the dive-bag. He recognised it. Last time he'd seen it, the Albanian gangster had been inside it. He helped Frankie the Fish lift the Big Shilling into the bag, after Frankie had duct-taped the little man's hands behind his back and his legs together. Frankie used a knife to cut the conductor wires, leaving the barbs in the Big Shilling's chest. Then he checked the little man's pulse. Satisfied, he zipped up the bag, hauled it to the truck, and swung it onto the back seat.

'You've been paid?' he asked American Troy when that was done.

'Yeah.'

'What about you?' he asked the van driver, who'd been quietly munching nuts and spectating. 'You've been paid?'

'I half been paid.'

'Right, you can go then. You've only done half the job, clear off.'

The van driver was about to object but, after seeing the look on the face of Frankie the Fish, thought better of it. Shrugging, he returned to his cab.

'What about me?' asked American Troy, as the wine van drove away.

'Please yourself, sport, Frankie doesn't give a toss.'

This was a new Frankie, a Frankie American Troy hadn't seen before, apart from that one time at the Killing House. Gone was the buffoonery and clown clothes, replaced by this professional killer in uniform.

When Frankie got behind the wheel of the police truck, American Troy hurried round to the passenger door and climbed in as well.

'Complicated, isn't it?' said Frankie.

'Yeah. I guess you're my way home now?'

Frankie didn't answer immediately. They'd driven a few hundred yards before he said, thinly, 'I suppose I am.'

'Where's the boat? You're not really working for

the Israelis, are you? What are you going to do with him?'

American Troy wasn't nervous, just pretending to be. He'd glanced at the bag on the back seat and seen a small, crooked finger emerge from the zipper. Somehow, the Big Shilling had worked himself free. And there and then Troy had made a decision. He couldn't trust Frankie. For better or worse, he was in this thing with the Big Shilling. So he kept up the nervous questioning. He kept it up right until the moment the little man pounced.

'Bottler,' said Frankie, in resignation.

He could smell a faint odour of faeces from the fingers which held the scalpel blade against his jugular.

'Pull over,' said the Big Shilling, triumphantly taking Frankie's pistol from its holster, 'pull over, turn around and take me to the airport.'

American Troy was wide-eyed with admiration. 'To bottle' was cockney cant, from 'bottle and glass,' rhyming slang. He remembered the lube, and the little plastic enclosure from a Kinder egg, on the bed at the apartment in Nicosia. But that 'me' sounded ominous. He glanced at Shilling. The little man's expression was uncompromisingly neutral.

It was only a short drive to the airport at Lefkosia in the powerful police truck. The Big Shilling directed Frankie to a side gate that gave access to the small terminal which serviced private jets and a flying school. The gate was guarded, but as soon as the security guard saw the police truck he merely waved them through and returned to his televised football game.

'There,' said the Big Shilling. 'Drive right onto the apron, Frankie, eh? Nice and easy does it, hey, nice and easy.'

The aircraft was a BAE 125, a mid-sized executive jet. The passenger door was open and the steps were down. South African Troy, dressed as a pilot in a peaked cap and a white shirt with four gold stripes on the shoulders, stood with his hands on his hips.

'This'll do, Frank, eh,' said the Big Shilling. 'Pull up, turn off the engine and give me the key.'

Frankie did as he was told, saying, 'It can go one of two ways.'

'No,' said Shilling, 'this is going to end one way. But hang on, hang on, hey? Maybe you're right, maybe you are right at that, eh?'

Frankie, who understood, managed to laugh. He looked at Troy, and said, matter-of-factly, 'He's going to tell you to do it.'

'Me?'

'Yeah,' said the Big Shilling. 'You got it in one. American Troy, wack Frankie the Fish.'

CHAPTER
TWENTY-SIX

'After the Turkish invasion of Cyprus in 1974, and the capture of the city of Famagusta,' said the Big Shilling, 'the suburb known as Varosha, home to the most exclusive hotels on the island, was fenced off by the Turks and allowed to fall into ruin.'

The two of them, the Big Shilling and American Troy, were standing on the concrete apron near the business jet. Frankie the Fish was in the police truck, dead.

'In the early 1970s,' the Big Shilling continued, 'the jet-set had come to Gazimagusa, as the Turks called the city: Richard Burton and Elizabeth Taylor, Steve McQueen and Ali MacGraw, Raquel Welch and Brigitte Bardot. It was the most important tourist destination in the world. But since 1974 it has been a ruin, eh. The high-rise hotels are derelict, windows smashed, concrete crumbling, and Nature has taken over, everywhere there are trees growing, bushes, plants and weeds.'

American Troy was looking at Frankie the Fish's pistol. He was looking at it because the Big Shilling was aiming it at his head.

'It was Ahmet Bey's dream to rebuild Varosha. Once again, he wanted the jet-set to promenade along JFK Avenue, George Clooney and his lovely wife, David and Mrs Beckham, Dame Helen Mirren, Charlize Theron.'

American Troy wanted to say something, anything. He was an intelligent kid, and he had the idea that Ahmet Bey's dream had somehow involved the assassination of the Russian exile. Had the Russian exile been a rival in the renovation of Varosha, and the Israelis and Brits as well? He wanted to say this, but words failed him. He stammered, and a single desperate word eventually came out.

'N-no,' said American Troy.

The Big Shilling didn't believe him. He signalled with the pistol again.

'On your knees.'

'No.'

'No?'

'If you're gonna shoot me, I'll die standing.'

'You're scared to die, kid. You saw how Frankie died, like a man, not a dog. You couldn't do it, could you? You couldn't pull the trigger. Because you don't have it in you, do you? You don't have what it takes.'

'No,' American Troy admitted with a gasp. 'I don't have it in me.'

'But Frankie's dead anyway, eh?'

American Troy didn't respond.

'You're going to beg.'

'No! I am not going to beg.'

'You're going to tell me to search my heart.'

'Fuck you, you son of a bitch! You don't have a heart.'

'Don't I? I'm heart, hand and head, my boy. Kneel!'

'No!'

'What have you learnt?'

American Troy couldn't think.

'W-what?'

'I'll send you back to the beginning,' warned the little demon.

'That's what happens?' whined Troy. 'You live your life over? When you die, you go back to the start?'

'But?'

'I don't know!' said Troy desperately.

'I showed you, boy, I showed you, in your coffin. If, but only if...'

Tory searched his addled brain.

'I told you,' warned the Big Shilling. 'You asked me, in Geneva, and I told you. I showed you.'

The 125 began to whine as South American Troy started up the engines. American Troy was shivering, and the shivers became the shakes. He couldn't think! What happened in Geneva? He couldn't remember, it was a blank. Tears wet his face.

'Do it, you bastard, do it, or let me go!'

'Bravado.'

The Big Shilling squeezed the trigger, he squeezed the trigger, and fired a shot past American Troy's left ear.

'No!' wailed Troy. 'No, no, no!'

He'd wheeled out of the way, and now he was pleading, pleading for his life, cowering in front of his cruel mentor.

'I don't have it in me,' said Troy, explaining. The engines were drowning out his words and he had to raise his voice to be heard. 'I'm not like you. I want to go home.'

'An honest man,' yelled the Big Shilling, 'an honest man, at least.'

Tossing the pistol over his shoulder, he ran forward and grabbed American Troy about the waist and bundled him towards the plane. Troy was a wreck. Shilling got him aboard, up the steps, and secured the door.

'Make yourself at home, kid,' said the Big Shilling, ironically. 'Make yourself at home.'

The jet began to move, inching forwards, then swiftly gathering speed as it taxied towards the runway. American Troy sank down at random in one of the cream leather seats. He'd seen video of biz jet interiors, but never expected he'd experience one in real life. The shakes subsided. He dried his eyes and his face, and violently sneezed once. The gleaming woodwork had recently been polished and the scent of lavender irritated his nose. With trembling hands, he fastened his seat belt and glanced out the oval window: cop cars.

The Big Shilling had seen them too.

'Amateurs,' he said, getting comfortable across the aisle. 'Rank amateurs, eh? Too little, too late.'

'We're through,' said American Troy as the jet hurtled down the runway. 'Are we through?'

The Big Shilling did not reply. He was looking out the window at the flashing blue and red lights of the police vehicles converging on the airport.

The 125 left the ground and ramped up into the sky. The Big Shilling sighed. It was over. He'd always said it would be difficult to get off the island, and he'd been right. Hell, believing was seeing, wasn't it? Of course it was. He giggled, stupidly.

When the jet had levelled off, he sent American Troy to the galley. He watched the kid search the cupboards and drawers, saw the look of sad satisfaction when he discovered the box of Havanas and a lighter, and the bottle of tequila in the fridge.

'We'll have a drink, eh, you and me,' said the Big Shilling, 'a celebratory drink and a smoke.'

'No,' said American Troy.

'I am what I am,' said the Big Shilling in explanation.

'Yeah,' agreed the kid.

Then the Big Shilling began to talk. He couldn't help himself, he loved to talk and he loved a captive audience.

He said, 'Georgii Georgiades must have been one of the most remarkable men ever to have lived, eh, one of the most remarkable men ever to have lived. He was extraordinary: so said Peter Demianovich, his errant disciple, who ended his days disappointed and pessimistic, haunted by Time and the notion of recurrence. He'd wasted his life teaching the System, a system he no longer believed in and that did not work. Why? Because he'd asked the wrong questions of the sly man, eh, he'd misunderstood, hadn't stuck around long enough to see the way forward. But you can hardly blame him, can you, hey? No, 'Sly Man' George was an ogre, he had the devil in him all right. Peter believed George had only two I's, one very good and one very, very bad. Now ...'

On and on he talked, the Big Shilling, on and on and on, and the jet cruised through the night skies over the Mediterranean Sea.

EPILOGUE

I t was August and London was suffering a heat-
wave. A record-breaking temperature of 41 degrees Celsius had been monitored at Heathrow
airport, and the city was blanketed by a lethal smog
composed not only of vehicle exhaust fumes but of
smoke from burning buildings as well, for there had
been three nights of rioting and arson. Urban youth
and trust fund anarchists had with disquieting ease
driven the police from the streets, and only now had
an uneasy peace been restored.

Petronella Plumleigh-Gorse looked around the
dining room of the National Liberal Club in White-
hall, at the shiny ceramic columns and pilasters,
and the impressive portraits of dead Liberal states-
men and politicians on the walls. The air conditioning had failed, and the portable fans that had been
placed around the room by an apologetic management weren't fit for purpose. Petronella might have
been perspiring, but inside she felt empty, and as
cold as marble. She fingered the clammy collar of

her shirt.

'So,' she said, 'you understand exactly what you are to do?'

'Yes,' said Sam, rather meekly.

Petra laid down her dessert spoon. She'd ordered the lemon sorbet. It was rapidly melting on the plate. The bitch troll from hell had ordered nothing, having hardly touched her main course of poached salmon and samphire. She was well into her second white wine spritzer, however. Drinking alcohol and hardly eating, this was a new Sam. Had she changed? She'd damn well better have.

'I want to make it absolutely clear, Sameerah,' Petra continued, 'what will happen to you if you let us down. You will be tried at the Old Bailey, in camera. That means there will be no media reporting of the case. You will be sentenced to at least ten years, if you are lucky. I'd do my damnedest to make sure it is double that. You know our reach. Prison won't be some holiday camp with an open gate, we'll make sure you serve hard time.'

Sam had bowed her head. Her long dark hair was uncovered, and she was wearing a summer frock and make-up. She'd lost quite a bit of weight as well.

'I won't let you down, ma'am,' said the traitress.

Petra leaned across the table, and hissed, 'You'd better fucking not.'

The bitch troll from hell began quietly to weep. After a few seconds, Petra, relenting, found a paper tissue and passed it to the girl.

'Ta,' she said, her accent that of any Londoner.

Petra was experiencing mixed emotions. Part of her was icily calculating how to play Sam back against the Turks, while another part, the compassionate, motherly part, felt a responsibility for the young woman's choices, as though she'd been let down, both by Petra herself, and by society as a whole. The nation too appeared to undergoing a similar soul-searching.

That morning, Petra had breakfasted alone, with the papers and BBC Radio 4. The question everyone was asking was what had gone wrong? No less than fourteen people had been killed and more than ninety injured, some seriously. Whatever it was, everyone was agreed that it was society's fault for failing the marginalised and the maligned, that much was certain. On the radio, a woman barrister had averred that criminals were made and not born, and it followed therefore that since a good citizen is one who is raised correctly and is properly educated, better education and earlier, more effective intervention were called for.

If only I'd spotted the signs, Petra chided herself, then perhaps Sameerah might have been brought back on track and this whole disastrous business could have been avoided.

'You'll be all right, dear,' Petra now said. 'Dry your eyes.'

Sam managed a smile, dabbing at her mascara with the tissue. 'Thank you, ma'am,' she said.

She was quite a pretty girl, really, what with her

hair down and having lost some of that puppy fat.

'Well, I think I'll get the bill,' said Petronella, feeling better.

She signalled to the waiter. One had to look to the positives. For instance, the news that the police officer and his father killed in the massacre at Paphos were both awaiting trial for bribery and corruption had drawn the sting somewhat. The death of dear old Frankie had also put an end to the child custody business. Yes, and there might yet be glory to be had from triple agent Sameerah Behgum.

While she waited for the bill, Petra turned on her phone and checked her texts and messages. There was nothing of much importance. A tweet caught her eye, some kind of spat amongst the chattering classes. Dreadful, horse-faced woman, thought Petra, branding community leaders 'rent-seekers.' Oh and what was this? 'Hand-wringing from authoritarian liberals who created the problem in the first place'? Delete your account, dear, that's quite out of order.

Bloody populists.

The waiter brought the bill, and Petra paid with her company card. She'd just put away her purse when the phone rang. When she saw it was Sir Mike, she experienced a frisson of alarm. The DG had gone away for weekend, to the Cotswolds. He'd said they'd speak on Monday, about how best to employ Sam.

'Hello, Michael,' she said, calmly.

'Petra? Can you talk?'

'We've just finished lunch, Sam and I.'

'Oh, I'd hoped to catch you alone.'

That sounded ominous. 'I'll call you back in two minutes, shall I?'

'No, don't do that. There's nothing to discuss. I've been speaking to my opposite number, Sir Tim.'

Petra's mouth had gone dry. Sir Tim was director general of MI5.

'He's very keen to have you as assistant director,' Mike continued, 'in charge of administration.'

Petronella swallowed hard. 'He's what?'

'It's for the best, Petra.'

'But I thought...'

'I'm afraid you thought wrong. Don't come in tomorrow morning. I'll have your things brought round to your house. Tim will be in touch. Sorry to do this by phone, but I thought it was best to make it short and sweet. You've been very loyal, and we shall miss you. I've spoken to HR, pay grade's the same and the transfer won't affect your pension.'

Petra didn't know what to say.

'Well, goodbye,' said Sir Mike, and ended the call.

'Bad news?' asked Sam.

It was only with a tremendous effort of will that Petronella did not start shouting.

ABOUT THE AUTHOR

Gomery Kimber

The Killing House is Gomery Kimber's first published novel and the first book in the Big Shilling trilogy.

The second book, The War Party, is due for publication in the summer of 2020. Book three, The Mad Man, will appear in 2021.

Mr Kimber is married and lives in the north of England.

Printed in Great Britain
by Amazon

47556862R00213